# All (DEAD) Girls Lie

PIPER L. WHITE

Library of Congress Cataloging-in-Publication Data
Available Upon Request

ISBN 978-1-955905-96-1 (TP)
ISBN 978-1-955905-97-8 (eBook)

Printed in the United States
Distributed by Simon & Schuster

First edition

1 3 5 7 9 10 8 6 4 2

*To my dad, who talks to everybody:*
*thanks for finding me my first book editor.*

*And to my mom:*
*thanks for funding my first book publishing journey and giving me an outlet to be the one thing I've always known I was meant to be: a writer.*

# CONTENTS

# CHAPTER ONE

November 13, 2004

What I wanted to say to the investigator was "Screw Marki Pickett!"—the first dead girl. Part of me loathed her for being murdered. Her death set off a chain of events I could've avoided if I'd minded my business. But when I saw her best friends in the cafeteria, solemn and martyred by everyone who thought their lunch table was now a bad omen, I couldn't help myself. Maybe the table *had* been a bad omen, and me going near its inhabitants cursed me. I certainly felt cursed as the only girl being questioned in this way, as if I was a suspect.

"It is November 13th, 2004, and I am here with Quinn Levi at the Boiling Springs police department," the investigator said into a tape recorder.

I tapped my foot, waiting to be questioned.

"Quinn." The investigator in front of me spoke slowly. "I need you to tell me anything you can about what happened on October 30th. Can you do that for me?"

The room was sterile, with nothing but a table and our chairs to occupy it. The investigator breathed heavily out of his nose as he tapped a pen on his notepad, the sound causing my irritation to rise. There was a camera in the corner as big as a robotic arm. I felt like I was under a microscope in biology class.

I stared down at the white table. The fluorescent light overhead reflected off the smooth, eggshell-white surface. It reminded me of the desks at school, only nicer. I caught my reflection: copper baby hairs in a crown around my sweaty face. I tried to match the blank stare of the investigator to seem innocent. But all that stared back was the face of a dead girl.

"I already told the police what I saw," I said. "I was told some things, but it's all hearsay at this point."

"We simply want to get an idea of what happened. Anything is helpful. Answer to the best of your ability," the investigator insisted.

My throat had gone dry the moment I entered the investigation room. They had been kind enough to give me a glass of water. I'd been questioned by the police before, but never by an investigator. I didn't like the feeling. I ran a hand down my messy ponytail, a few stray copper strands falling from my half-assed effort. They glided from my hand like autumn leaves onto the gray floor.

Two months ago, I'd dreaded school. My town of Boiling Springs, North Carolina usually only had a couple shoplifters to worry about, not a string of murders. *Murders.* Something I only knew about from my favorite slashers—which I doubted I'd ever watch again with the same intrigue. It was mind-blowing how much could change in two months.

I wasn't handcuffed; there wasn't any reason for me to be. They had to believe I was innocent. I took a sip of water, while the investigator slid a photograph in front of me. It was a photo of Marki Pickett—just the person I wanted to be looking at.

"Would it help if we started at the beginning of fall?" he asked.

Marki smiled, bangs cut across her forehead, golden curls to her shoulder. Her face was lively, smile bright, skin full of color. She was alive in the photograph, but I still only saw her as a dead girl.

I nodded my head, the investigator peeling the photograph away.

"I remember when the police announced her murder," I said. "We can start there."

## CHAPTER TWO

September, 2004

Fall slowly crept in, leaving its warning for the heat by the gray overcast and darkening trees. The weather was still kissed by summer, and the humidity still swept through, turning my arms sticky, my hair rolling in ringlets at the base of my neck like little orphan Annie. No matter how much I brushed it, the strands still collected sweat that stuck to them like tree sap.

There was something different in the air that Wednesday morning. Wednesdays were almost worse than Mondays. They taunted us with Thursdays and left the teachers packing as much lecturing as they could—no matter how restless we became. I leaned back on my desk chair, satisfied when my spine popped like a glowstick. My ears rang for a moment, and I blocked out the talk of algebra from Mrs. Lake in the front of the room. Then the door flew open, cutting the teacher off mid-sentence. My best friend Beck sauntered into the room, black hair halfway brushed, a spaghetti strap dangling off one of her shoulders. It was the third time that week she was late to class, so Mrs. Lake simply greeted her with a sigh before continuing her lecture.

"What did I miss?" Beck asked, unpacking a notebook she never opened.

"The first thirty minutes of class," I said.

"Asshole."

"What kept you this time?" I asked.

"The question should be *who* kept me," she said with a wink.

I chuckled, scribbling more next to my math notes from earlier. I wondered how many more tardies Beck would take before they finally suspended her. Her tardies were probably the most interesting thing about Putner High School. They threw out detention slips like candy, but never suspended or expelled anyone. Part of me believed they just didn't care enough; it was too much of a hassle.

Mostly, I managed okay enough. Lunch was the only time I dreaded—that and catching the bus. I was sixteen without a license, but taking the bus appealed to me more than sitting alone at lunch. Beck was supposed to have lunch with me, but she often skipped it to go to the gas station or smoke weed under the bleachers. That day, I chose the one table that had only one seat—the other broke a long time ago and nobody bothered replacing it. I put my headphones on and observed everyone. I bit into my ham and cheese sandwich, avoiding eye contact with the football players in their musty lettermans. Only a couple of them chose to sit in seats, most hovering over or sitting on the table, eating bags of chips. I nearly gagged when they sucked the remains off their fingers before reaching out and grabbing the cheerleaders' ponytails. Their brains couldn't have developed past elementary school.

My gaze shifted to Gilly Willis's table, where she sat with her four best friends. There was a gap between her and Sarai. Marki Pickett wasn't with them; it wasn't normal for any of them to miss school. They all packed their lunches in candy-colored boxes, probably bought from the same department store at the same time. The clique grew together like a cluster from elementary school and beyond. They were the girls who offered pens to people with moo-moo eyes for them or held the door with a kind smile. Everyone knew them, yet nobody *knew* them.

A whiff of skunk broke me from my observation.

"Do you have any chips?" Beck asked, eyes pink.

"You need perfume more than chips," I said, tossing her a bag of Fritos.

"Your mom never buys the good shit," Beck said. "Who the fuck eats Fritos?"

"Me," I said, "when I reach the end of the good chips I never bring you."

She dug into the chips, scowling at every bite. She sat at the table adjacent to me, kicking her feet on the ground.

"Marki's not here," I said.

Beck turned toward the table, accidentally making eye contact with Gilly. They stared at one another for a moment before turning back to their food.

"They're weird," Beck said.

"Because people like them or because they actually show up to school on time?"

Beck stuck her Frito-encrusted middle finger up at me. A beat later, she asked, "Why do you think perfect-attendance-princess-number-four didn't show up?"

I looked back at their table, and Gilly caught my eye that time. She was one of the prettiest girls in our school. I'd never had a conversation with her, but her voice was soft and lower than one would think. Every time she raised her hand in class, her feedback was calmly put together, lacking all the *ums* and *likes* that repetitively came out of her peers' mouths. I envied the way she always kept her composure. Even her honey-colored hair always fell into clean waves just above her waist. It never faltered, even in the humidity.

"Stomach flu," I said. "Or maybe her Yorkie finally cut its life cord."

"Morbid," Beck said, throwing her raven-black hair into a loose bun.

The bell rang, and everyone began flooding out of the cafeteria.

"Are you doing anything later?" Beck asked.

"Absolutely nothing," I said.

"Can I come over?"

"Sure."

We parted ways, and I pushed through the stampede of people. The fact that the day was only halfway over sent my body into exhaustion. I walked into my English class and pulled out my notebook. I doodled a flower in the corner when the scent of jasmine brushed past me. Gilly took a seat in front of me before turning around.

"Hey," she said.

"Hi?" It came out more like a question than I intended.

"I saw you looking over at my table at lunch," she said nonchalantly.

I lowered my face to hide my blush.

"Sorry about that," I said, returning to my flower.

"How come you eat by yourself every day?" she asked, leaning an elbow on my desk.

Bits of her sandy-blonde hair fell over my doodles.

I shrugged. "I prefer to observe things, I guess."

"I get that," Gilly said. "Sometimes it's exhausting talking through lunch. I barely finish eating every day. Those girls love to talk."

I couldn't understand why she was talking to me. In the years of being classmates with Gilly Willis, she'd *never* gone out of her way to speak to me. I didn't mean to stare as she sat there, fully turned toward me, but she held me captive. I knew Gilly

Willis was gorgeous—hell, everyone in the school knew it—but face-to-face, I noticed the softness of her powdered cheeks and pink-glossed lips.

*No; I couldn't think about the most popular girl in school this way.*

I smiled, not contributing anything to our conversation, so she turned around. I studied her during class. She was right-handed and used pink and purple ink pens instead of pencils. She kept a water bottle at the corner of her desk and sipped it quietly. Every time her head moved, I'd get a whiff of her perfume, and it'd make me dizzy—in a good way. The florals beat the smell of pencil shavings and stale classroom air I inhaled daily.

Halfway through class, the intercom sounded, announcing the principal.

"Students," he began, voice grim.

There was a pause, and some whispering from the intercom, before Mr. Leland continued. "It is my grave displeasure to announce the passing of one of our beloved students, Marki Pickett."

Gilly gasped, quickly covering her mouth. I stared at her back as her shoulders trembled, then bounced up and down.

"Due to the circumstances of her passing, school is canceled for the rest of the week," Mr. Leland said. "Details will follow tonight on the local news from our Sheriff's Department, so please keep your eyes out and stay safe. Your parents have all been alerted. School is dismissed."

A couple of students packed up, eyes on the ground, some traveling to Gilly who still cried in her seat, unmoving. I caught the eye of a few other students, their eyes wet. Losing Marki Pickett was like losing royalty around here. She was on all the committees, making sure everything ran smoothly for our dances or fundraisers. I couldn't imagine the blow it would take to Gilly's friend group.

"Everyone get home safe," Mrs. Ashley said, breathless.

I packed my things. Gilly still didn't move. I opened my mouth to express my condolences, but Mrs. Ashley cut me off as she approached our spot.

"Gilly, honey," Mrs. Ashley said, "we need to get you packed up and home. Your father will want you back immediately."

Gilly's father, Jon Willis, was the head of the sheriff's department. More charming than terrifying, I still wouldn't ever want to be on his bad side. Mrs. Ashley helped Gilly with the rest of her things and led her out the door.

"Freedom!" Beck said, crashing onto my bed.

"Don't say that," I said. "Marki is dead."

"May she rest in peace," Beck said, sending a kiss to the sky. "But thank you for getting school canceled."

I took out my algebra textbook, deciding to catch up on homework since I had the rest of the day off. Beck flipped through the TV channels until she got to the news.

"Want to watch it?" Beck asked.

"Sure," I said, abandoning the textbook.

Marki was the headline. *Local teen found dead in woods outside high school.* I stiffened where I sat, while Beck turned up the volume.

"We are here, outside of Putner High, where a local teen has been found dead in the woods that border the public school," the reporter said. "Foul play is suspected, but the police have not released a statement."

The TV cut over to Jon Willis speaking with another reporter.

"We don't have all the details yet, but we want everything to return to normal as soon as it can," the sheriff said. "As of right now, we are not enforcing a curfew, but we encourage everyone to be safe and mindful of strangers. School will return next week. These next couple of days are for grieving one of our own."

The news circulated the same facts over and over again, so we changed the channel. *Foul play is suspected.* I shivered. I finally felt summer go, leaving no trace of warmth behind.

# CHAPTER THREE

"Owen, can you grab some glasses, please," Mom said.

I set the salad bowl on the kitchen table while my mom took the rolls out of the oven. My little brother, Owen, flew into the kitchen, ready to eat. Ever since he'd turned thirteen, he was ravenous; he ate everything in the house. I had to fight to get seconds.

He filled three glasses with ice and set them at our places. We had a round table with three seats; we didn't need a fourth. My mom had been a single parent since Owen was born. I didn't remember my dad much, partly because he and Mom were never married. He had the same ginger hair that I did—that's the only thing I could remember. We'd seen her date here and there, but she didn't let anyone stick around. She focused more on us, and on her job as a nurse, than on anything else. I didn't mind. I liked our little family, even Owen on his good days.

He was at that middle-school age where he burped directly in my face and slammed the door on me if I interrupted his video games. Sometimes, I missed when he was little and sweet; every time his piggish behavior made way, I was reminded of just how annoying he was. Still, while we bickered, we'd never had any true angry outbursts with one another.

We had the news on low in the living room. There was a clear view from the kitchen table. We filled our plates from the serving bowls, staring at the TV for an update. The weather report showed it would still be hot next week but not as bad as it had been.

"How was work?" I asked Mom.

"The parents only talked about Marki," Mom said. "Even some of the kids were asking about her. It's horrible."

"At least it got us out of school," Owen said.

"Owen," my mom warned.

I kicked him in the shin. He was being so inconsiderate. I dug into my salad, watching as Owen absorbed his as if he were a vacuum cleaner. Every time we ate together, I was surprised he didn't choke.

"You could slow down," I said.

"You could shut up," Owen said, mouth full of food.

I stuck my tongue out at him, while Mom shushed us both. "Turn it up," she said.

I grabbed the remote, clicking the volume nearly all the way up. Jon Willis was on the screen in his uniform. It looked like they were reporting from our town hall. Camera flashes went off, and Jon Willis stood with a solemn look on his face. It had only been two days since the news of Marki's murder, yet there were already more cameras and people than the one time a president drove through our town.

"We finally have an update for everyone, but I'm sorry to report it isn't a good one," he said. "The coroner report came back to us this evening and, as we'd suspected, Marki Pickett's death has been ruled a homicide."

We all dropped our forks. Even Owen stopped eating.

"As I previously stated, this is a horrible tragedy, but we already have a list of suspects. Everyone should remain calm and go about their business. School will resume on Monday morning."

Reporters jumped to question Jon Willis about potential suspects and the nature of how Marki was killed. My body went hot, pinpricks tickling my neck as I thought about a murder in our town. Especially the murder of someone I saw every day in the cafeteria.

We didn't speak during the rest of the dinner, eating our food slower than normal. Owen shuffled his food around with his fork, taking smaller bites. My stomach refused any more food.

"I'll stick the rest in a container," I said, excusing myself from the table.

I grabbed some Tupperware from a cabinet and mindlessly shoved my food into it. I stared down at the puddle of mashed potatoes, gravy spilling off, creating a mote. It was mixed with turkey and peas. It looked like a mess. My mind slipped, and I caught myself wondering if when they found Marki, she—for the first time in her life—looked like a mess. I gagged.

"Quinn, will you please make sure all the doors and windows are locked?" Mom asked, grabbing the remaining dishes off the table.

I walked around the entire house, checking all the windows twice and making sure our front and back doors were double-bolted. She didn't really think the person who killed Marki would break in and kill us, right? For the first time, I didn't feel safe in my own home. I didn't scare easily; my idea of a perfect night was binging my favorite slasher films with the lights out. They didn't feel so fictional now.

Before I went to bed, I checked all the blinds with Mom and made sure each was tightly closed. I peered out one of my living room windows, finding the street empty, illuminated by the yellow glow of a streetlamp. The barren streets seemed more intimidating now as the town fell silent due to Marki's death. The shadows that danced in the darker part of the streets no longer felt innocent.

Whoever killed Marki could be one of those shadows, studying the suburban houses, picking their favorite, and deciding who would be their next victim. I hoped the ugly, paint-peeled lawn gnome on our front lawn turned them off from our house.

On Monday, the sun shone, and it felt like a slap in the face. The weather mocked the town of the news we'd received about Marki. Everything felt out of place. The same school I stared at every morning seemed to tilt slightly more to the right as if our world was close to tipping over. In towns as small as ours, everyone knew each other. Marki had been in my kindergarten class. We'd been partners on a group project before. Yet, we'd never spoken outside of school.

Even the school bell sounded ominous. The trill was clouded by what had happened. Barely anyone spoke.

Beck, for once, was on time. "Hey."

"Hey," I said back.

She looked paler than normal and didn't greet me with any snarky comment. She wore her hair down, which was unlike her to do.

"Are you okay?" I asked.

"This whole thing is freaking me out," Beck said. "I see those woods every day when I smoke under the bleachers. Last week I was under there when Marki was found. She was dead, and I was under the bleachers getting high."

I'd expected Beck to be more neutral to the situation, considering she didn't have any relationship with Marki either. Even I was taking the news better than Beck, which wasn't normal. She rarely thought about the negative. I wouldn't necessarily call her positive, but she didn't let things get to her.

"I think everyone is freaked out," I said. "But you heard Jon Willis. They have suspects already. I'm sure they'll find whoever did it."

"Did you hear how she died?" Beck asked.

I shook my head.

"She was stabbed."

"How do you know?"

"Everyone is talking about it," Beck said frantically. "Jason Mulley said his dad told him."

Jason Mulley's father was a deputy who worked with Jon Willis. Jason was a big mouth.

"That's awful," I said.

Mrs. Lake came in acting as if nothing had happened. It was probably an easier thing to do since the murder victim wasn't one of her students. She walked the rows, collecting the algebra homework from those who'd actually done it. A lot of people hadn't, me included. I never skipped my homework, but after the news from the weekend, I'd forgotten to finish it. My mind, like everyone's, was elsewhere.

Nobody sat still. Those who normally paid attention stared out the window, bouncing their legs as if whoever killed Marki watched them, promising they were the next victim. I tried copying down notes, but the only thing my pencil wanted to write were questions about the murder.

I ditched my usual spot at lunch that gave me a clear shot of Gilly Willis's table. She and her friends tried sitting closer together to cover the gap in their table where Marki normally sat, but the absence was still heavy and evident. Most of the time, people came and went by their table, making small conversations with the popular girls. They'd smile and engage, then turn to one another with their more intimate conversations when people left. But not today.

Everyone refused to even walk by their table. The remaining four girls were ostracized.

Beck and I sat in a two-seater across from one another. She used her wad of cash to buy some chips and a cookie instead of weed from the guys under the bleachers. Having her as my lunch company was the distraction I needed, though I also longed for my space alone away from everyone.

"I think Harry's giving me a ride home today," Beck said. "I don't want to take the bus."

"That's a good idea," I said.

I didn't understand why Beck was so freaked out over Marki's murder. She kept looking around the lunchroom, moving her leg up and down the way everyone in class did.

"Beck, it's going to be okay," I said. "Not to be morbid, but whoever killed Marki probably knew her or had a motive. That's how it normally is, isn't it?"

"Not if it was a serial killer," Beck said.

I'd told her not to watch so many true crime documentaries.

"Has anyone else died?" I asked.

"No," Beck said. "But killers always start with one; then they go from there."

I finished off my sandwich, gaze trailing over to where Gilly Willis sat. She sat in silence with her friends, nobody cracking a smile. Her hair was pulled back in a braid today, lips paler from their lack of lip gloss. She swirled her water around in its bottle but didn't take a sip. A few people finally approached them, placing hands on their shoulders, to which the girls mouthed "thank you."

In English class, Mrs. Ashley wrote on the board that we were to have a reading day. She had buckets of books at the front of class in case nobody brought any. I shuffled up to the front, finding Gilly sorting through one of the big gray buckets.

"Find anything good?" I asked.

"*The Virgin Suicides*," she said, holding up the book.

"Sounds like a good one."

It was all I could think to say, considering. I didn't get how a book about girls dying would appeal to someone whose friend just died, but people grieved in different ways. Death made people act differently.

"You don't have to be all timid around me," Gilly said. "Everyone has been watching the things they say to us today. Marki died and we didn't. It sucks and I miss her, but I'm already tired of everyone saying they're sorry."

Her hard voice sounded so un-Gilly like. I knew her as a calm-spoken girl who always raised her hand, but Marki's death had clearly hardened her.

"I noticed those people at lunch coming up to you," I said, trying my best not to say, "Sorry for your loss."

"People I've never said more than one word to," Gilly said. "It's weird how death makes people more approachable sometimes. You'd think the opposite were true."

I sifted through the book bucket, uncomfortable at her bluntness. Was this the real Gilly Willis?

"I get why people are scared," I said. "But it is a bit ridiculous. The police will find who did it, and then we will go back to being the same town who waits on news of lawn chairs being stolen."

This made Gilly smile, and I blushed. Stop it, Quinn. The girl's best friend just died, and I was blushing, because of a smile?

"There's going to be a candlelight vigil tonight," Gilly said. "Do you think you'll go?"

"I feel like I should since everyone is going," I admitted. "But I didn't know Marki like that. I'll feel weird."

"Well, I'm going," Gilly said. "And you know me, so by proxy, you know Marki. I think you should come. I could use someone real with me tonight."

I didn't understand what she meant by *someone real* when her friends would surely be there with her. But the thought of Gilly Willis inviting me to anything—even if it was her best friend's vigil—made me feel important.

"I'll meet you there," I said.

# CHAPTER FOUR

I sat in my bedroom, blasting music as I finished up my homework. I cracked my neck, fixing my posture, which immediately went back to a slouch.

"Are you going to that candle thing tonight?" Owen asked from my bedroom doorway.

I jumped. When would he ever learn to knock?

"Yes," I said. "Do you want to go?"

"Sure," Owen said. "Some of my friends are going, so don't expect me to hang out with you."

"Wouldn't dream of it."

Before we left, I grabbed a flannel in case I got cold. Nights had grown colder, even if the days didn't match. I ran my brush loosely through my hair, undoing any knots. I stopped at the mirror, checking myself over once and deciding I looked good enough. Besides, tonight was about Marki.

We had Mom drop us off by the football field at the high school. There was a large crowd of people lighting each other's white candles for Marki. Beck refused to come to the vigil with me. She claimed being there would bring us bad luck. She even thought that would be the place the killer was most likely to blend in. I let her ramble about the risks then ended the call with the excuse that I had homework.

A majority of the town showed up, even children who thought the candles were mini swords they could fight one another with. Owen ran off with his friends while I searched for Gilly.

"Over here!" Gilly said, waving me over.

She was with Sarai and the two other girls whose names I always forgot. They were twins, identical down to the amount of ear piercings they had, and I couldn't bother learning to tell them apart.

Gilly handed me a candle, lighting it with her own. She smiled slightly at me. She grabbed my wrist and led me to Marki's memorial. There was a large picture of her. She smiled wide, golden hair styled, bangs covering her forehead. She glowed, happy. Teddy bears and flowers were placed around the picture. I never understood why people brought such tangible things to a memorial. Flowers would die, but where would the bears go? They'd probably be shoved in a closet so nobody was reminded of their loss.

"I miss her," Gilly said. "She was so pretty."

The comment took me off-guard. It was evident Marki was nothing short of beautiful, but shouldn't an honor of her life consist of more than just her looks? I was surprised she hadn't mentioned something more personal. I let it slide when I looked at Gilly's face. She pulled her bottom lip in between her teeth to keep from crying. I didn't know how to console her.

Sarai and the twins came up to Gilly, hugging one another. They blubbered, but Gilly held her composure. I stepped off to the side to give them their moment while Mr. Leland approached the front of the crowd.

"Everyone, we are gathered here to honor the life of Marki Pickett, a life lost too soon," Mr. Leland said. "This memorial is for all of us to grieve together and remember the light that was

Marki Pickett. Anyone is free to come up and share any memories or offer any words about Miss Pickett."

He stepped down. Sarai was the first to speak. Gilly and the twins held hands, heads high while the first of their group took to the mic.

"Marki was one of my best friends," Sarai said through tears. "I remember the first time we met. It was preschool, and I forgot my snack at home, so Marki shared some of her cookies and grapes with me. She was one of the kindest people I knew, and I will miss her terribly."

Sarai stepped down with a broken sob while the twins pulled her in between them. Gilly looked at the ground, kicking a stray rock while another student took to the mic. One after the other, people came up to express their condolences, recounting surface-level memories of Marki that would never parallel the weight of the group of girls beside me. While Sarai and the twins stood with their hands over their hearts, nodding along to the words spoken of their lost friend, Gilly leaned in closer to me.

"Do you want to leave?" Gilly whispered to me.

"What?" I asked.

Gilly grabbed my wrist and led me through the crowd, not explaining any further. The voices of students trailed off the further we got from the stadium.

Gilly led me closer to the woods and I halted.

"Why are we going toward the woods?" I asked.

"I need to see where they found her," Gilly said.

I blinked. "Why? Gilly, I really don't think that's a good idea."

I heard Beck in the back of my mind, screaming that the killer was out there, waiting for another teenager to stumble into their trap.

"It will make it real for me," Gilly said. "Hearing Sarai talk about her up there made me feel nothing. It's like Marki is at home, and tomorrow I'll see her at school. I keep seeing things on TV that Marki would like, and I want to call her and tell her about them. I keep thinking she will answer. If you don't want to come with me, I won't make you, but I need to do this."

Gilly stared at me, waiting for an answer, her blue-gray eyes daring me to follow. When I didn't move further, she let go and made her way to the woods, the candle and moon her only sources of light. She walked with purpose, as if the woods would give her the answers and grief she wanted. When she crossed the threshold into the trees, I watched as her light was chewed up by darkness. My heartbeat sped up at the thought of her meeting Marki's fate.

"Shit," I said, following her into the woods.

I cupped my hand around my candle, careful so it wouldn't blow out. The trees loomed over me, darkened by the night. Every twig I stepped on made me jump. I was careful to watch my back. It was haunting in the woods, as if Marki's memory had broken apart in pieces and stuck to every inch of nature it could touch. Every pine needle reminded me Marki was found dead in these woods, and that I was walking across her grave.

"Gilly!" I called out.

There wasn't a single trace of her candlelight. I steadied my breath, trying not to panic. If anything, I could run back the way I came to school and leave Gilly to find her own way out. But doing that would keep me up all night wondering if she made it, and I wanted to save myself the peace.

I searched for her candlelight, but all I saw was darkness. My candle whipped in the breeze, and I tensed, hoping the flame wouldn't go out.

"Gilly!" I called again.

But nothing. I broke out in a cold sweat; I'd had enough.

With a breath, I turned to leave the woods—and found Gilly in my path. I jumped back, sending my candle flame into a frenzy.

"You scared me," I hissed.

"I found it," Gilly replied. "The spot where they found Marki. Follow me."

She grabbed my hand. Hers was warm with adrenaline and made me realize how frigid mine had grown in the chilly wind. I followed her a little further into the woods where caution tape lined a small clearing. On the ground were splotches of what I assumed were dried blood, and I shivered. Gilly knelt down on the pine needles, staring. I watched her back as her shoulders bounced again. When she sniffled, I knelt down next to her.

"Who would do something like this?" Gilly asked. "My dad tells me stories about this stuff, but none of them have ever phased me."

"I think that's because it's never been as real for you as it is now," I said.

She turned to me, tears flooding her blue-gray eyes. "Do you think they'll actually find who killed her?"

The truth was I didn't know how well our police would do on the case. There wasn't much crime in our town that involved intensive work, so I'd never seen it happen.

"I don't know," I said.

I probably should have lied to her, but I couldn't. Everyone sugarcoated everything for Gilly, and I didn't want to be like everyone else to her. We sat there and stared at the caution tape blowing in the slight breeze. It looked unnatural against all the wiry trees.

"Who do you think killed her?" Gilly asked.

"I don't even have an educated guess," I said. "Did Marki say anything about anyone that seemed off?"

Gilly shook her head. "Everyone liked Marki."

*Everyone liked the* thought *of Marki*, I wanted to say, but I held my tongue.

"She was probably in the wrong place at the wrong time," I said aloud.

"You think she was in the woods when she died?" Gilly asked. "Or do you think someone put her here?"

She stared at the ground as she asked the questions. If I were her, I wouldn't have wanted to speculate anything regarding the death of my best friend, but I guess being the daughter of the town sheriff could do that to someone.

"Have you ever known Marki to come to these woods at night?" I asked.

"No," Gilly said. "Well, maybe not. I don't think she would come alone, at least."

"It's a popular spot for people to drink," I pointed out. "Or have sex."

"Marki wasn't like that," Gilly said with a hint of irritation.

I nodded but thought about the times I'd seen Marki in the hallway, some guy's hands wrapped around her butt while they kissed as if nobody would walk by and see them.

"Then I think she was probably taken here," I said. Gilly only shivered, so I added, "We should get back."

"Good idea."

We walked close together, keeping our candles in front of us and stopping after every noise we heard. I'd never been one to spend time in the woods, but I knew Beck had before. I hoped never to return to them.

"Have you ever hung out in the woods before?" Gilly asked to distract us.

I shook my head. "Not really my thing."

"Yeah," Gilly said. "Mine either."

Our shoulders bumped together, but neither one of us attempted to give the other more space.

"I . . . like the way your hair looks in the dark," Gilly said. "It's very Jessica Chastain."

"Thanks," I said, a little softer than intended.

I figured I should compliment her back, but I couldn't think of anything to say. It didn't matter, though. By the time I thought to say anything else, we were back at the edge of the woods.

Jon Willis and a couple other deputies stood around. Their radios went off every other second.

"Gilly!" Jon Willis said. "What the hell were you doing in those woods? I've been looking all over for you."

"Sorry, Dad," Gilly said.

Jon Willis and I locked eyes, but I quickly averted them.

"Get back to the memorial," he said. "Gilly, I'll meet you back up there when it's time to go."

I followed Gilly back to the memorial, turning around to watch as Jon and the other deputies went back into the woods.

"I should find my brother," I said to Gilly.

"And I should go find Sarai, Alma, and Jen," Gilly replied.

Alma and Jen—the twins. Noted.

"I'll see you at school tomorrow," I said with a nod.

When she was gone, I set my candle down in front of Marki's photo. The light reflected off her eyes like little golden balls of fire. For a moment, I couldn't help but picture her eyes—glassy, as they might have been when she was found in the woods, all the golden hue drained, just like her life. I tore myself away from the picture and went to find Owen.

Gilly and I didn't speak much at school the next day. She sat with her friends at lunch and didn't look up at me once. Nobody bothered to stop and speak with them at all. They could pass by quietly, as they had already exchanged condolences for luck that they wouldn't become the next victim.

Beck still sat with me, her hollowed cheeks filling out now that she was finally eating fuller meals.

"Have you passed by the counselor's?" Beck asked. "The line has been long all day."

"For grief counseling?" I asked.

Beck nodded. "I think most of the people going are looking for a way to get out of class though. I didn't see any of *them* in the line at all today."

Beck motioned to Gilly's table, and I looked. Gilly and Sarai talked, but their conversation was hushed. They still weren't smiling as much as they normally did. Marki's spot was left to the air today. I didn't think anyone would ever get over the permanent gap at their table.

When the bell rang, I gathered my trash quickly, hoping to bump into Gilly, but she and her friends shot out of the cafeteria before I could catch her.

"I'll see you later," Beck said.

I waved her away while I headed to my next class, English.

Gilly was already in her seat in front of mine. My heart skipped, and I quietly made my way to my desk. When I sat, Gilly turned to me. I looked up at her and felt the heat rush to my cheeks.

"Want to hang out with me this weekend?" Gilly asked. "I'm partially under house arrest until they figure out who. . . ."

She didn't finish her sentence, but I understood what she was trying to say.

"Sure," I said.

"What about Saturday night?" she asked.

"That works for me."

I tapped my nails on the desk. Gilly Willis wanted to hang out with me? What had I done to get all this attention from her?

She placed her hand on top of mine to calm my fidgeting. Her touch sent another rush of heat through my body. I stiffened at the realization that she wasn't moving her hand.

"Bring stuff to sleepover," she said.

When the bell rang, Gilly finally released my hand, slowly. I noted how her fingers brushed sparks against my knuckles. When she turned fully, she fluffed her hair, and the lingering scent of jasmine enveloped me. There I went, another person wrapped around Gilly Willis's perfect little finger.

She uncapped her pen so she could take notes. I stared at the back of her head. When she wrote, the tips of her curls bounced the way her shoulders did when she cried. It took me a moment to realize I'd actually agreed to a sleepover at Gilly Willis's house. It was another place where the memory of death lingered like thick, unspoken gossip.

Beck swore Gilly's house was haunted. Her mother and brother died there two years ago due to a gas leak in the basement. Nobody knew much about the details except that Jon and Gilly hadn't been there. Gilly had found them first, dead in their bedrooms.

It was the talk of the town for a while. People tried not to stare at Gilly when she returned to school after her hiatus, but it was near impossible. Death around here attracted people to one another like magnets— or maggots. It wasn't out of sympathy, just pure curiosity. Especially when the people didn't die peacefully in their sleep the way a lot of grandparents did.

But I wouldn't let Beck's ghost sounds or nagging steer me from my plans.

After school, I found Beck standing by Harry Newman's red car. She leaned against it, tapping her foot on the passenger-side tire. While Harry unlocked the car, Beck looked up and saw me.

"One second," she said to him, approaching me. "What's up?'

"I think I agreed to sleep over at Gilly Willis's house this weekend," I said.

Beck laughed, but my face stayed neutral. "You're serious?"

"Do I try to get out of it?" I asked.

"Yes," Beck said, then stopped. "Actually, no. I want you to tell me if you see any ghosts."

"Beck," I scolded.

"Why did you even agree to it?" Beck asked.

I honestly couldn't answer that. Maybe it was my pity for her after she had just lost one of her best friends, or maybe she intrigued me. Maybe, deep down, I was like everyone else and couldn't believe the most popular girl in school had invited *me* to her house.

I shrugged. Harry beeped the horn for Beck, and she held up her finger.

"I've got to go," Beck said. "I'll be expecting a full report on this sleepover."

I watched her rush off and sighed.

Once I found my bus, I took a seat alone and put on my headphones. Gilly's face materialized in my mind—how she'd looked in the woods the other night, defeated, sad, yet stonelike. The dark had enveloped her and lived in her curls.

My thoughts lingered on the way her hand felt on top of mine. I rubbed the spot she'd touched. Had Gilly Willis actually *flirted* with me? Or was I reading too much into it? I wasn't the best in the flirting department. I stared at my faint reflection in the bus window. Plain blue eyes that lacked pigment and bright, copper hair that frizzed around my face. I didn't see any ounce of Jessica Chastain like Gilly had told me the other night in the woods. Maybe she'd just wanted to be nice, but I couldn't help but shake the feeling that Gilly could be interested in me as more than a friend.

Suddenly, I was excited for our sleepover.

# CHAPTER FIVE

When Saturday came, I woke up to the smell of bacon and eggs. My mom had Saturdays off and made sure to fix up a full breakfast for us. Owen was already eating his second serving; my mom had saved me a plate knowing his appetite meant the food was at risk of disappearing. I poured maple syrup over my bacon and nearly lost my appetite when I noticed the ketchup all over Owen's eggs. His taste was heinous. Ketchup was meant solely for french fries—sometimes chicken tenders if no other sauce was available. He made it even worse when he squished the ketchup into the eggs, turning his plate into a massacre.

He chewed with his mouth partially open; I could never look at him during meals for too long without wanting to gag. Mom joined us, reading the newspaper with her reading glasses on. Marki Pickett's face was plastered on the front. That same warm-eyed photo of her from the memorial. Would they ever use anything else, or would Marki forever be remembered by that one picture on every anniversary of her death?

"Do you have any plans tonight?" Mom asked both of us.

Owen answered first, sloppily. "Matt wanted to know if I could come over?"

"That's fine," Mom said, flipping the page in the paper.

My mouth felt thick before I opened it. A rush of heat reached my face at the thought of Gilly. I was starting to get used to that feeling. Luckily, Mom's was covered by the waif newspaper.

"I think I'm going to sleep over at a friend's house tonight," I blurted.

Mom moved the paper slightly so I could see her suspicious face. "Which friend?"

"Gilly Willis," I said, shoving a forkful of eggs into my mouth.

"Gilly Willis?" Mom echoed with a blink. "The sheriff's daughter? I didn't know you two were friends."

"New friends," I said. "We have a project for English class to work on together, so she invited me to stay the night so we could work on it."

The lie slipped from my tongue so easily. I almost applauded myself at my composure but stifled my mischievous smile with a sip from my orange juice.

"Wasn't she friends with the girl who died?" Owen asked, a crumb of food flying from his mouth onto the kitchen table.

I scowled at him, for both the comment and his lack of table manners.

"She was," I said. "I assume she could use our homework as a distraction."

"I think that's a good idea," Mom said. "But don't bring up her friend."

"I won't," I said, rolling my eyes.

I quickly finished breakfast so I could prepare for my night with Gilly. I had plenty of time before I was meant to get to her house. I told her I'd be there at seven that evening. In my room, I emptied my bookbag on my bed and grabbed a pair of sweatpants and a shirt to bring. I studied my pajama choice and wondered if it was too plain. I wanted to impress Gilly, but I didn't own any that would be considered *cute*. I opted for a pale blue tank top instead of my oversized t-shirt. I packed a hairbrush and my toothbrush then zipped up my bag.

I busied myself with random things around my room to make the time pass. I doodled in my notebook, shot some rubber bands across the room, and even played a game of MASH with myself, where I inevitably married Gilly. We had four kids, two pet gerbils and lived in a bungalow off the coast of Fiji. I crumpled up the piece of paper and tossed it in my wastebasket. This crush on Gilly-effing-Willis would be my downfall. I hated that my delusions sucked me into the belief that maybe she shared the same attraction for me. Or was I merely intrigued? The argument played out in my head, but when I thought of her sandy hair and the way she smelled like flowers, I knew it went deeper than curiosity.

At 6:45 that evening, I grabbed my backpack and left the house with a quick "goodbye." I hopped on my bike in the garage, not bothering to ask Mom for a ride. I needed to work the nerves out of my stomach and figured working out my legs and breathing some fresh air would suffice. The breeze was cool against my skin, and the sky was painted in periwinkle and tangerine. Nothing could beat a Southern sunset. The sky was handcrafted for our landscape with trees that surrounded the town like a shield.

I turned off my street, peddling down the lonely sidewalk toward Gilly's neighborhood. Hers was larger than mine, but only a few minutes away by bike. She lived in a big gray-blue house with white shutters. The home matched her eyes, and I wondered if she had spawned from it instead of her mother. It was painted in sadness, and I tried not to think of the tragedy that befell her mom and brother. I couldn't imagine how I would feel if I lost Mom and Owen. It would break me.

Jon Willis's sheriff car was parked in the driveway of their house. I threw my bike on her lawn and quickly pulled out the deodorant I stashed in the side pocket. I lathered my pits again, then spritzed myself with a perfume Mom gave me because it smelled too spicy for her. I tightened my ponytail before I approached her front door. With my heart in my throat, I rang the doorbell.

Gilly answered wearing black shorts and a lavender tank top. Her hair was down and messier than usual. But even as she stood in the threshold of her door, I got a whiff of her perfume. It was tantalizing. She pulled me into her house by my wrist. The inside smelled like a tropical candle mixed with whatever food was in the oven.

"We're making dinner in the kitchen," Gilly said, taking my bag from me.

"Hey, Quinn," Jon Willis said, cutting up asparagus.

"Hi," I said, staring at him.

He was out of uniform, wearing a white shirt and jeans. Seeing him be a dad was odd; I'd only ever known him as the sheriff.

"I hope you like pork chops," Jon said.

"I do," I said.

Gilly went to flip the pork chops in the pan. The popping sizzle made me jump.

"Want to help peel the potatoes?" Jon asked.

"Sure," I said, setting down my bookbag.

I took the peeler and placed it against the rough brown potato skin. It took me a minute to get the hang of the peeler. When I finally did, it slipped and knicked my knuckle, causing blood to pop up. I sucked on my knuckle and looked at Gilly who watched it all happen. While Jon had his back turned to us, she quickly grabbed my arm, leading me out of the kitchen.

"Where are we going?" I asked.

"My bathroom," Gilly said. "Where the cute Band-Aids are."

The walls inside were burgundy, and her shower curtain was baby-pink. She had a sweet-smelling candle lit, and it cast a dim golden glow. I ran my hand under the cold sink water and let it numb my stinging knuckle. Gilly rummaged around underneath her sink until she found a Band-Aid. It was pink with a strawberry print. I blotted my knuckle on her hand towel and let her fasten the bandage.

"This is why I never cook," I said.

"I didn't take you for someone clumsy," Gilly teased.

She rubbed her fingertips across the Band-Aid on my knuckle a few times to make sure it stuck. Her fingers were gentle as she held my hand in hers. My heartbeat sped up, and for a moment, I forgot the pain. It was the closest I had ever been to Gilly. She was slightly taller than me, but I still got a perfect view of her lips. I could've sworn I saw her lean in, but the bathroom was dark, and our shadows swayed with the candlelight.

"Maybe I should stick to observing you cook," I said, looking away from Gilly finally.

"I'll meet you back down there," Gilly said. "I'm going to put your bag in my room."

I descended the stairs slowly, not wanting to be caught alone with Jon Willis for an extended period of time. I couldn't make small talk with adults. Especially when that adult was the town sheriff. I took an awkward seat at their kitchen table while Jon popped the asparagus in the oven.

"Your cut alright?" Jon asked, slinging a hand towel over his shoulder.

I nodded. "Nothing a Band-Aid couldn't fix."

"I couldn't tell you how many times I've cut myself trying to peel all kinds of vegetables," Jon said.

I forced a laugh as Gilly appeared back in the kitchen. She took over the potato peeling before chopping them into thick strips. The two worked around the other, seasoning and checking the oven. Neither said a word as they worked in unison. I noticed a picture on the wall and squinted to make it out better. It was a photo of Gilly with her parents and brother. It was probably only a couple years old, considering Gilly didn't look that much younger. She shared her dad's features: sandy blonde hair and blue eyes that were borderline gray. Her mother and brother were brunette but shared those blue eyes—except theirs were deeper, darker even, and held more depth. If Gilly's features had been darker, she would have looked identical to her mother.

"Quinn, want to help pour drinks?" Gilly asked. "Or do you think you'll get cut on an ice cube?" She grinned mischievously as she pulled cups from the cupboard.

"I think I can manage a little ice," I huffed.

She pulled the ice tray from the freezer for me, bumping into my side as she placed it in front of me along with the cups.

"Extra in mine, please," Gilly whispered. "I like mine super cold."

Her whisper sent a shiver down my spine. Luckily, I was still in my hoodie, so she couldn't see the goosebumps that littered my arms. I filled the cups with ice and the sweet tea Gilly had retrieved from the fridge. The ice clinked and cracked like bones. I took a slow sip from my glass, the sugary liquid making me smile.

"This is good sweet tea," I said.

"I made it," Gilly replied.

When Jon and Gilly finished cooking dinner, they sat the food around the table so we could each plate our own helpings. I placed one pork chop on my plate along with some asparagus and potato wedges. I wasn't a huge fan of asparagus but knew I'd feel bad if I didn't eat any. I could hear my mom nagging in my head that I needed to eat more vegetables.

The only sounds at the dinner table were our forks scratching the plates and ice clinking around glasses as we sipped our tea.

Every time I accidentally made eye contact with Jon, he smiled, the sides of his eyes crinkling.

"Quinn," Jon said. "How is school going for you?"

"Good," I replied. "Math is pretty boring though."

Gilly looked at the two of us, casually sipping her drink. I pleaded with my eyes for her to save me from the conversation.

"Math wasn't my strong suit either," Jon said, taking a big bite of pork chop.

"Dad," Gilly cut in, to my relief. "It's really nice out tonight. Are you okay with Quinn and I eating on the deck?"

"Sure," Jon said, shrugging. "I get it, I'll stay out of your hair."

I followed Gilly onto the deck, smiling at the cool night air. I was able to eat at a normal pace away from the suffocating kitchen. I let out a breath.

"That was brutal," Gilly chuckled.

"I don't know how to do small talk," I said.

"Because you like to observe more, right?"

Gilly's eyes bore into mine, reading me like a book. Normally, I was the one studying other people. When it was done to me, I wanted to retreat within myself like a turtle shrinking into its shell. She continued to eat her dinner, the last light of day holding on by a single sliver in the distance. Her yellow porchlight made her hair look even more golden.

"Why did you invite me over?" I asked.

"Because I like you," Gilly mumbled.

My eyes widened. Did she mean *like* like me? There was no way. This was Gilly Willis, the most popular girl in school.

"You barely know me," I said.

"So? I want to get to know you more."

"Why?"

Gilly laughed. "Why can't things just be, Quinn? You're interesting, so I want to get to know you more."

I intrigued her? This whole time it felt like the other way around. I finished off the last of my tea. Nobody had ever called me intriguing before, but the thought of Gilly being interested in me made my stomach do flips.

We finished our food and left the plates for Jon to clean after he told us to enjoy our night. Gilly's room was the last one in the hall. All the doors to the rooms were open except for the one next to Gilly's. I assumed it was her brother's room.

Gilly's room had pink walls and a yellow duvet like a strawberry-banana smoothie. A carousel piggy bank sat on her dresser, which was scattered with makeup, a hairbrush teetering on the edge of it. I scooted the hairbrush over, meeting my reflection in the mirror. Photobooth pictures of her, the twins, Sarai, and Marki were shoved into the sides of the mirror, held in place by random stickers of sparkly animals. Bedrooms revealed more about a person than anything else did.

"Was this what you expected my room to look like?" Gilly asked.

"Yes and no," I said. "It looks more lived in than I thought it would."

Gilly laughed. "I'm not that organized most of the time."

"What's your favorite thing about your bedroom?" I asked.

Gilly scanned her room. "The window nook. Sometimes I'll read there, but most of the time, I sit and watch outside."

I walked over to the nook and took a seat. I saw my bike in the grass and Jon's sheriff car on the dark street. Some kids chased each other, giggling and yelling while their parents called them into the house.

"I got questioned by the police yesterday," Gilly said.

She was on her bed with her knees tucked into her chest. The position made her look smaller.

"What did they ask you?" I asked. I didn't move from the nook; I wanted to give Gilly some space.

"Basically asked me how well I knew Marki and if anything was going on with her that was concerning."

"And you told them no?"

"I did," Gilly said. "She was the same Marki as before. . . . Anyway, I think they're trying to paint this narrative that Marki got herself into the position to be . . . killed. But I don't believe that."

"What do you believe?" I asked.

Gilly smiled. "I believe that death has no motive, whether it's by someone's hand or God or whatever higher power there is. Don't tell my daddy I said that though. He'd have a cow."

Gilly spoke like she'd lived on this earth more than once. She spoke with acceptance of things I'd fight against if the conversation presented itself. But I didn't want to argue with her. I knew I shouldn't push the conversation of Marki further, but like gossip, once you start, you can't stop.

"Have you heard anything else about Marki?" I asked. "I'm sure your dad has some sort of lead."

"He hasn't said anything to me," Gilly said. "He's afraid it will upset me, all the talk of death."

"Because of your mom and brother?" I asked, then bit my tongue. I shouldn't have brought it up.

Gilly nodded and sighed. She walked over to her dresser and reached underneath the carousel piggy bank. There was a small photograph of Gilly with her family. It was similar to the one on the wall downstairs.

"It's been two years, but sometimes I feel like Daddy thinks they died yesterday," Gilly said. "He's always been protective, but it's changed these last couple of years. Now he won't let me go anywhere except school for the most part."

"How did it happen again?" I asked. "If you're comfortable telling me."

I already knew how it happened; the whole town did. But I wanted to hear the words from Gilly herself and not assume I already knew like everyone else. I didn't want to be that to her.

"Gas leak," Gilly said. "They died within two hours of it happening. Dad and I had gone out of town for lunch with my uncle. Mom stayed home with a cold, and Justin had a wrestling match earlier that day, so he was too tired to go with us. Dad found them when we got home and nearly dragged me out of the house. I didn't see them, but I smelled the house. It's something I'll never forget."

My ears pricked at the part about her dad finding them. The story I knew was that Gilly found them, but I kept my mouth shut. If her way of coping with the tragedy was remembering it differently, then so be it.

"That's awful," I said.

Gilly put the photograph back under the carousel. "Thanks for not saying sorry. That's all anyone said to us for a year. Now I'm listening to it all over again with Marki."

She flopped back on her bed, arms and legs spread like a starfish, and stared at the ceiling.

"Beck is scared there's a serial killer," I said.

Gilly sat up. "Beck Wood?"

I nodded. "She's my best friend. We don't have too much in common though."

"But I feel like those relationships can be the best," Gilly said. "I don't feel like *we* have that much in common, yet I still want to be around you."

I tried not to smile too big. Not knowing what else to say, I asked, "Well, what's your favorite animal?"

"A fox. You?"

"Otter."

"Damn, this is never going to work," Gilly teased. She joined me by her window nook. As she pushed open the window, the cool September breeze blew in on us. Gilly shivered, scooting closer to me. We looked out into the now-empty street.

"I don't want to be scared," Gilly said. "Of this shit with Marki's murder . . . or anything else."

"What else scares you?" I asked.

She turned to face me, lips inches from mine again.

"The way I think I want to kiss you," she said evenly.

My stomach lurched up, stealing my words from me. Part of me wondered if I heard her correctly.

Gilly's eyes were a hue of cool. Looking into them, I saw an imprint of the tragic events that had happened in her blue-gray house. But I still found myself wanting to swim in them. I wanted to know the Gilly that existed before everything that had happened to her. I'd never thought about kissing her until that moment. Two days ago, it wouldn't have felt like a possibility. But now? I wanted nothing more than to know what her lips felt like pressed to mine.

She moved her hands to my cheeks. My skin was hot, but her hands were icy. She leaned in closer, not quite touching my lips.

"May I kiss you?" she asked.

I nodded, not breaking eye contact with her. She leaned in and pressed her lips flush against mine. It was just our lips touching for a moment. My arms stayed limp at my sides while Gilly's thumbs brushed my cheeks. When she pulled away, emotion flickered in her eyes: longing and understanding. I knew Gilly more than I had before.

We sat pressed against one another, staring out of her nook. At one point, our hands collided, fingers intertwined around the other's.

"I've never kissed a girl before," Gilly admitted. "You were my first."

"I'm honored," I said, smiling victoriously.

"Have you always known you liked girls?" she asked me.

I shrugged. "I think so. What about you?"

Gilly turned back to the street. "Once I figured out girls smelled better than boys, I was pretty much sold."

I laughed, genuinely, nearly tipping backward off the nook's bench. Gilly reached for me, pulling me back to her. I leaned in to kiss her again, but a knock on the door tore us apart. We both stood up, creating a gap between us that felt too far apart.

"Gilly," Jon said, throwing on his sheriff jacket in the now open doorway. "I have to go down to the station. We might've found something."

"Did the officers say what?" Gilly asked.

Jon looked at me, and I averted my eyes.

"Something like a hair clip," Jon said. "I'll be home later. Make sure everything is locked."

He closed the door behind him, stomping down their stairs. Gilly's face twisted in confusion, her chest heaving with adrenaline or nerves. I couldn't tell.

"Marki hated hair clips," Gilly said. "She never wore them. She said they tugged at her hair too much."

## CHAPTER SIX

The DNA on the hair clip came back inconclusive, but the police figured it had fallen off of Marki in the woods. According to Gilly, Marki didn't wear hair clips, but maybe she had that night. Or she'd had it in her pocket for some reason. A hair clip didn't mean anything if there was nothing to support it. But it opened a whole can of worms in school after word got around.

"Does that mean whoever killed Marki was a girl?" I heard someone in the cafeteria say.

"Do you think it was someone at school?" someone else asked.

"I bet it was one of those weirdos who live deep in the woods," said yet another person. "They hate trespassers."

The theories circulated. It was all anyone could talk about. The shock and grief of Marki's death left the school and was replaced by people talking about her as if she were a new conspiracy. Her humanity was stripped from her once again by those who were still alive to speak about it. I hated that she couldn't defend herself.

Nobody from Gilly's table was at lunch. I figured they found somewhere quiet to sit so they didn't have to listen to the ramblings about Marki's killer. Everyone masked their edge with theories. The police still hadn't made any arrests, and it stressed everyone out. My mom continued to check the locks on the doors and windows three times before bed and even convinced Owen and I to lock our bedroom doors as if someone was going to choose our house and come attack us in the middle of the night. With no confirmed specifics about Marki's death, mom's paranoia had gotten worse. What little we knew wasn't comforting either. All anyone knew was she was stabbed and found in the woods.

"Are you going to the game Friday night?" Beck asked, gnawing on a french fry.

"You know I don't care about football," I said.

"Yes, I know that," Beck sighed, "but a lot of people are going, and it might be good. It might make things feel normal again."

"Do you want me to go with you?" I asked.

"Yes," Beck said. "It'll make me feel better getting out of the house. Harry said he could drive us."

"Are you two dating now?" I asked.

I pictured Harry Newman in his letterman jacket and fluffy brunette hair. He wasn't as much of an idiot as some of the other jocks, but he was still a jock. I couldn't picture him and Beck ever being a couple.

"He just gives me rides," Beck said. "Besides, I've known him since we were kids when he'd shoot me with his stupid water guns. He owes me for all the years of torment."

"As long as I'm not third-wheeling," I huffed.

"Invite Gilly," Beck said. "Speaking of, how was that sleepover?"

A flash of Gilly's lips came to my mind. The familiar flush crept back as I relived our first kiss.

"It was fine," I said. "Normal, I guess."

"That's all I get?" Beck said. "You go to the haunted old Willis house, and all you tell me is it was normal?"

Beck folded her hands together, staring into my soul to break me.

"Gilly kissed me," I blurted, shoving food in my mouth.

Beck dropped her pudding cup. "No shit."

"Keep it down," I said.

Beck's mouth fell open. "You kissed Gilly-fucking-Willis. The girl who color-codes her notes and always raises her hand in class?"

"Yes, that one," I deadpanned. "Thank you for the reminder."

Beck continued to stare at me while I ate.

"Stop looking at me like that," I whispered.

"I'm just in shock," Beck said. "I didn't know she was even your type."

"I don't have a type."

"Kirsten Dunst?"

I blinked. "You got me there."

"Anyway," Beck said, "come to the football game on Friday. We can pick you up at your house. And your new girlfriend."

I threw a grape at her. "Fine. But she's not my girlfriend."

"Yet," Beck said with a smirk.

In English class, I waited for Gilly. My legs shook under my desk; I tried not to stare as she appeared in the doorway. *My girlfriend.* I quickly brought myself down to earth. No, no, no. We had *just* kissed. Just hung out for the first time. We couldn't move that fast, right?

I watched her say goodbye to Sarai in the hallway, then saunter in, a pale floral skirt swaying around her legs. Her sandals clicked on the tile floor, and I scooted my sneakered feet under the desk.

"Hey," Gilly said, brushing her arm against mine.

"Do you want to go to the football game with me on Friday?" I blurted.

Her eyes widened as she took her seat.

I continued, more calmly. "I'm going with Beck and Harry Newman. I just figured I'd ask. I don't want to be a third wheel and all. I understand if that's not your thing."

Gilly smiled at me, pink lip glossed lips curving up at the corners. "I'm already going with Alma, Jen, and Sarai."

"Oh," I said. "Right. That makes sense."

"But can we meet at the game?" Gilly suggested. "We can all stand together on the bleachers."

"Sounds good," I said, returning the smile.

She turned around and ripped a piece of notebook paper from her journal, folding it and doodling. We still had a few minutes before class truly began. I sat back and tried to peer over her shoulder but could only make out her assortment of pens in a line on her desk. When she finished, she turned back to me, a fortune teller stuck to her fingers.

"Pick a color," she said, flashing the four colored circles on the top of the fortune teller.

"Blue," I said.

Her fingers moved back and forth as she spelled out *blue* in her head.

"Now pick a number."

"Three."

She moved the fortune teller three times before showing me another set of numbers.

"Seven," I said, as it was a lucky number.

She moved it seven times. "Last number," she said.

"Three again."

She opened the flap with the number three on it and smiled down at her own writing.

"It says you will live a long and happy life."

"Do another," I said. "Two this time."

She unfolded the "two" slot, and I could've sworn I caught her cheeks blushing a darker shade of pink.

"You will receive a kiss from Gilly Willis this Friday night at the football game," she read.

The bell rang, signaling the start of class. Gilly turned away from me, leaving the last words hanging in the air. Butterflies erupted in my stomach. Our second kiss? In public? Maybe I wasn't reading too far into this.

After school, I walked to the bus lot and sighed. I wasn't in the mood to ride the bus with its sticky seats and sweaty air. I walked around the school to the bleachers, finding Beck smoking with another boy. I didn't know his name and didn't feel like learning it.

"Are you riding home with Harry today?" I asked.

"Yes," Beck said, blowing smoke away from me. "He has to make up a quiz first, so it'll be about half an hour."

"Think I can convince him to take me home?" I asked.

Beck raised a brow. "No bus?"

"I'm not in the mood."

Beck handed the rest of the joint to the boy and stood to grab her bookbag.

"Sure," Beck said. "Let's go wait for him."

We walked back into school. It was a ghost town at that point of the day. Some teachers left; others stayed to catch up on work. There were only about five students we passed who were leaving late for the day. We stopped in front of the classroom where Harry was making up his quiz. It was Civics class, and the door was open. Beck stood in the doorway, making faces at Harry to throw him off. He held up his middle finger when the teacher wasn't looking, then got back to his quiz.

"Did you ask Gilly about the game?" Beck asked.

"She's going with Sarai and the twins," I said. "But she said we could meet up with them."

"I'm not sure if I can handle hanging out with all of them," Beck muttered.

I rolled my eyes. "We just have to stand next to Gilly. You and Harry can stand on the other side of me."

"*Fine*," Beck said. "But I get to call when we leave."

"Deal." I handed her my bookbag. "I'm going to the bathroom."

I turned down the hallway, pushing against the bathroom door. There was someone in one of the stalls, so I chose the one furthest from them.

"It all seems fishy to me," a girl said, although I couldn't pinpoint who the voice belonged to. It sounded familiar.

I listened intently, holding my breath to make my presence less known. I stood in the stall, peering through the lock when the girl emerged from the stall. It was Alma.

"All I'm saying, Sarai, is she was supposed to come study with us that night and didn't show up," Alma said over the phone. "The same night she would've been killed."

I tried listening through the sound of the sink water rushing.

"I don't know where she disappeared to," Alma continued. "She told me she would walk over around seven and then never showed. I tried calling her house, but she wasn't home. There's no way she wasn't kidnapped."

The word made my heart skip a beat.

"I don't know who would've kidnapped her," Alma said. "Probably just some weirdo. Unless it was Vance or whoever she was messing around with at the time."

I steadied my breathing.

"Sarai, calm down," Alma said. "Jon will protect us." Seconds later, she left the bathroom.

I opened the stall door, no longer feeling the urge to go. Vance Luther was a football player, that much I knew about him. We had algebra together. I never saw him with Marki, and I remembered how Gilly said Marki wasn't the type to hook up. I knew better than that. I wondered if Alma had told Jon Willis what I'd just overheard. I debated relaying the information to Gilly when I saw her next, but thought better of it. It wasn't my place.

I met back up with Beck just as Harry stepped out of the classroom, his bookbag slung over one shoulder.

"Can you also take Quinn home?" Beck asked.

"Sure," he said.

We walked out of the school, and I looked for Alma, but she had disappeared.

For the football game, I wore what I had of our school colors: red, gold, and white. I had one spirit shirt from middle school that still fit. When Harry arrived with Beck to pick me up, she handed me a gold bandanna, which I tied around my arm. Beck had red-and-gold glitter under her eyes, the most school spirited I'd ever seen her. Harry, as always, wore his basketball letterman jacket. He had on a gold bandanna I concluded Beck had forced him to wear.

Once we got to school and paid for our tickets, I glanced around, heart jumping at each head of hair I thought might belong to Gilly. The last time I hung out with her, she kissed me—and according to my fortune, I would receive another from her tonight.

"Quinn! Up here!" Gilly called from the bleachers.

She was in the middle of the crowd of students. Like Beck, she and her friends were covered in glitter.

"Gilly," I greeted as we squeezed through to reach her. "You know Beck and Harry?"

Harry threw up his hand, and Beck smiled forcefully.

"Hey! And nice middle school spirit shirt," Gilly said, nudging my arm.

"How did you know?" I asked.

"I remember when they sold them at football games in eighth grade," Gilly said. "It looks cute on you."

My cheeks burned, so I turned to the field and cheered, pretending I had a clue what was going on in the game. Sports were not my forte; Beck tried explaining certain things to me, but the cheering or booing of the crowd drowned her out. At halftime, we sat down, watching the band and cheerleaders do their routine.

"Be right back," Sarai said. "I'm going to get some water. Do any of you want anything?"

We all shook our heads. After a few moments of watching the cheerleaders' stunts, I changed my mind.

"Actually, I am kind of hungry," I said. "I'm going to get a snack."

I waited to see if Gilly would follow me, the promise of our second kiss a lingering thought. She didn't, and with no way to convey that all I wanted was for her to come with me, I left her behind. I pulled out the wad of cash in my pocket; I guessed I would have to buy a snack after all.

I watched my step, careful not to trip on the bleachers. There were parents standing around and mingling while teens bought weed by the brick wall of the stadium.

The line for concessions was long, so I watched the crowd while I waited for it to let up. Some middle schoolers chased one another while others stood around eating snacks, not paying an ounce of attention to what happened on the field.

I looked around some more and found Sarai by the gate, talking to Jon Willis. He was in uniform, his hat off and smiling at Sarai. She giggled and twisted her hair while she looked up at him. They talked, but I couldn't make out anything they said. Her body language—and how she leaned against the gate—made me doubt their conversation had anything to do with Marki Pickett.

I almost moved to eavesdrop or stop the conversation from progressing, but I stayed in line, observing them. As much as I wanted to drag my eyes away from the horrific sight, I couldn't. Soon the line grew shorter, and I lost my line of vision to the pair. I ordered a pretzel, trying to peer over the people while I waited for it. All I caught was a glimpse of Sarai walking back to the bleachers.

When I got back, Sarai sipped her water as if she hadn't just been flirting with her best friend's dad. The thought of Jon Willis feeding into it repulsed me. I couldn't imagine how uncomfortable it would have made Gilly feel if she'd seen Sarai practically drooling over her dad. I ate my pretzel sitting down while everyone around me watched the game once it resumed.

The crowd erupted, nearly sending my pretzel out of my hand.

"That's a touchdown for number twenty-eight, Vance Luther," the announcer called from the loudspeaker.

Vance Luther ran toward his teammates, getting high-fives. I looked over at Gilly's group. Alma nudged Sarai and motioned toward the field while they clapped. Gilly and Jen didn't notice. I stood up, leaving my pretzel carton on the floor of the bleachers.

I realized I didn't belong there. My stomach churned at the thought of Sarai flirting with Jon Willis. The whole situation had me out of sorts and Gilly seemed too into the game to pay me any more attention.

"I know you said you'd decide when we go, but I think I've had enough of the game," I said to Beck.

"We've already made it to the third quarter," Beck said. "Let's just stick it out."

"I'll just call my mom to come get me," I said, turning to Gilly's friends. "Do any of you have a phone with you?"

"I do," the twins said at the same time.

My brain spun as they both pulled them out.

"Use Alma's," Jen said. "She has more battery."

I took Alma's phone and hopped off the bleachers. I dialed my mom and asked her to come get me, promising I'd meet her in the parking lot. When she hung up, Alma's call log glowed on her phone. The top few calls were to Sarai, but two other calls caught my eye: a call to Jon Willis that had happened recently, and another call to Marki Pickett, which, by the looks of it, had been to her cellphone. The call was nine seconds long—and according to the police reports, around the time she would've been murdered.

## CHAPTER SEVEN

I rotted in a pool of my own nerves as I thought about Alma's call log. Police ruled Marki had died around 10:36 p.m. The call on Alma's phone was at 10:35 p.m. that same night. Was it possible Marki picked up before she was killed? Did Alma hear anything? If she had, her continuous poker face amazed me. I tried to steady my breathing.

The call to Jon Willis didn't alarm me as much. I knew Gilly didn't have a cellphone. But the call to Marki wouldn't leave my mind. I wanted to confront her about it, but she could turn it around and confront me for snooping through her call log even if it had been an accident. She did, after all, let me call my mom.

"I'm torn between saying 'this is crazy, Quinn' and 'calm down, Nancy Drew,'" Beck said to me.

I'd invited her over, and like always, she took over my bed, holding on to one of my pillows.

"Did you hear me?" I waved my hands in exasperation. "That call was made right before Marki *died*."

"Yes, I hear you Quinnie," Beck said, sitting up on my bed. "I'm processing it all."

"Alma has to know something," I said.

"Or the call was a dead end," Beck countered. "If the call picked up for those few seconds, whoever killed Marki probably hung up when they saw the call had connected. Or the call just failed."

"Wouldn't Alma have called back?" I asked.

"Not necessarily. She was probably annoyed that Marki hadn't come over. And if she heard something, it probably would have been a groan. It would have sounded like pleasure instead of pain to Alma. Nobody's first thought in this town is that their friend is being murdered."

Beck had a point. I picked at my cuticles—a habit I leaned into when I was antsy—and joined Beck on my bed. A pinboard appeared in my head connecting the elements of this murder, and I itched with the need to know—to snoop.

"Let the police handle it," Beck said. "Curiosity always kills the cat."

I laid back on my bed in silent agreement, staring at the ceiling. "I'm bored," I said, after a moment.

"Any interest in renting a movie?" Beck asked.

"Pizza and movie night?" I suggested.

"Fuck *yes*," Beck said, flying off the bed.

Borrowing Owen's bike, we headed to the movie store. I had a wad of ones in my pocket to rent the movie. Owen promised to order the pizza for us as long as we let him have some. The deal was made, and I hoped Owen wouldn't order a pizza with olives the way he always did.

Between the rows of movies at Karson's, we played rock, paper, scissors to see who got to pick the genre. Beck won and waltzed over to the horror section.

"Do we want gore, psychological thriller, or paranormal?" she asked.

"Whatever you want," I said.

She disappeared behind an aisle while I busied myself looking at other movies. Karson's was old; most of the movie names were taped to the side or written in Sharpie. I heard giggling from behind the aisle next to mine and peered around the corner. Alma stood next to Vance Luther. He held her waist, hands trailing down to her butt, and I cringed. Why would she be with him after what she said on her phone call with Sarai?

"Come on, Alma," Vance said, "let's go for a drive and skip the movie."

"But I really want to watch one," Alma whined.

"Why don't we compromise," Vance said. "We can watch a movie, but then we go for a drive. I know a cool spot."

"Deal," Alma said, pecking him on the lips.

The hair on the back of my neck stood at the thought of Vance killing Alma. Did she suspect him? If she did, why was she with him? Didn't she mention Marki hooking up with him? Boy-swapping friends never made any sense to me.

"I'll go pick out some candy while you look," Vance said.

Alma nodded and looked through the movies. This was my chance. I approached her, pretending to check out a movie a row down from her. When she didn't notice me, I cleared my throat.

"Hi Alma," I said, throwing my hand up.

"Quinn!" Alma said. "What's up?"

"Just here with Beck to get a movie," I said. "And you?"

"Surprisingly, I'm here with Vance Luther." Alma grinned. "You know, the football player. He scored a touchdown on Friday."

"Right, him," I said, wanting nothing more than to roll my eyes at her gloating.

I ran my finger along one of the movie spines while Alma smiled at me. She was too polite to tell me to piss off.

"Alma, can I ask you something . . . confidential?" I asked.

"Sure?" She took a step back from me.

"I heard you talking in the bathroom the other day," I said. "You mentioned Marki and . . . Vance."

Alma froze for a moment, then laughed almost mechanically. "You heard that? God, I didn't think anyone was in there with me. I didn't mean anything by it. I think it was just jealousy."

Jealous? Of her dead friend? She tried to walk away from me, but I stopped her again.

"I saw your call log," I admitted. "When I used your phone at the game. When my mom hung up."

"What about it?" Alma asked, her tone sharpening.

"I saw a nine second call from Marki the night she died," I said. "Alma, if you heard anything—"

"Listen," Alma said, not letting me finish. "You need to keep your nose out of mine and my friends' business. I understand you and Gilly are 'friends' now, but that doesn't make you mine. You aren't one of us. So keep your mouth shut."

I grabbed her wrist without thinking, and she halted.

"Alma, if you know anything you need to tell Jon Willis," I began, looking into her eyes, hoping to communicate some sense into her.

She shook out of my grip. "Freak," she mumbled as she walked away.

My skin grew hot at the word. I wasn't the one who was on a date with my dead friend's ex. Now *that* was freakish behavior. I felt bad for interrogating her, but I couldn't let the questions simmer anymore. I could only hope what happened between Alma and me wouldn't get back to Gilly.

"Ready?" Beck called from somewhere behind me.

"Yeah," I said. "Let's get the movie and go."

Back home, the pizzas had already arrived; Owen was kind enough to order Beck and I our own without the nasty olives he preferred. Beck handed me her movie of choice, *Final*

*Destination 2*, and I put it on. Owen joined us. I focused more on the pizza than the movie. What would I tell Beck about Alma? I knew she would scold me, and I also didn't want to escalate the situation anymore. Hopefully, the moment would stay at Karson's.

About halfway through the movie, there was a frantic knock on the front door.

"Not it," Owen said, touching his nose.

I groaned, pausing the movie, and stomped to the door. I opened it to find Jen, fist raised as if she was about to knock again. Gilly stood next to her, arms on her shoulders. My body grew cold, already aware of where this was going.

"Do you know where my sister is?" Jen asked, tears pooling in her eyes.

"Why would I know where your sister is?" I asked.

"Alma said she ran into you at Karson's," Jen said. "Did she say where she was going?"

Jen's hands shook slightly, and I hated that she was left to worry. Alma was probably fine and not answering because she was locking lips with Vance.

"I don't know," I said. "I overheard Vance say he wanted to take her to a secret spot or something. Did she not tell you?"

"I left for Gilly's before she told me," Jen said. "I tried calling her, but she hasn't answered."

"Do you know where he takes girls he hooks up with?" I asked.

"The only place I know of is the woods," Jen said. "But there's no way she would go there. That's where they found Marki!"

"Maybe she's not exactly in the woods," I said. "Vance does have a car."

Jen gasped and grabbed my hand, pulling me out of the door and toward her car.

"Where are you taking me?" I spluttered, pulling back.

"You're coming with us," Jen said. "I need a witness when I castrate him."

"But Beck is here!"

Beck appeared in the doorway, squinting to see who I was talking to. She threw up her hands, as if to ask where the hell I was going as Jen and Gilly practically kidnapped me.

"We are going to castrate Vance Luther!" Jen called.

"Shit, that's cool," Beck said. "Let me put my shoes on."

I rode in the backseat with Gilly while Beck awkwardly tried to talk to Jen from the passenger side. Gilly stared at me until I finally glanced at her. She smiled.

"Hi," she said. "I tried to say it earlier, but it's hard getting a word in with Jen."

"Is she actually going to castrate Vance Luther?" I asked.

"She's all talk," Gilly said. "She's protective of Alma."

Jen drove carefully but with purpose. Gilly silently slipped her hand into mine, clearly not wanting to make a big deal out of it. While Beck and Jen fell into conversation about their shared hatred for their world history teacher, Gilly leaned in to whisper in my ear.

"I'm sorry your fortune didn't come true at the football game."

Her warm breath made my ear tingle. "I wanted it to," I whispered back.

"Next time, don't leave early," she said.

She slid away from me, checking out my lips before returning her gaze to the window. I steadied my breath as Gilly rubbed circles on the back of my hand with her thumb.

We pulled into the parking lot at school. Jen whipped into a spot, crooked, and got out. We all followed her as she ran across the field to the edge of the woods. Sure enough, there was a car running with its low lights on. Stupid mistake. The police would find them and bust them in a second if they drove by.

"Hey!" Jen yelled, approaching the car.

Alma emerged from the car, shirt hanging off her shoulder, with Vance practically stuck to her side. She pushed him. "Get off of me, you prick."

Vance lost his footing, snapping a "Bitch!" as he fell.

"Do *not* call my sister a bitch," Jen fumed.

She went to Alma and pulled her away from Vance. It was like watching one of those reality shows.

"What are you doing here?" Alma asked.

"You didn't answer, and I got worried," Jen said. "Come on. We're sleeping at Gilly's tonight."

Jen walked Alma to the car. Alma looked at me once but didn't react. Beck, Gilly, and I watched Vance scramble to get up.

"Marki was so much easier!" he sneered.

Everyone froze. My mouth fell open as I watched Alma and Jen turn around. Gilly was the only one to react. She marched up to Vance and punched him square in the face. I swear I heard a crack as her fist made contact with his nose.

Vance whaled like a baby. "My nose!"

"*Never* speak about Marki ever again," Gilly said.

She walked past me and turned with a stern expression. "Let's go."

Beck and I stared at one another, amazed at what we'd just witnessed. We left Vance to clutch his bloody nose and scramble to get into his car. The car ride was silent except for Alma who complained about Vance the entire ride. She never directed anything at me.

I sat in the middle of Beck and Gilly. Gilly stared out the window with her arms crossed, knuckles red from where they'd collided with Vance's face. I wanted to reach out and hold her hand, but knew better than to bother her. Never once had I imagined Gilly as someone who would punch a football player in his face. On the surface, she was so pretty and put together. Clearly, I didn't know her as well as I wanted to.

Back home, after an awkward car ride, Beck and I locked the door and slid onto the couch. Owen had finished the movie without us and fallen asleep, snoring.

"I didn't realize how crazy they were," Beck whispered. "I take back everything I said. I love them."

Not too long after, another knock on the door sparked my annoyance, and I debated taping a sign outside that demanded nobody bother us. I opened the door to find Gilly illuminated by Jen's headlights.

"Sorry. In the car . . . I needed a moment," Gilly said. "I just want to make sure you're okay."

I stepped out so I could face her better. "I could say the same for you. How're your knuckles?"

Gilly rubbed them and shrugged. "I didn't want you to view me differently. I've never done anything like that, but hearing him talk about Marki like that got me so mad."

"I would've done the same," I said.

Gilly stepped closer to give me a kiss on the cheek before jogging back to Jen's car. My lips ached. I wanted Gilly to kiss me again, fully. I watched them leave before closing the door and turning off the porchlight. No more visitors tonight; it was for the best.

# CHAPTER EIGHT

Vance had a bandage on his nose come Monday—Gilly had indeed broken it. He seemed pissed all through algebra. Whenever Beck or I accidentally caught his stare, he looked as if he could kill us.

"Damn, she really did a number on him," Beck whispered. "I didn't know she had it in her."

"Adrenaline," I replied, still staring at the equations on the board.

The remainder of the weekend, I thought about Gilly and I's first kiss—and the lack of a second one. She kissed my cheek, but it didn't feel the same. We didn't have plans to see each other outside of school, and I couldn't help but wonder if that one night was all she and I would ever get. It put me in a bad mood; all I wanted was to see her and get some kind of confirmation that "us" wouldn't just cease to exist.

At lunch, I sat with Beck and spotted Gilly with her knuckles bandaged. When she saw me, she waved but made no move to leave her table with her friends. She turned her attention back to whatever story Sarai was in the middle of.

To my surprise, Alma approached our table a few minutes later. She took a seat next to Beck, who stared at her like she had two heads.

"Quinn," Alma said, "I wanted to say I was sorry for calling you a freak. I was wrong."

"It's fine," I said.

And yet, she still didn't say a word about the call made to Marki. She nodded, satisfied with my answer before getting up, not acknowledging Beck. She left the table to join her friends again.

"Did I miss a chapter, Nancy Drew?" Beck asked.

"I may have confronted Alma when we went to Karson's," I said. "I saw her and Vance together."

"About the call log?" Beck asked.

I nodded, biting into my sandwich while I waited for Beck to yell at me for not telling her.

"I told you to let Jon Willis handle it," Beck said. "You can't go around talking crazy. It'll give people the wrong idea."

"What? You think people will suspect that I killed Marki?"

"I don't know." Beck gave a helpless shrug. "But Lisa Crest has already been ostracized in biology because of her roadkill obsession. People say she probably did it because of that."

I didn't respond. I couldn't let Beck know she had a point.

"What did Alma say when you asked her about it?" Beck asked.

"She told me to keep out of her business," I said. "And just now, she didn't even acknowledge the call log."

"That's suspicious."

"I'm not going to worry about it anymore." I looked down at my food. "She's never going to tell me about it."

Gilly laughed at her table, a genuine one, and it made me smile, but a sting of jealousy quickly followed. I wanted to be the one to make her laugh like that.

In English class, Gilly took her usual seat in front of me, turning to begin the class with a conversation. It had become our usual routine. I closed the notebook I doodled in to give her my full attention.

"On Saturday, Sarai is having a kickback at her house," Gilly said. "A few people we know are going, and I wanted to see if you and Beck would want to come?"

I thought about it for a moment. Hanging out in a small space with Gilly sounded like a great idea, but I wasn't so sure about her friends. Granted, it was the "in" I had waited all weekend for. Maybe we would finally get our second kiss.

"We'll be there," I said, fiddling with my pencil. I hoped Beck would agree to it because there was no way I could go alone.

"Cool," Gilly said. "I really want you to come.

"Oh, really?" I pressed, leaning forward.

"Yes."

Gilly reached for my hand and stroked her fingers along the top. I focused more on her pearly pink polish than the bandages covering her knuckles. I almost brought up Vance and his broken nose, but the bell rang. Gilly turned from me to focus on today's assignment, and my hand grew cold where her fingers had been seconds ago.

Beck was game for the kickback and came over to get ready with me on Saturday. She put eyeliner on me while I lazily brushed through my hair.

"Hold still," she said. "You'll smudge it."

"Well, hurry up," I said. "I can't sit here any longer."

When she was satisfied with her work, she set down the eyeliner pencil. She reached into her bag and pulled out a black tank top, which she threw at me. The fabric hit my face in a heap.

"Wear it," Beck said. "You'll look hot."

I put it on, self-conscious about how it hugged my frame. Beck made an *ooh* sound and fluffed my hair with her fingers. I stuck on a silver necklace and applied a small bit of lip gloss. I blotted most of it off because I couldn't stand the sticky feeling. I did one last take in the mirror. I actually felt pretty with my makeup done and hair out of its normal ponytail. I was excited for Gilly to see me like this.

Jen picked us up. Alma and Gilly were already in the car. I sat in between Beck and Gilly, getting a whiff of that familiar perfume.

"You look really pretty," Gilly whispered to me.

She had on a yellow top and jeans. Her hair was in a half-up hairstyle, held in place by a banana clip. Her lips sparkled, and I could almost feel them against my own. I had a plan to get her alone somewhere in the party and make the next move.

"So do you," I said, staring at her lips.

She smiled and slid her hand into mine as Jen drove off. Sarai's house was near Gilly's. It was a big half-brick house with black shutters. Lights in the lawn shone directly on the house, almost as if to prove its importance.

"Who will be here?" I asked.

"People," Gilly said, leading me out of the car. "But don't worry. I'll stay close to you."

Inside Sarai's house, pop music played and people I'd never seen drank from red cups. Most people sat around and talked while others made their rounds. Sarai approached us with two drinks in her hands, screaming when she saw her friends. She sloppily hugged Alma, Jen, and Gilly. Her chocolate hair was pinned back, and she had on a baby-blue dress. She was already past tipsy.

"Come in and mingle," Sarai said far too happily.

We walked in, and I immediately tensed up from the amount of people in the house. I found a spot on an empty chair, with Gilly and Beck following close behind me.

"Do you want a drink?" Gilly asked.

"If you can find a soda, I'd rather have that," I said.

Gilly noted my request and disappeared to find me a drink. Beck sat on the arm of the chair.

"Beck?" someone asked.

He approached us, long hair tied back in a low bun and a long-sleeve shirt on.

"Rink!" Beck said. "I didn't know I'd see you at your stepsister's party."

"I didn't think I'd see you at a party like this . . . ever." Rink smirked.

"Have you met Quinn?" Beck asked.

I recognized Rink as one of the people Beck smoked with under the bleachers sometimes. He was a senior. I waved to him.

"You two want to smoke?" Rink asked.

"Sure," Beck said.

"I won't smoke, but I'll come outside," I said, relieved to get away from the crowd.

I bumped into Gilly, who handed me a can of ginger ale.

"Where are you going?" Gilly asked.

"Outside with Beck and Rink," I said. "Want to come with us?"

"Maybe later," Gilly said. "I'm going to go hangout with Sarai for a little bit."

My heart sinking, I left to follow Beck and Rink to the backyard. The air was chilly, causing goosebumps to arise on my skin. Beck noticed and handed me her flannel. Rink had set up a water bottle contraption to smoke out of. I studied the mechanics as he lit it. He smoked first, not coughing once, and Beck followed. I looked out into the backyard. Darkness and trees covered a majority of the space. I took a seat on one of the chairs, sipping my ginger ale. The chill made me want something warm, but I doubted anyone drank hot chocolate at parties.

"How does it feel to be Sarai's stepbrother?" I asked.

Rink blew out a puff of smoke. "It happened around ten years ago. I honestly sometimes forget we're stepsiblings. She's always felt like my real sister, surprisingly. We're different, but it's nice that way."

"She can be a lot sometimes," Beck said.

"For sure," Rink laughed. "That whole group is trouble."

Rink took another hit from the water bottle, ignoring the weight his words held.

"What do you mean they're trouble?" I asked.

"Not to be sexist," Rink began, "but there's something about girl groups in high school that radiates trouble. I've been around them all enough to see it. I think they love each other, but you know how it can be. Everyone's insecure at sixteen. Everyone is always looking twice at one another. That's how it goes."

"Wow," Beck said. "Weed makes you smart."

Rink blew smoke right in her face. I sipped my ginger ale slowly. Marki and Alma . . . both of them seemingly had flings with Vance. The phone call between Alma and Sarai entered my mind next, along with Alma's call log. The urge to ask Gilly about it rose again, but I swallowed it down with my ginger ale. It wasn't my place to say anything—even if I desperately wanted to.

A girl slid the door open. Her brunette pixie cut was splattered with shades of aquamarine. She wore a black sweater, and I cursed myself for not thinking to bundle up.

"Christine," Rink said. "Want to smoke?"

"You know I do," she said, approaching us.

She took the water bottle before she even acknowledged Beck and me.

"Beck, right?" she said, blowing smoke.

Beck nodded. "And that's Quinn."

I raised my ginger ale to say hello. She smirked when she saw the soda but kept smoking.

"Needed to escape?" Rink asked.

"You know I can only handle crowds in bursts," Christine said. "She's with the other girls anyway."

"Good luck getting her away from them," Rink said.

"I was the one having to make the grand escape," Christine said. "She's drinking, so she's being clingy."

Christine pulled up a seat next to me. I wanted to scoot further away, unsure of how I felt about her yet.

"How's Jen doing anyway?" Rink asked.

I stopped sipping my ginger ale to listen closer.

"Fine, I guess," Christine said. "We just started seeing each other. You know it's nothing serious."

"I know," Rink said. "But she loves to talk."

I stayed outside with Beck while they smoked some more. I actually liked the smell of the chilly air mixed with the weed. It was a smell I associated with Beck.

Sarai broke the silence when she opened the door. "Some of us want to play a game, y'all. Come to the den."

After Rink threw the ashes out, we all went inside. He led us to the den, which had a couple of bean bags, chairs, and a long couch. Gilly patted the open spot beside her, and I took a seat. Beck sat with Rink on a giant bean bag. Christine joined Jen, who kissed her on the cheek. Alma and Sarai sat together, snuggling on the far end of the couch.

"What game does everyone want to play?" Rink asked.

"Never have I ever," Sarai said, making Alma giggle into her hair.

"Five fingers up, then," Rink said.

I held my hand up, planning to target Beck to get her out. Judging by her facial expression, she had the same idea.

"I'll start!" Sarai sang. "Never have I ever kissed a girl."

Everyone except Alma and Sarai put their finger down. Beck and I met eyes and giggled. We had been each other's first kiss when we were seven. We played "wedding" in Beck's garage and kissed every time we said, "I do." It went on for a month until her parents yelled at us for kissing. Beck liked to tease that I made her realize she liked boys; I always fired back that she made me realize I liked kissing any girl *but* her.

"Never have I ever smoked weed," Alma said.

Beck, Christine, and Rink put a finger down. I followed, remembering the time I tried to smoke with Beck but nearly coughed up a lung after one hit.

"Never have I ever lied to my friends," Christine said.

Everyone except Christine put a finger down.

"That's such a lie!" Jen said. "There's no way you've never lied to your friends."

Christine shrugged. "That's all I could think of."

I studied Christine and her body language. She seemed tense, trying her best to scoot away from Jen, but it didn't work. Something about what she said rubbed me the wrong way, as if she was trying to accuse someone without actually saying it. I didn't like pot-stirrers. I nearly missed what Gilly said due to my concentration on Christine.

"Never have I ever been in a relationship," Gilly said.

Everyone except Gilly and I put our finger down. We looked at one another. She smiled, and my face heated up. Had that been Gilly's subtle hint for me to make a move? I seriously needed to get some alone time with her.

"Never have I ever been drunk," I said.

Christine, Rink, and I were the only three who didn't put our fingers down.

"Don't you dare target me," Beck threatened Rink.

She had one finger left. Rink looked at me, and I nodded, wanting him to get her out. Watching Beck lose games was funny.

"Never have I ever been inside Beck's house," Rink said.

She slapped him on the arm, angry at being the first one out. I put my finger down and so did Gilly.

Beck's eyes locked on Gilly's hand. "When have you been to my house?"

"It was a long time ago," Gilly said. "My mom worked with your dad, and I guess she had to get paperwork from him this one time."

"Wait, I remember," Beck said. "End of middle school. You still had braces."

"Hey, they're gone now," Gilly said, flashing straight white teeth.

This made Beck go into a frenzy of laughter, taking Rink along with her.

"I need chips!" she said suddenly, clambering to her feet.

Rink followed her—probably to make sure she found the pantry—thus making him the second person out.

"I'm not waiting on him," Sarai sighed. "Never have I ever walked in on my parents, doing . . . you know."

Alma and Sarai giggled. Gilly and Jen were the only two to put their finger down. Gilly seemed to shut down at the mention of parents. All of her fingers were down, leaving Alma, Christine, Sarai, and I in the game.

"When did you walk in on Mom and Dad?" Alma asked Jen.

The two went back and forth about how Jen walked in on their parents when she was ten. Alma grew offended that her twin never told her. I watched Gilly, switching my hands so I could hold her free one. When she noticed, she smiled, and a sparkle returned to her eye. Jen slumped back and folded her arms.

"Never have I ever been named Sarai," Alma said.

Sarai pushed her, and Alma laughed.

"That's so not fair," Sarai huffed. "No more targeting!"

I held my breath when it got to Christine's turn.

"Never have I ever been in the woods behind the school," Christine said.

Sarai rolled her eyes as she got out. I was also out as I remembered when Gilly and I went into the woods. The nature of the memory haunted me.

"Do the outskirts count?" Alma asked.

"No," Christine said, looking at me. "Only if you've been completely in the woods."

I didn't like her stare. That accusatory tone was back, and I wanted to ask what the hell her problem was. Why was she even here? What did Jen see in her?

"Never have I ever flunked a class," Alma said.

Christine sighed, putting a finger down. Both of them had one finger left.

"Never have I ever been to a funeral," Christine said.

Alma slowly put her last finger down as the tone shifted darkly in the den. Sarai stopped giggling, Jen looked mortified, and my hand gripped Gilly's harder.

"What the hell is your problem?" I spewed before I could stop myself. "Seriously, why would you say that?"

"I really didn't mean it," Christine said, her cocky expression fading to that of embarrassment.

I stood to face her. She looked at me with apologetic eyes, but there was something insincere there. I was certain of it.

"You know you're dating one of Marki's best friends, right?" I said. "Someone who just went to her funeral."

"Quinn, really, it's okay," Jen said. "Christine didn't mean it like that."

"I'm sorry," Christine said, glancing sheepishly around the room. "I'm . . . gonna go." She left quickly, ignoring Jen as she called out to her. Jen ran after her, sounding as if she were about to burst into tears.

"Well, I need another drink," Sarai said. "Come on, Alma."

Sarai reached out her hand, pulling Alma off the couch. The two left Gilly and me in blistering silence.

"I don't know what came over me," I sighed. "I didn't mean to snap like that. She just hasn't given me the best vibe tonight."

"You did what all of us probably would've done if the situation wasn't still so fresh," Gilly said. "So maybe I should be thanking you."

I helped her off the couch. We stood face-to-face. Our eyes met, and she pulled me under once again. I understood her. While it was only us left in the den, I let my hands reach out for her waist and pull her closer. She leaned in, and one of my hands found her cheek, truly feeling her. I squeezed her waist with my other hand as our mouths connected, hastily, as if we both longed for this. Her face beneath my hand was warm and soft like peach skin. We stood there and kissed, gripping one another to not let the moment go, until the sound of sirens broke us apart.

"Shit!" Gilly froze. "I snuck out tonight. My dad's gonna kill me."

"The sirens could be for something else," I offered, hoping to calm her down.

"Cops!" someone shouted upstairs.

The back door slid open and slammed as a few people fled from the house. Gilly and I stayed stock-still as the front door opened and the house fell silent. After a moment, heavy footsteps and murmurs drove us from the den. I peeked around the corner and saw Jon Willis walking into the house.

"Just stay here," I whispered to Gilly.

I strode out of the den, fixing my hair to look more presentable. In the living room, there were a few people I didn't know, along with Alma, Beck, Jen, Sarai, and Rink. Beck slowly ate her chips while Jon Willis looked around.

"Jon, uh, Mr. Willis," Sarai said. "Long time no see."

He studied Sarai's drunk-flushed face. He looked past her at Rink, who avoided his gaze.

"Rink," he said, tone threatening.

"Mr. Willis," Rink replied.

"You've got about a month before I can take you in for this," Jon said. "I won't be so kind once you turn eighteen."

"I know, sir," Rink said.

"Party's over," Jon yelled. "Everyone out of here."

I stayed in the corner while Beck handed Rink the bag of chips. She snuck over to me, halfway hiding behind me so Jon wouldn't notice how high she was. She nudged me to leave; I didn't want to without making sure Gilly was able to get home safely.

"Where is my daughter?" Jon asked Sarai.

"She told me she couldn't come tonight," Sarai said.

Jon Willis finally turned to me, and I stood up straighter. Meeting his eye was the most intimidating thing to happen to me.

"Quinn?" he said.

Before I could find a lie that wouldn't rat out Gilly, she appeared from the den. Her dad sighed.

"Hi Dad," Gilly said with a wince.

"Get in the car," Jon replied. "Let's go."

"Mr. Willis, can I stay the night?" Sarai asked.

He looked at her as if she'd lost her mind. But Sarai's puppy dog eyes worked their magic.

"Fine," Jon sighed. "Both of you, in the car."

Sarai grabbed Gilly's hand and led her out the front door. Beck and I followed, along with Rink who promised to give us a ride home. I watched Sarai twirl her hair again for Jon Willis as he scolded both her and Gilly. Gilly turned and waved at me, forcing a smile as her dad spoke. Alma and Jen followed behind us, Jen complaining because Christine wouldn't answer her calls. Maybe Rink was right about their group being trouble.

# CHAPTER NINE

Monday felt like purgatory. Zombified versions of the partygoers walked to class, and Sarai was one of them. She looked dejected, purple bags under her eyes like two deadweights. Even Alma seemed less perky. I could've sworn I still smelled the alcohol on both of them.

Before I walked into algebra, I saw Christine. The apologetic eyes I'd seen on Saturday still stuck to her, and I wondered if that was actually how she looked at times when she didn't put up the asshole front. I normally tried to see the good in people. Maybe I had been harsh, but I didn't have time to contemplate it. Beck was late to class, and for the first time since Marki Pickett's death, things felt a little more normal.

When the bell rang, I put my headphones on to walk to my next class but found Gilly waiting for me. I immediately threw the headphones off, not bothering to pause my music.

"Hi," I said, voice cracking.

"I'm sorry I didn't get to properly say goodbye this weekend," Gilly sighed. "My dad can be so annoying."

I nodded. "At least he seemed pretty calm."

"Only because it was my friends," Gilly said. "Besides, he gave me 'the talk' about sneaking out and scolded Sarai for drinking too much."

"I'm surprised he let her stay over," I said.

"He knows that if one of them is at the house with me then I won't sneak out," Gilly said. "Besides, he doesn't like Rink."

"Why not?" I asked.

"He's the town weed dealer—and the only action the cops ever truly get, so he puts them on edge."

"I know what you mean," I said quickly. "I'm assuming you're grounded?"

"Unfortunately," Gilly said. "But I'm trying to convince him to let me go to the game this Friday. If I can somehow strike up a deal with him, then we should meet up again."

"Want me to come over sometime this week and help you convince him?" I asked. "Or did he veto you having friends over after Sarai?"

"I'm sure you could come over," Gilly said. "I think he likes you."

She quickly kissed me on the cheek before going the opposite way. I pulled my headphones back on. I wanted to kiss her again the way we had in Sarai's den, without interruption. On my walk to class, I pictured us going on a date together. I'd never done the relationship thing, but it seemed like something I could be pretty decent at. I did watch a lot of romance movies with my mom on nights she needed a good cry. I reflected on all the stops: flowers, chocolates, and the occasional plushy. I'd get Gilly a fox, since that was her favorite animal. I chewed the sides of my nails to keep from smiling.

The rest of the day dragged on. I liked that there was routine, but I felt stuck in the hamster wheel of high school. Beck and

I barely talked at lunch. There wasn't anything new to discuss and when one of us brought up a random topic, the conversation fizzled. Over Beck's shoulder, I caught Rink floating into the cafeteria. He immediately glided to our table.

"What's up," Rink said, taking a seat next to Beck.

"When have you ever come to the cafeteria for lunch?" Beck raised a brow.

"I make my rounds sometimes." Rink shrugged, then winked. "I got a new order if you're interested."

"I only have a twenty," Beck said. "I'm saving it for a rainy day."

Rink looked appalled, gripping his chest. "Did Beck Wood just refuse to buy my weed?"

"I'm a changed woman," Beck said, finishing off a cookie.

Rink looked at me, and I immediately shook my head.

"I guess I'll have to take my business elsewhere," Rink said. "Have either of you seen Christine?"

Beck shook her head, and a flash of Christine's droopy eyes entered my mind.

"Earlier," I said. "She looked sad."

Rink shrugged. "Weed will pick her up. I'll go find her."

He patted Beck on the head before leaving. When lunch ended, I rushed for the hallway, Gilly's eyes flashing in my mind. The last time I had a crush like this was in middle school. There was a girl named Roxanne in my eighth-grade science class. She would secretly snack on almonds during class, and one day, she offered me one. I took it as flirting. Our relationship never went anywhere past sitting next to each other and sharing almonds. She moved after middle school, and I haven't seen her since.

"I'll see if Daddy will let you come over tomorrow night for dinner," Gilly said. "Or homework. He may be more inclined to say yes if we lie and say we have a project to do together."

"I'll bring my best markers to make it believable," I said.

During class, I played with Gilly's hair, braiding it and combing my fingers through it. She nearly fell asleep, head accidentally tipping backward when I hit a sweet spot by her ear. Mrs. Ashley didn't call us out for it, even though her eyes trailed over to us multiple times.

At the end of the day, I decided to suck it up and take the bus. I really needed to get my license, but then again, I didn't have a car to drive. On the bus, someone tapped me on the shoulder; I turned to find Christine watching me. I pulled off my headphones.

"What do you want?" I asked.

"To talk to you," Christine said.

I tried to walk away from her. "I really don't have anything to say to you."

"Quinn, stop," she said. "I've heard some talk from people about Marki. You know your name is being tossed around?"

I wheeled around, getting as close to her face as I could.

"What the fuck is that supposed to mean?" I asked, my tongue a heated pistol.

"*I* know you didn't have anything to do with Marki's murder," Christine said. "Unlike some people."

I couldn't think of anything to say. I simply stared at her, wondering what sort of brain damage she went through over the weekend. My name? Not a whole lot of people knew me, so I doubted it was true.

"I'm sorry," I said. "I think I misheard you. Did you say you know I have nothing to do with Marki's murder? Do you know how insane you sound?"

Christine rolled her eyes. "I'm just trying to warn you."

"Why?" I asked. "And how do I know you're not just bullshitting me to make up for our disagreement this weekend. I have no connection to Jen; I won't put in a good word for you just because you screwed up at the party."

I tried to walk away again, but she reached for my wrist. Her grip was hard, nails digging into my skin. I winced.

"I'm not bullshitting you," Christine said. "Even my name has been tossed around. I just wanted to let you know before you hear it from Jon Willis."

I shook myself from her grasp. "Why would I hear it from Jon Willis?"

"Word on the street is he wants to question every name that's been fed to him," Christine said. "I suspect that somehow your name has gotten to him, and you will eventually go in for questioning. I just wanted to prepare you."

"Have you been questioned?" I asked.

"Not yet," Christine said. "But I suspect I will too. Especially now that I've been hanging with Jen."

I didn't think about how my new tie to Gilly could look for me, especially in the wake of Marki's still-fresh murder.

"I'm innocent," I insisted.

"I know," Christine said. "The way you got so angry about what I said on Saturday, it made me realize you really have no idea what's going on. The others said nothing."

"Because you shocked them all by bringing up their dead friend's funeral!"

People stared at us, and Christine tried to hide her face.

"All I'm saying is there is something suspicious going on, things that factor into Marki's death," she said, almost whispering. "We can talk about it more, if you want?"

"Save it for the police," I said.

I placed my headphones back on but didn't play any music. I was too shocked to press play. When I got on the bus, I chose a window seat by myself and watched Christine. She stared after my bus, and I sank down so she couldn't see me. I didn't want to feed into her delusion about Marki, but I was curious about her findings. Who did she think killed her? More importantly, who thought *I* had anything to do with it, and why?

Gilly had the porchlight on for me when I arrived at her house at dusk the following day. She must have been watching for me because she opened the door before I could knock. I walked inside and followed Gilly to the staircase. Jon Willis made dinner in the kitchen.

"Hey Quinn!" he called.

"Hello!" I called back, already at the top of the staircase with Gilly.

"Good luck with your project," he said from downstairs.

Gilly and I giggled at his naivety. She pulled me into her room, barely giving me enough time to shut the door before her lips were on mine again. We stood in her room, kissing, before she pulled us onto the bed. We were on the edge; if one of us made any slight movement, we would tumble off. Gilly moved her lips to my jaw, my neck. I had never been kissed like that before. Her lips were pillow-soft against my throat. I wanted to try it on her. I pulled her face up to meet my lips, taking my time before trailing my own lips lower to her neck.

"Be careful," Gilly said. "I don't need a hickey to flaunt."

I stopped. "I'm sorry."

"It's okay," Gilly said. "It can happen sometimes."

I shrugged. "I have zero hickey experience."

Gilly giggled. "Do you want me to give you one?"

I hesitated, then nodded. "Just not on my neck."

Gilly pushed me down so I was on my back. She unzipped my jacket slightly, revealing the blue tank top I had on underneath. She pulled the neck of my tank top down slightly. I was self-conscious at the fact she could see the top of my bra. She kissed down my neck again until she got to my chest. Her teeth grazed my skin, stinging a little. Goosebumps rose over my flesh. I wanted to linger in this moment forever. My stomach tightened at the feeling. It hurt, slightly—the soft bite— but it wasn't a bad pain. When Gilly was finished, a red spot was left where her mouth had been.

"There," Gilly said. "Now when you see it, you'll remember you're mine." Her face lit up red at her own words, and she looked away from me. We hadn't discussed what we were to one another; she had no idea I had fantasized about her saying those exact words to me from the first night we kissed.

"Well, I'll be yours if you are mine," I said.

Gilly grinned widely and kissed me again. Jon called us down for dinner, and I zipped my jacket up to my neck, careful not to expose the fresh hickey. We ate casually, talking about school and the approach of October.

"There's a game on Friday," I said. "The theme is decades. I think it'll be super fun."

"Really?" Gilly said, acting as if she had no idea. "Can I please go! I promise I will only go out on Friday, and you can give me a curfew. Please!"

Jon looked between Gilly and I. Her puppy dog eyes were quite convincing.

"Fine," Jon said. "But I want you home by eleven. No later."

Gilly flew up and hugged Jon, kissing him on the cheek. She even helped him with the dishes after dinner to show her gratitude, while I awkwardly left the kitchen to wait in her room. I studied the trinkets on her dresser again, reaching for the carousel piggy bank.

"Hands off, sweetheart," Gilly's voice came from behind me. I turned to find a finger gun pointed at me.

I backed away with my hands up. "Oh, won't you please forgive me?"

She narrowed her eyes, then pretended to shove the fake finger gun back in the pretend holster on her hip. "I'll let you off, just this once."

"I'm so relieved I could kiss you!" I laughed.

We collided again, but only briefly, as we decided we should probably at least start our homework. We kept quiet, but I didn't mind. I could be with Gilly in silence and still feel comfortable.

Eventually, Gilly fell asleep, but I stayed awake to keep watch of time. When it was nearly nine, I woke her up with a gentle nudge. Her blue-gray eyes fluttered open, lazily looking up at me. She walked me out, and I gave her a quick kiss before hopping on my bike.

"You need a license!" Gilly called to me from the porch.

"One day!" I said back, peddling away.

Euphoria fizzled through my body as I rode home, tilting my head back to let the wind wash over me while I relished in the way I felt.

I took a shower when I got home and stopped in front of the mirror afterward to see where Gilly had marked me. A small bruise appeared on the top of my right boob. Gilly was mine. My first relationship was with Gilly Willis—the most popular girl in school. After changing into my pajamas, I called Beck to tell her the news.

"I never thought you would say Gilly Willis is your girlfriend," Beck said. "But I'm happy for you, dude."

"I guess that's what makes it interesting," I replied, preening. "They say opposites attract."

"They do."

## CHAPTER TEN

Beck agreed to go with me to the football game to meet up with Gilly. Harry Newman would pick up Owen and me, then we would meet Gilly, Sarai, and the twins at the game. I wouldn't have classified us as part of their group, but it felt nice having more friends to hang out with.

The theme for the student section was decades. Sorting through my closet, I found a Nirvana t-shirt and one of the flannels I practically lived in when the weather was colder. I dug an old choker out of my jewelry box and decided to go with a nineties theme.

When I heard Harry Newman's car horn outside, I grabbed some money from my dresser and went to get Owen from his room.

"Hey little Levi," Beck said as Owen and I got in the car.

"How are you, morning wood?" Owen asked Beck.

"Owen," I scolded.

"What's up, Quinn," Harry said, pulling out of our driveway.

Harry, of course, wore his basketball letterman jacket. Beck had teased her hair and thrown on a neon-patterned top with big neon-green hoop earrings. Unlike us, Owen hadn't dressed for a decade. He and his friends normally hung out around the snack court like all the other middle schoolers.

"No Gilly?" Beck asked.

"We're meeting at the game again," I said. "She went with her friends."

We bought our tickets when we arrived. Owen promised we would meet by the snack court at the end of the game. There was a sea of people dressed in clothes from different decades. Most were dressed in the style of the seventies or eighties; peace signs and bright colors were everywhere. I searched the student section until I found Gilly. She was in a pink lady's jacket, matching Alma and Jen. Each had high ponytails with black and white polka-dotted ascots tied around their necks.

"They look like a cult," Beck whispered to me before we ascended the bleachers.

"Quinn!" Gilly called, waving us over.

We squeezed in between sweaty students screaming in our ears. Gilly grabbed my hand and pulled me next to her. Beck and Harry followed, squeezing in next to me.

"Where's Sarai?" I asked.

Gilly shrugged. "She called us at the last minute and said she didn't want to come anymore."

"Hi Gilly," Beck said, smiling.

She looked at me, wiggling her eyebrows, and I nudged her side.

"How are you, Gilly?" Harry asked.

"I'm perfect," Gilly said with a smile.

Jen and Alma waved at us, then continued cheering for our team who were getting ready to begin the first quarter. Beck and Harry cheered loudly beside me. The buzzer went off, and the game began. Our team got the ball first.

I tried keeping up with what was going on. It was easier to tell when our team was doing well by the cheers. Beck, once again, helped explain some things before she was sucked into the uproar of the student section.

"After the game we should all go to Lonny's," Harry suggested.

"We'll have to bring Owen," I warned.

"Fine by me," Harry said.

"He's such a little shit sometimes," Beck huffed.

Harry smiled at her. "That's why I like him."

She caught his eye and rolled hers, but a faint smile stayed on her lips. Harry noticed, and his face flushed before his attention was also taken by the game. Harry Newman had always been Beck's annoying neighbor growing up. He'd grown taller and grown his black hair out—honestly, he was pretty attractive. Watching the two of them, I knew they both had feelings they were too proud to admit.

"Want to go grab a corn dog?" Gilly asked. "I'm starving."

"We'll be right back," I told Beck.

After we made it off the bleachers, Gilly grabbed my hand for a moment, pulling me under the silver seats. It was dark, and the grass beneath the bleachers smelled wet.

"What are we doing?" I asked.

Gilly grabbed my face and kissed me. I let myself go and grabbed Gilly's waist. Our lips moved together, heads tilting to the left and right, pausing only for a second to breathe. Her lips tasted like citrus and made me want lemonade. We pulled away when the students started stomping on the bleachers, being led in a fan chant. We covered our ears, laughing, and went back out into the crowd.

While Gilly ordered two corn dogs, I watched Owen with his friends. They were standing around with a few girls, awkwardly trying to speak. Owen flipped one of the girl's braids, and she playfully slapped his hand. This led to them play-fighting, but really, they just wanted to touch one another.

Gilly handed me the corn dog, along with a packet of mustard. We found a bench and sat with our backs leaning against the table. I squirted some mustard on the corn dog and took a bite. Somehow, game food was always the tastiest, even if grease oozed out of it.

"That's your brother over there, right?" Gilly asked, motioning her head to Owen.

"Yeah," I said. "He's at *that* age, but he's not too bad most of the time."

"Justin was older than me." A wistful smile lit Gilly's face. "Sometimes I wonder how our dynamic would have been if he had been younger."

"He probably would have annoyed you in a different way," I chuckled. "I couldn't imagine if Owen was older than me."

"The older sibling privilege must be nice."

"It's real with everything except food." I look down at my corn dog. "Owen inhales everything. I have to fight to get one chip out of the bag."

Gilly laughed. She laughed how she cried, with her shoulders bouncing up and down.

We finished our corn dogs, tossing the sticks and empty mustard packets into the trash can before heading back to the bleachers.

"Harry invited us to Lonny's after the game," I said. "Do you want to go?"

"Sure," Gilly said. "Jen drove us here, so I'd need a ride home. And I have to 'be home by eleven.'"

Her impression of her dad was spot-on.

"I'm sure Harry wouldn't mind giving you one," I said.

Back at the bleachers, I turned to Harry while Gilly was busy talking to the twins.

"I invited Gilly to Lonny's," I said. "She might need a ride home afterward if that's cool with you."

Harry shrugged. "I don't mind. I love driving."

Beck started making ghost noises, and I glared at her.

"I'm only messing around," Beck said. "You'd probably be haunted by now anyway if there were ghosts in her house."

The game dragged and nearly ended in a tie until we scored the winning touchdown. The student section erupted, people jumping up and down, screaming.

"Let's go before it gets too crazy," Harry said.

"I'll go find Owen," I said. "Meet me at the gate."

I power walked back to the snack court and found Owen talking to the girl with braids. She twirled one of them while he talked. I stopped in my tracks, waving my arms to get Owen's attention. When he looked up, I motioned for him to follow but turned so he could say goodbye to the girl in privacy.

"Don't say a word about it," Owen said when he reached me.

"My lips are sealed," I crooned, only to make kissy noises in his ear a second later.

Beck, Gilly, and Harry found us, and we left together. I sat in the middle of Owen and Gilly, Harry fighting through the flood of people walking back to their cars.

Luckily, we were able to find a parking spot at Lonny's before the rush arrived. It was a diner everyone hung out at after the games. The diner had a black-and-white checkerboard floor with teal seats that were cracked, but the owner would probably never replace them. Their cherry vanilla milkshake was my favorite.

We ordered our food. I got cheese fries along with a cherry vanilla shake. Everyone else got burgers. We chose the booth next to the jukebox, and Beck and Harry went to flip through it.

"No, we should play that one," Harry said.

"That song sucks," Beck argued.

"*I'm* the one with the quarters for the machine, need I remind you." Harry shook his fistful of change, smirking.

Beck gave up her argument while Harry chose his song. Just as it started playing, a rush of students came in, drowning out the song.

"They'd be cute together," Gilly whispered to me.

"They're both too stubborn to do anything about it," I said.

The waitress brought out our food, her uniform matching the teal seats.

"I wonder how many times food has been dropped here," Harry said, sitting back down. "It can't be easy carrying those big trays around."

"Why don't you get a job and test that theory out," Beck said, dropping into the seat next to him.

Harry mocked her before digging into his burger. I gave Beck a look, and she subtly shook her head.

"What milkshake did you get?" Gilly asked.

"Cherry vanilla," I said. "You can try it."

Gilly grabbed the straw, taking a sip. Her eyes lit up. "This is the best milkshake I've ever had."

"We can share it," I said. "If you want to."

"Are you sure?" Gilly asked.

I grabbed a stray straw from the table and stuck it in the milkshake. When I looked up, Beck, Harry, and Owen were staring at us.

"Am I missing something?" Harry asked.

"Keep up, Harry," Beck drawled. "Gilly obviously really likes the milkshake."

We all busted out laughing, the joke going over Owen's head. Our laughter was cut short when Jon Willis approached our table. He was in his sheriff's uniform, hat off, holding it in his hands. I checked the clock; it was only 10:15.

Gilly sat up straighter. "Dad? What are you doing here?"

"I hate to cut your fun short, honey," he said. "But I need you to come home, now."

"Why?" Gilly asked.

"Just come with me," Jon said. "We will talk about it at home. Sorry, everybody."

A moment passed before Gilly stood and grabbed her jacket from the booth. "Bye, guys."

Jon put his arm around Gilly, but she shimmied out of his grasp, throwing her jacket on before leaving.

"What was all that about?" Beck asked.

"I'm not sure," I said.

I turned back from the door and stared at the milkshake. Gilly's straw sunk to the side, and I no longer wanted any.

Harry dropped Owen and I off in the driveway. All the lights were on in the house, and when we came into the door, Mom approached us. Her expression was grim, and we stopped taking our shoes off.

"What's wrong?" I asked.

"The news," Mom said.

She paused, seemingly unable to finish her sentence. I walked into the living room and saw police lights on the screen. There was caution tape and a headline underneath. *Local teen found dead.*

"Who is it?" I asked.

"They haven't released a name yet," Mom said. "Owen, make sure the door is locked, please."

The red-and-blue lights on the TV assailed my eyes, mixing into a painfully bright streak.

"Is this not a replay of when Marki was found?" I asked, hopeful.

"No, sweetie," Mom said. "It's not."

Another teen found dead? The cherry vanilla milkshake crept up my throat, but I swallowed the sickly feeling down. The woods, the caution tape, the police officers searching with their flashlights—it all played like a reel on the screen. I knew Beck and Gilly were safe, but it still didn't quiet the thought of who could've possibly been the next victim.

Maybe Beck was right about there being a serial killer.

On Saturday, I woke up early to the smell of coffee. I let the scent pull me downstairs and into my slippers. Mom poured us both a cup, and we sat in front of the TV together. The cup burned my fingers, but my eyes stayed glued to the screen. I was frozen as I waited for Jon Willis to announce any updates on the newest death.

"It is with heavy hearts that we are here again with tragic news," Jon said. "Last night, at around 10:00 p.m., dispatch alerted us of a body found in the woods. Another one of our own taken from us too soon. I would like us to take a moment of silence for Sarai Matthews."

The screen went silent as if we had muted the TV. I looked at Mom whose hands shook as she sipped her coffee. Another teen girl my age, murdered.

"We suspect foul play once again," Jon Willis said. "We are not sure if this is connected to a previous crime, but we will update with any and all information as we receive it."

Mom turned the volume down, gripping her chest.

"Honey," Mom said, "I would appreciate it if you only left the house during the day for a while. And don't go alone, please. Bring Owen if you have to. I don't want to take any chances."

"Sure, Mom," I said, staring at the now silent TV.

My body felt like lead. I couldn't move, nor could I blink. The coffee mug scorched the pads of my fingers. Sarai hadn't gone to the game last night. If she had, would her fate have been different?

My instinct was to call Gilly. I left the couch and hesitated when I picked up the phone. I stared at the numbers, all of them swirling together, but finally dialed. Gilly answered, voice strained.

"Gilly," I breathed. "I just saw the news."

A barrage of sobs met my ear, and I felt horrible for being the one to set her off.

"She could've been safe." Gilly's voice trembled. "She should've stayed home or gone to the game like she planned to."

"Can I . . . do anything?" I asked.

"What if Alma or Jen are next?" Gilly went on, ignoring me. "What if it's just our group being targeted?"

I didn't want to think about it, but the fact Marki and Sarai were the victims made me think twice. I assumed Gilly was protected having Jon as her father, but Alma and Jen? What if it was all a plan? I didn't have any more words for Gilly, so I let her cry on the other end of the line. I pictured her shoulders bouncing and wished I was there to hold her. She was the one who finally hung up after a sheepish goodbye. I let the tone sting my ear until I finally placed the phone back on the dock.

I stayed home the majority of the day, staring at the wall or napping. I wanted to keep my hands or mind busy, but I still felt as though I couldn't move. When the evening came, there was a hard knock at the door.

"I'll get it," Mom said.

I held my breath and peered over the couch, straining to see.

"It's Beck!" Mom called.

Beck came into the living room with her bookbag, dropping it.

"My parents are gone for the weekend, and I can't stay there by myself," Beck said.

"You're free to stay here any time," Mom said.

Beck joined me on the couch. She wouldn't stop bouncing her leg and picking her nails. When the news came on, it was clear there weren't any new leads about Sarai, just the same footage on repeat.

"She was found in the woods too," I said.

Beck turned to me. "Are you worried about Gilly?"

"More than you know," I said.

"What about us?" Beck said. "We technically have ties with them now."

I blinked. "I don't know."

Jon Willis instilled a curfew on the town strictly for teens at Putner High School. We had to be in our houses by 8:00 p.m. for at least two weeks. If anyone was out afterward, they would be charged. He promised the curfew was only temporary while they looked deeper into Marki and Sarai's murders.

School felt the way it did on Mondays. Nobody talked. Everyone grabbed stuff from their lockers and went to class silently, not waiting on their friends and slumping in their seats. I kept my headphones on, but the music was down low. I could still hear sneakers squeak against the floor, and the bell signaling for us to get to class.

I scratched notes into my notebooks and paid more attention than I normally did. Anything to keep my mind off what was going on outside of school. Gilly wasn't here—a fact that made my heart drop. I firmly reminded myself Jon was probably keeping her under stricter house arrest.

On the way to lunch, Alma and Jen stopped me.

"What is it?" I asked, heartbeat speeding up.

"Gilly wanted us to tell you she's staying home for a couple of days," Alma said. "Her dad doesn't want to let her out of his sight."

"Okay," I said. "Thanks for telling me."

I walked away from them, relieved Gilly was safe. Beck motioned me over at lunch to sit with her. She was drinking a red bull, shaking.

"You need to eat actual food," I said.

"The line is long," Beck countered.

"You're shaking."

"I'm on edge." Beck blinked. "How are you not?"

"What exactly could happen to us at school?" I said, pulling out my sandwich.

Harry came over to us, tossing a bag of chips in front of Beck.

"You look jittery," Harry said. "Eat these."

"Told you," I said.

Beck opened the chips and dug in, finishing the bag in under a minute.

"I'm getting you lunch," Harry said, leaving before Beck could oppose.

She poured the rest of the crumbs from the bag into her mouth, chasing them with a sip of her red bull.

"I know what you're going to say," Beck said. "And the answer is no."

"Come on," I whined. "Harry is the most normal guy I've ever seen you around."

"He's *Harry*."

"And you're Beck."

"You just want to go on double dates," Beck huffed.

"Maybe I do," I fired back.

Harry returned with a plate of food for Beck and set it in front of her. He sat at the table adjacent to us and watched expectantly, waiting for her to take a bite.

"Thanks," Beck said, forking a mandarin orange.

"How's Gilly?" Harry asked.

I shrugged. "We talked on the phone the other night, but she wasn't doing well. Her dad is keeping her out of school for a couple of days."

"I can't even imagine," Harry said. "They're dropping like flies."

We looked over at their table. Only the twins sat there, across from each other. The gaps around their table in the cafeteria would become a lasting memory.

English was lonely without Gilly. I imagined her sitting in front of me, laughing, her shoulders bouncing up and down from joy instead of tears.

"A reminder that grief counseling will be available all week for those that need it," Mrs. Ashley said. "If at any time you feel overwhelmed and need to get out of here, please let me know."

Nobody reacted, so we started the lesson. We read *The Scarlet Letter* and discussed the chapters we read for homework. A couple of people tried to contribute to the discussion, but Mrs. Ashley did most of the talking. Nobody felt like speaking—that would mean acting as if everything was normal.

When the bell rang, I packed up slowly, dreading going to my last class of the day but ready for it to be over.

"Quinn," Mrs. Ashley said. "Could you come here for a second?"

I approached her desk slowly, and she handed me a stack of papers. "What are these?"

"Homework for Abigail Willis," Mrs. Ashley said. "Would you mind running them by her? She emailed and said I could ask you."

"Sure," I said.

I was taken off guard by the use of Gilly's full name. For as long as I'd known her, she was strictly *Gilly*. I stuffed the papers into my bookbag and left. The bus ride was excruciating. I wanted to get home and get to Gilly's before curfew.

I got home before Owen and Mom. I went straight to the garage to grab my bike and head over to Gilly's before Mom could oppose me doing so.

Jon Willis's car wasn't in the driveway when I got to her house, and I was relieved. I wanted my moment alone with Gilly. When I knocked on the door, she answered with a sad smile.

"I brought your homework," I said.

"I hope you don't mind. I asked Mrs. Ashley to give it to you," Gilly said. "Honestly, I just wanted an excuse to see you."

"I don't mind," I said.

I followed her upstairs to her bedroom. She had the window cracked open, the air in her room less fragrant with the fresh air. Her hair was in a messy bun, strands sticking out as if static pulled at them.

"When will you be back at school?" I asked.

"Why?" Gilly replied, a teasing lilt to her voice. "Do you miss me?"

"Maybe," I said.

"Hopefully next week," Gilly said, laying on her bed. "I had to argue with dad about it. He doesn't want me setting foot outside the house."

"Has he said anything?" I asked, leaning against her dresser.

"They're going to block off the woods by school," Gilly said. "He's going out there today to look around some more."

"Do you think that'll do anything?' I asked.

Gilly shook her head. "I love my dad, but he has no idea what he's doing. None of them do. They haven't had a murder case in nearly twenty-three years, Dad said."

We let the conversation evaporate, and Gilly motioned for me to join her on the bed. I did, laying down next to her. Our bodies molded together as Gilly kissed me. Her duvet smelled like lilac. She crawled on top of me, and I placed my hands on both sides of her hips, letting my hands creep under her shirt. Her skin was warm and plush under my fingertips, reminding me of how alive both of us were.

With her permission, I lifted Gilly's shirt over her head. She had on a pink-lace bralette, and the straps were already falling off her shoulders. She helped me out of my jacket and pulled my own shirt off. I grew self-conscious at the fact that I smelled like school. That and my bra was plainly nude—one my mom got on sale for me from the department store. I should've changed before I came over.

Gilly stopped kissing me to run her finger along the hickey she left me. She was in a trance, the soft feeling of her fingertip tickling me.

"We should go on a date soon," I said.

Gilly's bun fell to the side of her head, and she pulled out the scrunchie holding it up. Her hair cascaded down her shoulders like woven gold.

"I don't think Dad will like that very much," Gilly said. She leaned down until her lips touched mine again. My skin grew hot under hers as she kissed me with ferocity, like it was the last time we'd ever get to do it again. The thought made me shudder, and it felt as if Gilly was thinking the same thing.

# CHAPTER ELEVEN

The local news station released a statement Sunday morning that Sarai had been found with a candy bar wrapper in her pocket along with a wad of cash, which, it was assumed, she would have used for the football game. The candy bar had been some sort of chocolate from Germany, which led the police to question Alma and Jen first. They had gone to Germany over the summer and brought back dozens of snacks. I pictured their eyes, wet with tears as they swore up and down they had nothing to do with Sarai's murder. Part of me wondered if they were next, and if they felt the same threat of becoming victims too.

Gilly sat alone at her lunch table while Alma and Jen went along with Jon Willis. I left Beck and Harry to sit with her.

"What's going on?" I asked.

"Dad said they were coming to question people today," Gilly said.

"Does he think they did it?"

"No way." Gilly scowled. "There's no way."

"Does he think a student killed them?" I asked.

Gilly sipped her juice pouch, not meeting my eye. Something nagged at her. I didn't push. After a few seconds, she leaned in.

"Can I tell you something? But you can't say a word of it to anyone."

I nodded.

"I heard Dad talking on the phone to someone," Gilly said. "He thinks both Marki and Sarai were killed with a pocketknife. Based on that, he's questioning everyone who lives near the woods. Anyone is a suspect now."

Two other policemen came into lunch to collect more students. A couple were volleyball players Sarai had been on a team with. When Jon Willis came back with Alma and Jen, he approached our table.

"Quinn," he said. "Will you come with me, please?"

I looked at Gilly, who shot daggers at her father. He kept his poker face while I stood up to follow him.

Beck and Harry stared at me while I followed Jon Willis out of the lunchroom. There was a group of boys waiting in the lobby, trading game cards while others waited for the bell to ring so they could beat the rush of students to class. There were policemen standing around, waiting to question more students and keeping surveillance.

Jon Willis closed the door when we got to the guidance counselor's office and sat in the chair across from me.

"Quinn," Jon said, "I'm not here to question you about Marki or Sarai."

I let out a breath I didn't realize I'd been holding in.

"I want to talk to you about Gilly," Jon clarified.

"What about Gilly?" I asked.

"I'm worried for her safety." Jon crossed his arms. "Two of her closest friends have been found dead. Murdered. I can lie and say it won't happen to her, but I just don't know that. Is there anything you can tell me that might help me ensure my daughter's safety?"

I didn't look at Jon Willis as the sheriff at that moment. For once, I saw him as Gilly's concerned father. His worry loomed over us, matching my own.

"I'm worried about her," I admitted. "Not because she told me anything or because I know anything about Marki or Sarai. But two of her best friends turning up dead doesn't feel like a coincidence to me."

"I don't even want her coming to school anymore," Jon said, leaning back in his chair. "But she'll resent me if I keep her home."

"Just make sure she doesn't go anywhere alone?" I suggested.

This conversation with Jon sent unease worming into my gut. Was he asking me for advice on what to do about Gilly? Any answer I gave would be like betraying her.

"Keep an eye out for her, will you?" Jon said. "I've met all of her friends, but I trust you the most to keep her safe."

"I will," I promised.

Jon walked me out of the counselor's office where Rink stood with some police officers. One had a white-knuckle grip on his skinny forearm. Rink tried to pull away, hissing from the pressure. But the officer wouldn't release him. I stepped forward to intervene, but Jon patted my shoulder and motioned for me to get back to the cafeteria.

"Would you let me go?" Rink snapped.

"We need you for questioning," the officer holding his arm said.

"I've already been questioned," Rink shot back.

"We need you for questioning *again*," the officer said. "Now, let's go."

Begrudgingly, Rink complied, following the officer, who finally let him go. Jon cupped the back of Rink's neck like an old friend, but it made Rink tense.

Back in the lunchroom, Alma and Jen were sitting with Gilly, so I went back to Beck and Harry who were basically foaming at the mouth with questions.

"Did they cuff you?" Beck asked.

"Yes," I said. "They let me keep the pair, want to see?"

I reached into my pocket and pulled out my middle finger, flashing it at Beck.

"Are they planning on questioning everyone?" Harry asked. "Because I don't even remember Sarai's last name."

"Jon Willis asked me about Marki and Sarai because I hang out with Gilly," I said. "I could barely answer anything."

"Does that make you a suspect?" Beck asked.

I rolled my eyes and didn't answer her question. But a little piece of doubt gnawed at my stomach. Jon hadn't insinuated he thought I could be guilty, but was I still on the suspect list? Christine's words swam back into my mind. I wondered who tossed my name around as a possible suspect. Studying the lunchroom, I found the jocks and cheerleaders more quiet than normal. Could it have been one of them?

The bell rang, and we flooded out. The police were gone by the time lunch ended. Rink sat on the steps outside. I tore away from the crowd and slipped outside. He stared straight ahead, watching cars pass by.

"Rink?" I said, standing over him.

"Hi Quinn," Rink said. "Did they question you too?"

I nodded, taking a seat next to him. "Are you okay? I saw them hounding you."

"There's no way to answer that question," Rink said. "No offense, but I'm tired of hearing it."

"Right," I said. "Sorry."

Rink played with a keychain on his backpack. It was a skull with a cigarette in its mouth. His backpack was partly opened, a bag of weed evident.

"Be careful," I said, pointing to it.

He shoved the plastic baggy further down so it was covered by some crumbled pieces of paper.

"Did Gilly mention anything about Sarai acting weird?" Rink asked. "This all seems so random. I don't know who would've wanted to hurt her."

"All I know is Sarai was supposed to go to the game with them on Friday but bailed," I said.

"I know," Rink said. "I was supposed to drive her that night, but she told me she'd rather walk instead."

I processed Rink's words. Sometime on Friday, before the game, Sarai had been killed and dumped in the woods. What a perfect night to do it when everyone would be at the stadium, distracted by one of the only fun things to do in town.

"Did you tell that to the police?" I asked.

"About five times," Rink muttered. "But since Sarai didn't go to the game, neither did I. I told those assholes over and over that I was at home all night playing video games. There's nothing else I can say or do."

I placed a hand on his shoulder. He patted my hand as he looked at the ground, a tear falling down his cheek.

"I'm really sorry about Sarai," I said.

"Me too," Rink replied.

I left him on the steps to be alone but stopped for a moment to watch him. He looked off into the distance, still playing with his keychain. His grief hung around him like a dull shadow. The way he spoke about Sarai the other night made it seem like they were close. Part of me wished I could've seen the two of them interact more. Rink no longer had a sibling, and now he was being questioned about her murder.

He was older than Sarai, much like I was to Owen. My throat tightened at the thought of not being able to see Owen anymore. It almost made me sick putting myself in Rink's shoes. I made note to give Owen a hug when I got home from school.

In my last couple of classes, I thought about the murders. Coincidences be damned. If someone was targeting Gilly's group, what was it for? There were things I didn't know about them but what secrets did they have that were worth murder? In a lapse of judgment, I considered going to Christine after class to drink up whatever new theories she had regarding Sarai's murder. But I couldn't bring myself to do it. I wanted Sarai to hold onto a little more of her humanity before the theories flooded in and she truly felt like another case.

Beck's eyes followed me as I paced around her bedroom, spilling my guts about Christine's confrontation on the bus lot as well as my brief conversation with Rink.

"Calm down, Nancy Drew," Beck sighed. "Christine seems paranoid about everything. I wouldn't listen to her."

"I think I want to talk to her again," I admitted.

Beck scowled. "Please don't let her suck you into her bullshit. She has no clue what she's talking about."

"But what if she does?" I said. "What if she has an idea of who might be a part of this? If she knows something the police don't, wouldn't that be helpful?"

"For Gilly?"

"Exactly," I said. "And Alma and Jen."

Beck lay on her stomach while Harry sat at the headboard of her bed. Beck's parents weren't home, and she didn't want to be by herself. We shared a bag of chips, passing it between the three of us. Harry took handfuls and shoved them into his mouth.

"Sarai was killed before the football game," I said. "What if whoever killed her *is* targeting Gilly and her friends? They could've known they were all going to the game, and Sarai happened to be the one by herself."

"*Everyone* goes to the football games on Friday nights," Harry pointed out. "There's nothing else to do. I think Sarai was just in the wrong place at the wrong time."

I still paced, using the chips as fuel. "We need to go to the woods."

Beck and Harry looked at me as if I'd just confessed to both murders.

"No," Beck said.

"Absolutely not," Harry agreed.

"If the three of us go together we will be fine," I insisted. "Besides, it's still daylight out. We can take some weapons too."

"Like Harry's sad little pocketknife?" Beck said.

He rolled his eyes at her.

"We have a hammer in the garage," I said.

Beck flopped back onto her bed. "This is insane."

"I know it *sounds* insane, but I need to do this," I said. "For Gilly."

"Her dad's the sheriff," Harry huffed. "If anyone is safe, it's Gilly."

"We don't know that," I said. "The police barely have any leads. If we can maybe find *something* out there, it will give me peace of mind."

Beck and Harry looked at one another, contemplating the idea. When Harry pulled his keys out of his pocket, I smiled, heading for the garage to find the hammer.

Yellow caution tape still lined the perimeter of the woods, but no police were out. Harry parked close to the edge of the woods in case we needed to make a run for it. He had his knife, Beck had an old flashlight, and I had the hammer. The three of us could easily take someone down if they tried to attack.

Harry lifted the caution tape for Beck and I. Even at midday, the woods were dark—as if the trees could sense what had happened and were poisoned by it. Sarai had been found a little ways away from where Marki had been. It was easier finding the caution tape around two big trees than it had been to find Marki's spot in the dark. There were a bunch of leaves and pine needles, but nothing out of the ordinary. No ghosts of the crime committed—it looked like any other part of the woods.

"This is useless," Beck said. "The police already searched here."

I shot her a pleading look. "Just look around, okay? Let me know if you find anything."

Carefully, I pushed some pine needles around with my foot while Beck and Harry did the same. I could all but feel Beck's frustration when all we found were more pine cones and leaves.

"I'm going to try looking further down there," Harry said, gesturing to a small trail.

"Be careful," Beck said.

"Aww," Harry teased, "are you worried about me Becky?"

Beck glowered at him. "Call me Becky again, and I'll personally be the one to kill *you*."

Harry threw his hands up, walking away and down the trail. Beck and I moved forward, heads down, feet shuffling pine needles out of the way.

"I wish you two would just get it on already," I sighed.

Beck rolled her eyes. "You have become significantly nosier in my life these past couple of weeks."

"What can I say, your life is just so *interesting*."

There was a scuttling noise behind a nearby tree, and Beck and I both jumped, moving closer together with our weapons drawn. A squirrel appeared, scurrying off as soon as it saw us.

"Guys!" Harry called from down the trail. "I found something."

Beck and I power walked down the trail to Harry, who was staring down at something shiny. He pointed, and the two of us scoffed as we looked.

"A condom wrapper?" Beck said. "You called us all the way down here because you found a condom wrapper."

"Yes," Harry said. "But look over here too."

We followed him to a patch of pine needles that looked like they'd been bunched up to bury something. Harry dug his handle under the needles and pulled up a dirty towel. It was green with navy blue stripes on it.

"So, some people screwed in the woods and hid the towel for next time," Beck said. "Great discovery."

"It's something," Harry said.

The two of them continued bickering while I caught the sound of something in the distance. The trees blew in the breeze—and there it was again, a distant tinkling. Wind chimes.

"Listen," I said.

They stopped speaking as we tried to listen again for the wind chimes. I followed the sound down the trail, Beck and Harry following closely behind. Every time the breeze hit, the sound of wind chimes grew closer until we saw them. They swung on the back porch of a house where Rink sat, lighting a joint. We ducked behind the trees as we watched him blow smoke in our direction.

"That's Sarai's house," Beck said.

"Harry, we might actually need that towel and condom wrapper," I said.

"I'll go get them," he said, quietly shifting from behind the tree.

I watched Rink blow another ring of smoke before retreating into his house. There was a slim chance this evidence could help him, so we had to give it a shot.

# CHAPTER TWELVE

Our discovery that Sarai's house connected to the woods—close to where her body was found—left me both on edge and satisfied. I knew we would find something, even if it had been just the towel and condom wrapper. Gilly had once told me anything could be evidence.

Harry drove us to Gilly's house. The towel and condom wrapper were next to me. I hoped to show it to Gilly first before handing it over to Jon Willis.

When we arrived, Gilly was the only one home. She opened the door cautiously until she saw it was me. She smiled softly.

"What are you doing here?" she asked.

"Nancy Drew here might be onto something about Marki and Sarai," Beck said, holding the towel bunched up with the condom wrapper inside.

Gilly waved us in, and we followed her up to her bedroom. I took the evidence from Beck to show Gilly more closely. Beck hesitantly sat on the edge of the bed, supporting most of her weight with her legs. She wrapped her arms around herself and looked around, as if waiting for the ghosts of Gilly's mom and brother to appear.

"Don't worry, Beck," Gilly said. "Nothing will get you in here. Not even my dad; he's out at the station."

Beck faked a laugh while Harry played with the carousel piggy bank. Gilly watched him carefully until he shyly stepped away from it with a smile.

"I think I found something today," I said, holding out the items.

"A towel and a condom wrapper?" Gilly asked.

She hesitated before taking them into her arms. She inspected them, careful to keep the condom wrapper inside of the towel as she turned her nose up.

"Remember when you said anything could be evidence?" I gestured to the items. "It could be something."

"Did you go into the woods?" Gilly asked.

I nodded.

"Quinn!" Gilly scolded. "You can't do that."

"I know, and I won't do it again," I said. "But I think it gave me a lead."

"How?" Gilly asked.

"We found the condom wrapper and towel on a trail that leads to the back of Sarai's house," I said. "Only a few steps away from where they found her body. Granted, the physical evidence could be nothing, but the fact Sarai's house is close to where they found her could mean something."

Gilly gave me a sad smile. "The police already know Sarai's house is by the woods. But I could bag the other evidence. It might mean something?"

I nodded, trying not to let my face fall at the information everyone but me seemingly knew.

Gilly left the room without saying anything and returned with a plastic bag. She shoved the towel into it then stopped before putting the condom wrapper in the bag.

"I've seen this same wrapper before," Gilly said.

"I think everyone at Putner uses that brand," Harry said.

"You included?" Beck asked.

We all glared at him as he shrugged. Beck scowled.

"I've definitely seen it somewhere recently," Gilly said.

"Got around with anyone before Quinn, Gilly?" Beck taunted.

Gilly threw her a look. "No. I think I've seen it in Marki's waste bin in her bathroom."

"Do you know who she used it with?" I asked.

"I don't remember," Gilly said, defeated. She tossed the wrapper into the plastic bag with the towel and tied it off.

Swallowing my disappointment, I added, "By the way, I talked to Rink at school today."

"Did he say anything?" Gilly asked.

"Only that Sarai told him she wanted to walk to the game instead of having him drive her. If she was on her way to the game, she probably went through the woods."

Gilly sat on her bed next to Beck. "That doesn't make any sense."

"Unless she was meeting someone?" Harry suggested.

"I don't know who, though," Gilly said.

"You can't think of anyone?" I pressed.

"The only name I truly remember hearing from any of them was Brady Simpson," Gilly said. "And, well, Vance Luther. But we've been there, done that."

"Simpson the swimmer?" Harry asked.

Gilly nodded.

"That's who I caught Marki in the hall with one time," I said. "Could he know something?"

Gilly looked taken aback. "Caught in the hall?"

I shut my mouth; I forgot I hadn't disclosed anything about my secret sightings of Marki with her.

"There was this one time I saw them in the hall together," I said. "Just . . . kissing."

Gilly nodded, a wave of hurt hitting her face. I didn't mean to be the catalyst for her dead best friend's betrayal.

Gilly quickly snapped out of it. "It would be worth a shot to speak with him."

"I could talk to him tomorrow?" Harry said. "See if I get any intel."

I gave Gilly a quick kiss before the three of us left. She set the bag of evidence on the kitchen table to give to Jon once he returned home. I waited on the doorstep until I heard the click of her front door lock before I joined Beck and Harry in the car. When I walked up, I noticed the two of them gazing at one another, pushing each other's arms playfully. They froze and snapped out of it once they heard me reach for the door handle. Typical.

After school the next day, Beck and I waited by Harry's car while he snuck into the pool room to find Brady. Neither of us knew how long it'd take him, so we climbed onto the back of the trunk and sat there. The parking lot cleared out, leaving only the athletes' cars and one beat-up, brick-red car with dents in the front. Rink walked out of school, flipping his keys in his hand.

Suddenly, a sheriff car pulled into the lot, driving up in front of Rink. I could see Jon Willis's head and tried my best to listen but couldn't hear them. When Jon drove off, Rink watched him, flipping up his middle finger when he was far enough away. I hopped down from the car.

"Where are you going?" Beck asked.

"I want to find out what Jon said to him."

Beck hopped down from the car and walked with me. We approached Rink as he stuck his keys in his truck door.

"What?" Rink said. "You need to buy more weed?"

"No," Beck said. "And drop the attitude."

Rink rolled his eyes.

"We saw you talking to Jon Willis," I said.

"Quinn," Rink sighed, "just let it go."

"Was he questioning you?" I asked.

"What does it matter?" Rink said.

If the purple bags under his eyes drooped any further, his eyes would surely pop out of their sockets. He looked exhausted, defeated. Rink opened his car door, but I stopped it with my hand.

"I think I found something that could help you," I said.

"I'll keep that in mind if I ever need people to testify in my favor," Rink replied, probably only half-joking.

"Your house connects to the woods," I said. "And you said Sarai didn't want you driving her to the game the night she died. I think she met someone in the woods."

Rink clenched his jaw and looked at me with his bloodshot eyes.

"With what the police *think* they know, that information will only hurt me," Rink said. "Bye now."

He tore the door from my hand and slammed it, driving away with screeching tires.

"What does he mean?" Beck asked.

"The police have him as a suspect," I said. "They just don't have enough proof."

"Rink wouldn't kill Sarai," Beck said. "He gets high all the time and reads Stephen King on the bleachers most of the day."

"It sounds sketchy when you say it aloud," I pointed out. "He has no good alibi. I wouldn't be surprised if they tried to convict him."

"You don't think he killed them?" Beck said. "Right?"

"I think I will have a better answer to that question once we get some intel from Brady," I said.

We waited on the back of Harry's car and watched as some teachers left for the day. When he finally jogged out of the building, it was nearly four.

"Took you long enough," Beck said. "Anything?"

"Well, I saw him," Harry said. "But I had to wait until he got out of the water to talk to him."

"And?" I pressed.

"He didn't have much to say to me about anything," Harry said. "He seemed pretty confused."

Beck rolled her eyes, marching to the building Harry had come from.

"Where are you going?" I asked.

"Never send a man to do anything," Beck said. "Come on."

The indoor pool smelled like sickening chlorine melted by the humidity. We'd probably suffocate if we stayed in there too long. Most of the swimmers were drying off and fleeing to the locker room to change. Their wet feet slapped against the ground.

"That's Brady," Harry said from behind us.

He pointed to a brunette boy with dripping hair who was shoving a swim cap into his bag along with some goggles. Beck approached him first, throwing her hand out to introduce herself. She motioned for Harry and me to follow, so we did.

Brady rolled his eyes when he saw Harry. "Dude, I just talked to you. I already told you I barely knew either of them."

"I've seen you with Marki Pickett in the hallway before," I said. "By the vending machine near the math hall."

"The fact you remember something like that is a little creepy," Brady huffed. "Maybe find another hobby other than stalking people. It's not a good look. Especially now with all that's going on."

He tried to move past us, but Harry threw his arm against the wall, blocking him.

"Someone's defensive," Beck said.

"I don't have time for this," Brady shot back. "I have other stuff to do today."

I peeked over his shoulder at where his bag was on the bench. Next to it sat a folded towel. I shimmied away from the three of them to get a closer look—green with navy stripes. It was identical to the one in the woods. I grabbed the towel, holding it up for Beck and Harry to see.

"You might as well sit down." Beck gave Brady a cold look. "If you're honest, this won't take long."

"Are you the police now?" Brady asked.

"We have our connections. Now sit."

Brady, finally giving up, took a seat on the bench. I held up his towel.

"Is you holding that supposed to mean something?" he asked.

"We found a towel just like this one in the woods behind Sarai Matthews's house," I said.

"It's a towel from Big Lots," Brady deadpanned. "Do you know how many people shop at Big Lots?"

"Just tell us how well you knew Marki and Sarai, and we will leave you alone," Beck said.

Brady crossed his arms and tapped his foot, glaring up at the three of us. He stayed silent, and Beck tensed beside me the way she did whenever she was staring daggers at someone. Eventually, Brady couldn't take it anymore.

"Fine! Marki and I hooked up on and off last year until I called it quits over the summer. For the most part, it stayed just a hookup. I truthfully didn't know that much about her."

"And Sarai?" I asked.

"We started hooking up at the end of summer," Brady said. "Same as with Marki, I didn't know too much about her. But I already told the police this."

I looked at Beck, who shrugged.

"When was the last time you saw Sarai?" I asked.

"As in the last time we hooked up?" Brady said. "Wednesday before the football game."

"You weren't planning to meet her the night of the game were you?" I asked.

"I had a swim meet out of town that weekend," Brady said. "In Raleigh. The team can tell you I was there. Came second on butterfly if you need specifics."

Asshole. But I knew he was telling the truth.

"Fine," I sighed. "Sorry we bothered you. See you around I guess."

"Whatever," Brady said, shrugging.

With the three of us leaving empty-handed, my next task was to call Gilly and tell her to forget the evidence we'd found. It was useless, just like our trip to see Brady. Any spark of hope I had fizzled out like one of those sad fireworks that leap into the air just to do nothing. We were back to square one—back to uncertainty and danger for Gilly. We wouldn't run out of time. We couldn't.

# CHAPTER THIRTEEN

Gilly and I had to sneak around on the nights Jon wouldn't let her out past sunset. He still didn't allow visitors at night. I rode my bike down her street, careful to let my feet off the pedals when I neared her house. I kept my bike light off and wore black so I wouldn't stand out to passersby. The curfew was still intact, and sneaking around could get me caught, but I wanted to see Gilly any way I could. I stopped one house down and walked next to my bike, cringing as the chain clicked. If Jon heard it, Gilly and I would be screwed. Still, she seemed to like the thrill of it all.

The light in her room was on, her silhouette a looming shadow waving to me as I arrived. Gilly let me in through the back door. Jon was watching TV, the volume seemingly too loud for him to notice the door close behind me. His back faced us as he reclined in his chair; Gilly tiptoed forward with my hand in hers.

"Gilly?" Jon called. "Did you need something?"

"Grabbed a snack, Dad," Gilly said.

I held my breath as we walked up the stairs. Sneaking me into the house was harder than sneaking me out. Jon liked to go to bed early. When Gilly closed her bedroom door, I collapsed onto the bed.

"That will *never* get any easier," I breathed.

Gilly crawled in next to me. "It won't be like this forever."

She kissed me, and her lips tasted like chocolate ice cream she must have had for dessert after dinner.

"We talked to Brady yesterday," I said. "But it didn't get us anywhere."

"I appreciate you talking to him," Gilly said. "But you should just let Dad and the police figure it out. I want you to be safe."

Gilly's pupils expanded as she looked at me, making her eyes look even bigger. I placed my hand on her cheek, which was soft and warm.

"I promise I'll be safe," I said. "Besides, that towel and condom wrapper we found in the woods was his. He and Sarai were hooking up, but they didn't meet the night of the football game. He was at a swim meet."

Gilly looked taken aback.

"Brady and Sarai?" Gilly said. "She never mentioned him once."

"Maybe because of Marki?" I suggested.

Gilly nodded, but her face fell, brows furrowing together. She got off the bed to sit at her window and look out at the streetlamps illuminating the dark street.

"What's wrong?" I asked.

"I feel like I didn't know them as well as I thought," Gilly said. "I know I shouldn't be upset about the Brady thing, but I am. If they were being secretive about that, then what else could they have been secretive about?"

I didn't move from the bed but sat up to face Gilly. The window was her sanctuary. She sat in the glow of the moonlight, knees tucked to her chest so I could see her toes, the nails painted pink.

"I think that goes for everyone," I said. "I consider Beck my best friend, but there are things she's secretive about. But I don't think that means I know her any less. I think people keep things, even from those they care about, because they're ashamed or just want to have something strictly for themselves."

"I barely talk to the twins anymore," Gilly said. "In the past week, the only time we've spoken is at lunch, and even then, it doesn't feel the same. I never thought I'd lose all my best friends."

Despite her words, Gilly didn't cry; maybe all her tears had been shed already. I remembered her crying in class, shoulders trembling; now, her shoulders sagged downward in stillness.

"Come here," I said.

I laid back down, and Gilly joined me. While I laid on my back, she tucked herself into my side and rested her head on my chest. I placed an arm around her waist while I stroked her hair. It tangled around my fingers and tickled them. We didn't speak. We simply existed with one another, hyperaware of our closeness, our breaths, our warmth. I didn't want to let her go. Jon's protectiveness made sense. Gilly could easily be a target after Marki and Sarai. Alma and Jen too. I squeezed Gilly tighter, her breaths deepening as she fell asleep on my chest.

I shimmied out from under Gilly when I heard Jon's bedroom door close. Before I left, I placed a blanket around her and turned off her light. I closed her door as quietly as I could before I tiptoed downstairs. Somehow, I made it out of her house without making a sound. I retrieved my bike from the road and didn't stop to look back at Gilly's. It was late, and I needed to get home, but I wasn't worried about getting in trouble with Mom. My thoughts were only on Gilly and how she felt in my arms. Alive, safe, protected. I was only 5'3, but felt in that moment that, if adrenaline kicked in, I could easily overpower someone. Maybe. Gilly had a couple inches on me, but I was the one who needed to keep her safe.

When I got home, Mom was asleep on the couch, so I locked up and headed upstairs. Owen was still awake, his door cracked.

I knocked before pushing it open. He was listening to music and doing his homework.

"What?" he said.

He looked at me, annoyed and tapped his pencil on the page. Always doing things at the last minute. I smiled at him.

"I'm glad you're my brother," I said.

"You're acting weird," he replied.

"I don't tell you that enough."

"Whatever you say."

He moved his headphones back on and continued scribbling on a worksheet. I closed his door, going to my own room.

I dialed Beck's phone number and waited on her groggy "hello" from the other end of the line.

"Hey," I said.

"Quinn, for once, I'm trying to sleep," Beck sighed.

"You would say we know each other fairly well, right?" I asked.

"I know you have a freckle on your left middle toe," Beck said. "So, I'd say well enough. Why?"

"I went to see Gilly," I said. "I told her about Brady and Sarai, and she got upset about it because Sarai never told her about him. It got her thinking about Marki and everything. I don't know. She's still sad."

"If it makes you feel any better, I can't recall anything I haven't told you," Beck said. "And in case you're wondering, if I really did anything with Harry, I would tell you immediately."

"Sometimes you aren't such a shithead," I chuckled.

"Right back at you, Quinny the Pooh."

"*And* you've ruined it."

"I'll see you tomorrow," Beck said. "Goodnight."

"Goodnight."

—

The four of us sat in the center of the cafeteria, Gilly and I on one side, Beck and Harry on the other. Alma and Jen had left the original table they sat at with Gilly, Marki, and Sarai to sit with a couple girls from the tennis team. The table stayed empty; the only empty one in the whole cafeteria. It was a landmark of what once was the oasis for the most popular girls in school. Three were left, no longer the powerful clique they once were.

I caught Gilly staring at the table, eyes glazed in memories, but it didn't last long. She turned to me with a smile. "I'll be right back," she said, standing and weaving into the lunch line.

"Look at the table," Beck said. "It's like they never existed."

"I don't like how empty it is," I said. "It's too loud."

"Do you and Gilly want to switch spots with us?" Harry asked. "I can't imagine having to stare at it the whole time."

"If Gilly ever mentions it, yes," I said. "Until then, we can just continue to ignore it."

Gilly returned with a brown-spotted banana. Rink passed us smelling like weed and Kit Kats. Two of his friends followed him out of the cafeteria.

"They're off to smoke," Beck said.

Beck met my eyes, and we held contact.

"Shit," I blurted. "I forgot I have to pick up study cards from Mr. Henderson."

"Well, I'm going to buy more weed," Beck said, gathering her bookbag and leaving the cafeteria.

"I can wait for you if you want?" I said to Gilly. "I don't think he'll mind if I get them later."

"No, go," Gilly said. "It's fine. Harry can keep me company."

Harry looked at me wide-eyed, before turning to Gilly with an overly cheery smile.

"Of course I can," he said, voice cracking.

Unconvincing—but Gilly didn't seem to notice. I left the cafeteria and found Beck waiting for me. She pulled my arm out the side door and we power walked to the football field.

"We can't just bombard him with more questions," I said. "We already tried that."

"That's why we are going to let his ding-dong friends spill some information for him," Beck said. "And we're going to smoke."

We found Rink and the ding-dongs under the bleachers lighting their joints. The smell of weed filled the air as one of them blew smoke in the direction of Beck and me.

"What's up, boys?" Beck said.

"Yo, it's been a while Beck," one of them greeted, eyes already red.

I guessed it wasn't their first time smoking that day.

"What the hell are you two doing here?" Rink asked.

Beck grabbed the joint from his fingers and inhaled, blowing it in his face. "Smoking."

I took the joint when Beck passed it to me and inhaled, coughing immediately. I'd smoked with Beck once and hated it, nearly throwing up from how much I coughed. I took my water from my bag and chugged while Beck handed Rink a wad of cash.

"You could always outsmoke everyone, Beck," the one with the bloodshot eyes said.

"Out of you guys?" Beck scoffed. "Of course."

"Seriously," Rink said. "Why are you here? To interrogate me some more?"

The two boys passed the joint back and forth while Beck stared at Rink.

"Like I said," Beck began, "I just wanted to smoke."

When the joint came back to me, I inhaled enough to keep in my mouth before blowing it out quickly. It was too quiet under the bleachers. Rink refused to speak while his friends dicked around with one another. I sat in the corner with my water while Beck stood between all of us.

"Just ask what you need to so we can all get on with our day," Rink said.

"I don't have any specific questions," Beck said. "Only that it seems to me you don't care that you have the biggest target on your back."

"So, you don't think I did it?" Rink asked.

"I don't think you're dumb enough to have killed two best friends, one of them being your stepsister," Beck said. "Especially two girls loved by the whole fucking town. I've known you for years, Rink. I *know* you."

"As your weed dealer," Rink said.

"You're not helping your own case." Beck sighed.

"Rink wouldn't ever hurt them," the other meathead piped up.

"Thanks for the input, PJ," Beck sighed.

"*Forreal*," Bloodshot Eyes said. "Why would he kill his best-paying customer?"

Beck turned on her heels to face Rink. Even my attention was back on him. He rolled his eyes, cursing his friends.

"You said I was your best paying customer?" Beck said.

"Things change," Rink said while he ashed the joint.

"You told me only family got weed for free," Beck said. "So, who is he talking about? Marki?"

"Did you not hear about Jon Willis busting him and Marki for weed a few weeks ago?" PJ asked.

Rink only shrugged at Beck's expectant stare. "I didn't know Marki was into this sort of stuff," Beck said.

"There's a lot you don't know about Sarai and her friends," Rink muttered. "I've told Jon Willis this. I wouldn't be surprised if they got themselves into trouble."

At that, I spoke up. "How could you say that about Sarai?"

"I considered Sarai my sister," Rink answered. "We never had problems with each other. We didn't really talk at school, but she was my sister. I knew her. I probably knew her better than Gilly or Marki or those twins. She never knew how to get herself out of situations. She hated confrontation. Marki, on the other hand, was a secret troublemaker. She came around through the woods for weed deals all the time, and Sarai never even knew. I have nothing to hide. They did."

Rink grabbed his bookbag to leave, followed by PJ and Bloodshot Eyes.

"Did he just say he used to meet Marki in the woods?" I asked.

"Yep," Beck said, staring as they walked away. "He sure did."

Beck sprayed me with some kind of peach perfume before we walked back to class. I wasn't high, but I still smelled like weed. It peeked through the peach smell, and I tried walking as slowly as I could so I didn't waft too much air. When I sat behind Gilly in class, she turned to me with her nose wrinkled.

"You smell like skunk," she said. "Did you smoke with Beck?"

"I was . . . present," I replied, the lie already halfway out, "but I didn't smoke."

"Did you get those study cards?" Gilly asked, arms folded.

I debated carrying on with the lie, but Gilly seemed like the type to ask for proof if she didn't believe me.

"No," I said. "Beck insisted I come with her, and they slipped my mind."

"There were never any cards, were there?"

"No." I dropped my head. "I'm sorry I lied, but I didn't want you to think I was hanging out with . . . Rink."

"I don't care about that," Gilly said. "I just wished you didn't lie to me. Anyway, Harry wants us all to go to the arcade together this weekend."

She turned around without letting me agree to the plans. I pulled out my notebook as class started. I wanted to tell Gilly about what Rink had said but decided the information would stay with Beck and me unless it absolutely needed to come out. I didn't want to upset Gilly any more with the secrets her friends kept.

I digested Rink's words, breaking them down to figure out everything. One thing was for sure: Marki had regular meetings in the woods with Rink, the same way Sarai had with Brady. The woods were the focal point to everything, and I figured that whoever knew about the girl's use of the woods was the one who killed them. So far, the only person I knew of was Rink. Things weren't looking good for him.

# CHAPTER FOURTEEN

There were certain things I wouldn't tell Gilly. One of them was how Harry drove Beck and me down Sarai's road to find Marki's house even after I promised to be safe. I knew they were neighbors, but I wasn't sure how many houses down Marki lived. I couldn't ask Gilly. It would lead to questions, and I knew she'd figure out what we were up to—being the daughter of the sheriff and all.

The second secret I kept was how, slowly, I took over the case. As much as I trusted Beck, I had to figure everything out *my* way—at least for my own peace. I'd promised Beck I'd let it go, but I couldn't. Part of me was too curious; the other part of me wanted to protect Gilly. I had also started to suspect Rink Matthews myself, and for my own sanity, I needed to debunk any theories I had related to him.

And so, I found myself in the back of Harry's car, Beck in the seat in front of me, scanning the houses that flew by. "Marki's house has a white cross on the mailbox," I said.

"How do you know that?" Harry asked.

"Heard people talking about it in the cafeteria after she died," I explained. "They wanted to drop off stuff for her family."

My observations came in handy sometimes. We all searched the mailboxes, Harry driving so slowly that he gained looks from the neighbors. He waved, trying to be friendly, and Beck slapped his arm.

"You look like you're about to offer every kid in this neighborhood candy before you throw them in the car," she groaned. "Be more discreet."

When we passed Sarai's house, Rink's car was in the driveway. I got goosebumps looking at it. We neared the end of the street and didn't find a mailbox with a white cross.

"Drive back," I said. "It could be on the other side."

Harry turned the car around and slowly drove down the street again. None of the mailboxes at the end of the street had the cross. We passed Sarai's house again, and Rink was outside, getting something from his car. Beck and I ducked down while Harry sped up, but Rink didn't notice. When we got to the start of the street, Harry pulled over.

"I didn't see anything," Harry said.

"Neither did I." Beck turned to me. "Are you sure this is the right street?"

"I'm positive," I said. "Sarai and Marki lived on the same street."

"What do you want to do?" Harry asked. "We can't keep driving aimlessly."

"I guess we can leave," I sighed. Another defeat.

I leaned against the window and watched the houses go by. I remembered Marki's mailbox had a white cross on it.

Harry drove us back to his house. We quietly filed out of the car and into his living room, not mentioning our second fail since we'd taken up the case together. We hung out at Harry's house until dusk, watching movies and eating junk food. Beck sat in between Harry and me, though I could've sworn she scooted closer to him.

Harry dropped me off before his parents got home, not wanting to explain why he had not one but *two* girls in his house on a school night. Before I went inside my house, I grabbed my bike. Sarai's house was probably ten minutes away. It was stupid to go alone in the near-dark, but I was desperate. I had to prove myself right about Marki's mailbox.

"Where are you going?" Owen asked, appearing in the garage. He had his headphones on, grabbing a soda from the fridge in the corner.

"A bike ride," I said. "I could use some exercise."

"Mom won't let you go alone," he said.

I rolled my eyes. "Then come with me."

"No way."

"I'll pay you."

"Deal!"

Mom gave us a curfew. We had one hour before she wanted us home, and if we didn't arrive, she would call the police immediately. The problem could have easily been solved with letting me have a phone, but since she didn't feel Owen was responsible enough for one yet, she wouldn't let me have one either. "One more year," she told me when I whined about it. I wondered if she would change her mind soon with everything going on.

Owen and I biked at the same pace. I didn't tell him my plan, but he halted before we turned down Marki and Sarai's street.

"Isn't this . . .?"

"Oh," I said. "I didn't notice. Want to go down it anyway?"

He shrugged and followed. I kept my eyes on the mailboxes. The white cross was out there, somewhere. Like earlier, we biked up the street until Owen slowed down. I put the brake on my bike while he stared at a house a few down from Sarai's. Rink's car was back in the driveway, and the lights were off in the house.

"Isn't this Marki's house?" Owen asked.

I looked at a brick house with one singular downstairs light on.

"No idea," I said.

"It has to be," Owen said. "Look at the mailbox."

On the side were small angel wings. The mailbox had a white base that reached up into what looked like a cross.

"White cross," I whispered.

"I'm creeped out now," Owen said. "Can we go home?"

I nodded, still staring at the mailbox. From Marki's house, I got a clear shot of Sarai's. When we biked away, I peered into Marki's backyard. There was a cover of trees, identical to the ones in the woods behind school.

I didn't pay attention to a single thing at school on Thursday. Not even Gilly's silly doodles of us with hearts for eyes drew me in. I smiled and drew her a flower back, but all I could think about were Marki and Sarai.

Harry, Beck, and I waited until the parking lot had cleared out before we drove to the edge of the woods. Harry stayed behind to keep watch while Beck and I went into the woods. I carried a flashlight while Beck took Harry's pocketknife. We walked back to the trail that led to Sarai's house and went right to find Marki's.

"Your determination these days is very un-Quinn like," Beck said.

"Hey," I pouted, "I've always been this way."

"You gave up the recorder in fifth grade because your Hot Crossed Buns sounded too squeaky," Beck said. "The recorder, Quinn. The freaking recorder."

"I get it." I rolled my eyes. "I just want everyone to be safe."

"You know," Beck said, "I'm starting to think this is less about Gilly and more about . . . me."

I stopped in place to stare at her. Beck offered me a sad smile and halfhearted shrug.

"You aren't in their friend group," I pointed out. "There's nothing to worry about."

"I know you worry about my antics," Beck said. "I know you think I get into trouble, and I do put myself into some questionable situations, but I'm not stupid. If all of this isn't a coincidence, I have no connections with Marki or Sarai. But I do with Rink."

"I thought you didn't believe he's the killer," I said.

"You can't trust anyone these days," Beck replied.

I didn't say anything because Beck was partially right. But I would never tell Beck she was right. Sometimes Beck called me late on weekends when we weren't together, slurring her words. Most of the time giggling about her scraped knees from hopping fences to run from the cops. Meanwhile Gilly had the most protection out of everyone at our school, but she seemed like the perfect target, being the center of her group of friends.

"I think Marki's house is coming up," I said.

Beck stopped me. "Just promise me you'll be careful if you keep sticking your nose in all this."

Beck held up her pinky finger, and as if we were little girls again, I locked mine with hers. We walked, crunching leaves and kicking pine cones. I counted the house's backyards. Marki was six down from Sarai. On the sixth, we saw Marki's backyard from a distance. There was a gazebo with pine needles on top as if nobody had cleaned it off in months. Her house was quiet, and I shuddered as I imagined the inside—the silence.

"Are we supposed to look for anything while we're here?" Beck asked.

"I don't know," I said. "But it does prove my point that their houses both connect back here."

Beck and I kicked around but didn't find anything out of the ordinary. The creak of a door hinge and voices flooded from Marki's back porch. Beck pulled me behind a tree, and we squatted. I had to squint to see who the voices belonged to. One was Marki's mother, the other was Gilly's. We could barely hear what they were saying but both smiled sadly at one another, drinking from mugs. They sat and talked, Marki's mom tearing up. Guilt washed over me.

"We should go," I whispered to Beck.

In my heart, I knew this would be the last time I'd go in the woods. I had infringed on Marki and Sarai's privacy, and neither of them were there to defend themselves from my snooping. It was also an infringement of Gilly's privacy. They had been best friends since they were children, like Beck and me. They were practically family to her. I wanted to get some answers for her, but well, maybe that wasn't my job. It was up to me to help her have fun and be there when she missed her friends, not remind her of who she lost by snooping into a case I had no business being in, even if it felt like the right thing to do.

"Find anything?" Harry asked.

"Nope," I said. "Let's go."

School was chaos the next day. I turned my music off when I saw Harry standing with Beck. He towered over her, smiling down, and I almost didn't want to interrupt them.

Rink ran past us and out the school doors.

"Someone's in a hurry to smoke," Beck said.

I couldn't help but suspect that wasn't what he was doing. The warning bell rang, and Harry went off, leaving Beck and I to walk together. Before we walked into class, Christine crossed our path on the way to the bathroom.

"I'm going to pee real quick," I said, handing Beck my bag.

She took it without arguing. In the bathroom, Christine leaned into the mirror, touching up her lipstick. When she saw me, she didn't say anything, avoiding my eyes.

"You got me thinking about the murders," I said.

She capped her lipstick and finally turned to me. "Yeah?"

I nodded. "But I've come to the conclusion that getting involved isn't going to help, especially if it's for personal gain. I know you want to protect Jen, but if we only focus on them, we can help by keeping them safe."

"I'm not doing this to protect Jen," Christine said.

"Then who are you doing it for?" I asked.

"Marki," she said.

The light above us buzzed.

"Marki?" I repeated.

"I didn't stutter," Christine snapped. "Let's see if you can figure that one out, sleuth."

Too taken aback to respond, I let Christine push past me, the bathroom door slamming shut behind her. I stood there, the buzz growing, until the light died.

I shut down after that. How had I let Christine slip through my fingers? After she'd namedropped Marki in the weirdest way possible? I couldn't find her the rest of the day, but Christine and Marki already sat together on a pin in my head. How were they connected?

I didn't speak more than a few words the rest of the day. My mind was too caught up in the new information. At home, I opened a notebook and wrote down my own set of clues, including the names of everyone surrounding Marki and Sarai's murders. By association, Beck, Harry, and I were on the list. My head spun at the amount of people grouped with the two dead girls. Their popularity spanned the page, existing even after their deaths. My skin prickled in discomfort. Here I was, ripping the humanity from Marki and Sarai, two students who'd become "dead girls" overnight.

# CHAPTER FIFTEEN

I woke up clutching my notebook. Memories drifted back: how, the previous night, I'd chicken-scratched nearly everything I knew onto its pages in a frenzy. I didn't have any leads. To me, everyone was innocent—though in times of murder, the opposite was usually true. Everyone was a suspect, especially when murders were few and far between.

Our town was small: everybody knew everyone. People would stop in the grocery store to chat while blocking the cereal shelves, but nobody really had anywhere to go, so it was never a problem. But now? I worried lingering too long anywhere in town might put a target on my back. I made a note to myself not to stay anywhere too long, even the school bathroom.

I threw the notebook in a drawer and dragged myself downstairs for some breakfast.

"Good morning," I grumbled.

"Good morning," Mom said, pouring herself a cup of coffee. "Gilly called for you about an hour ago."

I gave her a thumbs-up before I poured myself a bowl of cereal. Owen was still asleep, and neither of us bothered waking him up.

I ate my cereal slowly, the crunch of flakes quickly turning soggy. After I finished, I called Gilly back.

"Hi," Gilly said, sounding slightly dejected. "What are you doing today?"

"Nothing," I said. "Sorry I missed your call earlier. I was still asleep."

"It's okay," Gilly said. "Can you come with me to Sarai's funeral?"

I'd completely forgotten the funeral was that day.. I hadn't been invited. Sarai's family had decided to keep it small, only for those who truly knew her.

"Am I allowed to?" I asked.

"I don't really care," Gilly said. "I need you there today."

My heart skipped a beat. Gilly needed me. It felt wrong to smile, but the fact that she wanted me there with her, on a vulnerable day, made me feel wanted.

"Of course I'll go," I said. "I'll go anywhere for you."

I borrowed a black dress from my mom because I didn't have one. I never had any use for a black dress or funeral attire. I brushed my hair and fastened it in a low bun with a lot of pins to keep it from falling out of place. I put on lip balm and mascara with a bit of blush. I'd never been to a funeral; I had no idea how I was supposed to present myself.

Jen picked me up. Alma was in the passenger seat, Gilly in the back. None of them had makeup on. Their eyes were peppered red from their premature tears. I didn't say anything when I got in the car. I didn't need to walk on eggshells today.

Sarai's parents decided to have an open-casket funeral, and it took all of me not to turn around and walk out of the church. I gripped Gilly's hand tighter than she had mine. I'd forgotten that she'd already gone through this before with Marki, not to mention her mom and brother. I looked at her and saw her blue-gray eyes steady ahead as she approached the casket with me. Was she used to this? Could anyone actually get used to this?

Sarai looked peaceful, her makeup and hair done. There was pink back in her cheeks. Her hands were folded neatly across her chest. Alma choked when she saw Sarai. Her parents pulled her away from the casket so she could catch her breath. Gilly shed a tear and wiped it away quickly. When we passed the casket, I finally let out a breath. We took a seat next to Alma and Jen. Rink was in the first seat with his dad and stepmother. His leg bounced as the silence stretched on before the service started.

I drowned out a lot of the funeral. I couldn't sit still for most of it and played with my fingers. Gilly didn't seem to notice but grabbed my hand every now and then, either to steady them or to steady herself. Rink spoke a few words, and I turned to find Jon Willis in the back. He kept his eyes set on Rink as he talked. At any moment, he would stand up with his handcuffs ready—I just felt it. When Rink was finished speaking, Jon turned and met my gaze. I threw my hand up, casually, and he nodded to me.

"Gilly Willis," the preacher said. "Would you like to come up here and say something?"

Gilly nodded and released my hand. I felt barren without her next to me.

"I would like to read a poem I wrote for Sarai," Gilly said. "Not many people know this, but she loved to read, especially poetry. She hated sonnets but loved haikus because she thought it was interesting how much could be said in so few words. I'm no poet, but I did my best."

Gilly reached into her jacket pocket and pulled out a piece of paper. She unfolded it slowly, sniffling. She scanned the page to get a sense of her words before she started.

"Friend, forget me not. Your missing presence lingers. My tears stay faithful," Gilly read.

The second she finished folding the paper up and putting it back in her pocket, she cried. She left the podium with her head up, tears streaming down her face as she sat next to me.

Alma and Jen followed with their own words. Neither went with a poem; instead they expressed their favorite memories with Sarai and shared how much they would miss her. Sarai's mother sobbed a few times, trying to hide the noise with her wad of tissues. Rink and his dad rubbed her arms to calm her down. I hoped to never know her pain.

I accompanied Gilly to the lowering of the casket. It was windy; Gilly was lucky to have a jacket. The sun beat down, impairing my vision. Most of the funerals I had seen were in movies, where it usually rained, but this was real life. Sarai was dead, and the sun still came up because the rest of the world had gone on with its day. Millions of people had no idea we were lowering a sixteen-year-old into the ground at that very moment. After Rink and his parents threw in some soil on top of Sarai's casket, Alma, Gilly, and Jen followed. When all had gone, the earth seemed to hum. Everyone was silent across the crowd. Shoes shuffled, and we walked back to Jen's car.

Our last destination of the day was Sarai's house for refreshments. There, Gilly sat thigh-to-thigh with me on a couch. She handed me an old photograph.

"We took this picture on the last day of second grade," Gilly said.

All five of them wore tie-dye shirts and matching gap-toothed smiles, their hair in pigtails.

"You were so little," I said.

Gilly's hair was much lighter back then, her eyes bluer.

"I'm going to go talk to Mrs. Matthews for a little bit," Gilly said. "Will you be okay?"

"Go," I said. "I'll be fine."

I ate a plate of cheese and crackers, balancing it on my knees. I was grateful nobody was focused on me. The last time I had been there was for a party where Sarai was giggling, bouncing around, and mingling with everyone. Her house seemed dull now. I looked around and found Jen in Christine's arms, crying. She had on a black blazer, hugging Jen tightly. She looked up at me and motioned for me to follow her upstairs. Christine released Jen, who probably went to find Alma.

I set my crackers down and followed her up the stairs.

Upstairs, the hall was wide. Sarai's bedroom door was cracked, so I pushed through it. Christine sat on Sarai's perfectly made bed, not caring if she wrinkled it.

"Don't you feel weird being in her room?" I asked, closing the door.

"She's dead," Christine said. "This is just a room."

"But it's *her* room," I insisted.

"It was."

Giving up, I asked, "Why didn't I see you at the funeral?"

"I had to work," Christine said. "But I promised Jen I would come here."

I leaned against Sarai's desk. Books were scattered around, some with bookmarks still inside.

"How long are you going to keep bullshitting her?" I asked.

Christine chuckled and closed her eyes. "You don't even know the half of it."

"Then enlighten me," I said. "What exactly are you trying to do? And what ties do you have to Marki?"

"I am trying to figure this whole thing out because the police are doing a shitty job," Christine said.

"And what have you figured out so far?" I asked.

Christine reached into her blazer pocket and handed me a piece of paper. Her address was written on it in green marker.

"We can't talk now. Whenever you want to know, just swing by. I work on the weekends, but I'm free after school. Sometimes even during school if I don't feel like going."

With that, she left Sarai's room. I stuffed the small piece of paper in my sneaker so I wouldn't lose it. Still no answers about her relation to Marki. I discreetly left Sarai's room and went back downstairs.

"Hey," Gilly said. "I was looking for you."

"I was also looking for you," I said. Another lie.

"I said goodbye to Sarai's parents." Gilly tossed her head in the direction of the door. "I'm ready to go if you are."

"*Yes*," I said in a rush. "Sorry, that came out wrong."

Gilly smiled weakly. "I'll go find Alma and Jen."

While Gilly left me again to find her friends, I saw Rink out back through the screen door. He ate alone, staring at his plate. Had the people here exiled him on purpose? I moved to go talk to him, but Gilly found me with Alma and Jen in tow.

The car ride was silent, apart from a couple of hiccups from a still-crying Jen. Alma took the wheel for her a couple of times, steadying the car. Queasiness filled me from the jerky motions, but I refused to complain.

Gilly walked me to my door once Jen dropped me off.

"I have to get home," Gilly said. "I promised Dad I'd come home after the funeral, but I want to see you again soon. Just the two of us. I need it."

"Let me know when you can," I said. "We can do anything, as long as it's something you like to do."

Gilly kissed me before she jogged back to Jen's car. Back inside, Mom was on the couch watching a movie with Owen.

"There was another call for you," Mom said. "I don't remember who, though. Some boy."

The only boy I knew was Harry, and I doubted he would leave a call for me. If anything, he'd use Beck as a middleman. I picked up the phone and dialed the number back.

"Hello?" a woman's voice said. She sounded sad.

"Hi," I said. "I got a call from this number earlier. I'm Quinn."

"I'm sorry, I don't know you," she said. "Whoever called must've had the wrong number."

"It was a boy," I said.

There was whispering on the other end of the line. I considered hanging up before the phone clicked again with someone picking it up.

"Quinn?"

Rink's voice jolted me to attention. Stunned, I replied, "Rink? You called me?" Sarai's mom had been the one to pick up, then. I should've recognized her voice.

"I meant to talk with you at our house, but you left before I got the chance," Rink said.

"How did you get my number?" I asked.

He hesitated. "From . . . Beck."

Was that a lie? Beck wouldn't just give him my number without telling me.

"Why did you call?" I asked aloud.

Rink sighed. "I've noticed Jon Willis poking around here. I saw him at the funeral when I was talking. I think he truly suspects I killed Marki and Sarai. I can sense it."

My heart raced at the mention of my girlfriend's dad. If the town sheriff thought Rink was guilty, then there was no hope for him. Still, I couldn't bring myself to dash whatever hopes Rink held.

"There's no concrete proof," I told him. "Nothing can happen if there's no concrete proof."

"I wouldn't be surprised if they found a way around it," Rink muttered. "But I didn't call to tell you that, because you already know about it. I really called to ask that if I do get convicted, will you testify for me in court?"

I must have stopped breathing, because suddenly, the world around me went out of focus. Puzzlement filled me. How could I testify if *I* wasn't sure whether Rink was guilty or not? Like Jon Willis, I really had no concrete proof either way.

"Of course I will," I said, and I left it at that.

It was a half-truth—not quite powerful enough to be a lie. I just hoped it wouldn't come to that. There was no way in hell I could help in Rink's testimony, not with my ties to the Willis's.

# CHAPTER SIXTEEN

On Saturday, Jon Willis dropped Gilly off at my house. He spoke with my mom before driving away—small talk, parent stuff I didn't care to eavesdrop on. Harry and Beck were picking us up for the arcade within the hour. Owen begged us to come, too, so he could meet up with his friends. I sat squished in the middle of Gilly and Owen, elbowing him for more room.

The arcade's sign was lit up in red and purple, much like the inside with its multicolor lights and loud machines. Owen met up with his friends while we traded in cash for coins. I shoved as many as I could in my jean pockets.

"I challenge you to my favorite game," I said to Gilly, leading her to the Skee-Ball machine.

We picked two lanes side by side and began. The balls clinked together as they rolled toward us. We rolled the first one together. Gilly was slower than I was. I aimed for the 1000 points but missed every time, so I settled for the 400 and 500 points. Gilly rolled a ball that didn't make it into the slots and instead slid back to her.

"I win!" I said when our scores were tallied.

"That's not fair," Gilly pouted. "I didn't know I was going up against the Skee-Ball champion."

"I think you might just be really bad at it," I teased.

Gilly stuck her tongue out at me. We found Harry and Beck playing basketball against one another, Harry beating Beck. She punched his arm when he flexed his muscles and gloated.

"What's something we could all play against each other?" Gilly asked.

"Foosball?" Harry suggested.

Gilly and I were red, while Beck and Harry were blue. I showed Gilly how to control the little people, and she halfway understood, making our players do flips. We let her throw the ball in first, but it immediately rolled into our goal, giving Beck and Harry a point.

"I'll take over from here," Beck said, the next to retrieve the ball.

As the game went on, I found myself working up a sweat. Beck and I were competitive; we always had been. Both of us were sore winners, and I didn't want to hear about how she'd beaten us the rest of the night. We were tied until Harry hit the winning shot. He and Beck danced and laughed in our faces. I rolled my eyes, scoping out the arcade for our next game.

"Anyone want to see me wipe the floor at Pac-Man?" Harry asked.

"Never say that out loud again," Beck said.

Harry put his coins in the Pac-Man machine, and the electronic music began. As soon as the countdown stopped, Harry's focus centered on the little yellow Pac-Man. He kept his eyes glued to the screen, moving the joystick around precisely like a surgeon. He flew through the levels until he finally lost his life to the pastel-pink ghost. His score jumped to the top of the leaderboard.

"Easy," he said, cracking his knuckles.

"I have to say, I'm impressed," Beck said, drinking a Coke slushy.

"Nobody can beat me," Harry sighed, leaning back to stretch like a king.

A bit of his stomach showed, and I watched Beck nonchalantly look down. She just as quickly looked away to not make it obvious. I bit my tongue to stop a smirk from rising to my face.

After Harry's win, we sat at some of the tables to get a bite to eat. Gilly and I shared a basket of nachos while Harry ate a corn dog. Arcade food tasted plastic, but it was the exact greasy thing I needed after over an hour and a half of games.

"We should place a bet," Harry said to Beck.

"On what?" Beck asked.

"If you beat me at Pac-Man, I will take you out on a date," Harry said.

Gilly and I looked at one another and grinned. It was about time the two quit being in denial.

"And if I don't beat you?" Beck said, sizing him up.

"Then *you* get to take me out," Harry said, smirking.

He stuck his arm around the back of Beck's seat, staring at her with an intensity that would surely melt anyone in his line of vision. But not Beck—she was better at hiding it.

Beck seemed to think about it for a moment before sticking her hand out to shake Harry's. "You have a deal. But regardless, you'll be the one taking me out. I don't have a car."

We all laughed until Rink and his two friends I'd met under the bleachers walked by us.

"Hey Rink," Gilly said.

"Hi Gilly," he replied, voice softer than when he'd talked to Beck and me.

He didn't give Beck or me a glance and went to order his food. Although Rink was still on my radar, it didn't seem like he was on Gilly's. I let my negative thoughts go. He was her best friend's stepbrother; I didn't need to look any deeper into it.

"Come on," Beck said. "Pac-Man round two."

Beck died once within the first thirty seconds of playing Pac-Man, but she didn't give up. While Beck played, Harry cheered her on. My attention was torn from them when Jon Willis along with two other officers walked into the arcade.

"Dad?" Gilly said. "What are you doing here?"

"Just making my rounds," Jon said. "I'll only be a moment."

Jon Willis walked around, intimidating everyone in the arcade. Harry started another round of Pac-Man while I kept my eye on Jon. He said "hello" to a few people, including some of the arcade workers. Rink noticed Jon was there and pulled his hand into a fist at his table. I slowly moved closer to where Rink was.

"How are you doing today, Rink?" Jon asked.

"Fine," Rink said.

The hostility between the two was palpable, tension suffocating the entire arcade.

"Just wanted to see how you were doing following the funeral," Jon said.

"Why?" Rink asked. "So you can convict me for not crying like I should have?"

Jon chuckled and leaned down so he was face-to-face with Rink. "You better watch how you talk to me, boy."

His voice was a growl that made me take a step back. Jon Willis had become someone else, not the warm father of Gilly, but his true self—whom I hadn't seen before—the town's cold sheriff.

"Or what?" Rink said, standing.

His fist twitched at his side, dangerously close to throwing a punch.

"Rink!" I blurted.

Both of them turned to me, and I shook my head at Rink. He unclenched his fist. Jon Willis smiled before walking off and through the doors of the arcade. Rink's chest heaved up and down, his two friends sitting with their mouths open. Grabbing his drink from the table, Rink stomped out of the arcade, avoiding me.

"I won again," Harry said, approaching me with Beck in tow.

"What happened?" Beck asked.

I looked at Gilly who hid her face in shame at her father's actions.

"Rink stirring up trouble," I said, trying to make her feel better.

Beck nodded. "Well, guess I'll be taking Harry on a date."

Harry dropped Gilly and I off at my house. Jon had agreed to let her sleep over after speaking with my mom, to both mine and Gilly's surprise. Gilly Willis, sleeping over at my house. I imagined the only other people she'd had sleepovers with were within her friend group. But now my house was graced with her presence. Everywhere she walked, I hoped her perfume latched to my furniture, locking in the memory of her being there. Who knew if Jon would ever agree to it again with everything that had been going on.

Gilly laid against my chest that night while I played with her hair. Her arms were bare, and goosebumps would occasionally raise along her skin. I was in a big t-shirt, and our legs rubbed together, soft and warm. Even though our night hadn't ended how I wanted it to, I felt comfortable and safe. Nothing could hurt either of us here.

"Can I ask you something?" I said.

"Are you going to ask me if I think Rink killed Marki and Sarai?"

"Yes," I said. "But if you don't want to talk about it, we don't have to."

Gilly shifted so she could look at me better.

"I've known Rink basically my whole life," Gilly said. "He and Sarai became stepsiblings when we were six. We would make him play dolls with us when we needed someone to play the boy, and he would do it without argument. It just wouldn't make sense if it were true that he killed them. He's gentler than people give him credit for."

But Rink had called Gilly and her whole group trouble. Would he have the same opinion if he knew Gilly had defended him?

"Is that a no?" I asked aloud.

"My dad has told me that people do things without any implication or good explanation," Gilly said. "So I don't know how to answer that question."

The words burned in my throat like acid, trying to crawl out from my tongue but I couldn't let them. If I unloaded everything I'd found out to Gilly, a plethora of feelings could bubble up. Anger at me or her late friends. Hurt that I didn't tell her sooner. I wanted Gilly to feel peace, so instead, I settled in and pulled her closer to me before I closed my eyes, signaling we should sleep.

In the morning, we put strawberry cream cheese on bagels my mom got from the local bakery. They were still warm and buttery; the cream cheese had whole chunks of strawberry in it.

I promised Gilly she would have me for the whole day, and I kept that promise. We even got ready next to one another, brushing our teeth to the same rhythm. Normally, I liked my weekends to myself, unless Beck wanted to have a movie night. But this? I could have done this any day of the week.

For lunch, I planned a picnic in the park. My mom dropped us off, and I let Gilly choose our spot by a gazebo. It was white and next to the pond where geese swam with their threatening gazes. I tried not to make eye contact; geese were vicious. We ate chicken salad sandwiches, grapes, pickles, chips, and snickerdoodles. Mom had packed us fruit punch and disposable cups as well.

"I don't think I've ever been on a picnic," Gilly said. "But I like it."

"I thought you might." I let out a breath. "It's peaceful out here."

"It's a good place to clear your head," Gilly agreed.

I dug into my sandwich. Mom made the best chicken salad. She used to make it with raisins until Owen and I complained about it. Now, the recipe was perfect without them. We watched kids run around with their tired parents. Geese ate the bread-crumbs thrown for them. A colorful leaf fell from a tree. My excitement for October grew. I caught Gilly looking at me and leaned over to kiss her cheek.

"So can we consider this our first official date?" Gilly asked.

"I was planning on it," I said.

Gilly leaned into me, and I placed my arm around her shoulders. There was a chill in the air, but we kept each other warm. More leaves fell, signifying what was to come.

# CHAPTER SEVENTEEN

October, 2004

Mom forced Owen and I to help her decorate for Halloween—her favorite holiday. It was our tradition; when October 1st came, we had to spend the day decorating. My favorite part was spreading fake spiderwebs on the bushes. Owen stuck fake graves in the ground with green hands sticking out from them. Our yard could easily have won a contest for "most spirited." When the decorating was over, Mom made caramel apples with cider, and we watched an old Halloween movie of her choosing. It was our own small holiday routine.

The town's curfew died down as the police grew busier in their search for the person who killed Marki and Sarai. It was never officially called off, but everyone was too busy and wired to care. Jon took in more people for questioning, according to Gilly, and it looked like he had a lead on the case. Not much was released about it to the town. Things felt more in place finally. Gilly still sat with us at lunch, and we tried to hang out after school at least once a week. Sometimes, Beck and Harry tagged along; other times we were alone. After a few dates, it finally felt like Gilly and I were a real couple. I had the label, plus the most pretty and popular girl in school; what more could I want?

Rink stopped coming to school. Beck claimed his friends had told her he needed a break. Worry for him gnawed at me. It sucked that Jon Willis seemed set on intimidating him, plus the fact that a lot of people at school looked at him like he really was the killer. It was still hard to believe, but I found it best to keep my mouth shut and go along with what everyone else thought. Any difference in opinion could put a target on your back; theories would circulate that those who didn't agree were Rink's accomplices.

"I may go by Rink's after school," Beck said at lunch before Gilly and Harry joined us.

"Do you want me to come with you?" I asked.

"We'll have to walk there," Beck said. "Neither of us have a car."

"Why don't you see if one of Rink's friends will take us?" I suggested. "Or Harry?"

"I don't think Harry should go," Beck said. "Rink won't talk in front of him."

I hadn't told Beck about my phone call with Rink. Or the fact that Christine had slipped me her address. I'd moved the slip of paper to my desk drawer and hadn't opened it since the day of Sarai's funeral. Whenever I saw Christine in school, she barely acknowledged me. She was still waiting on me to figure out her ties to Marki, but I couldn't figure it out without asking people questions, and those always led back to guilt or conviction.

"We can go," I said. "But you have to find an excuse for Harry not driving you home."

Harry and Gilly joined us at the same time. Gilly lit up whenever she spoke to Harry. He had a charm to him that made being in his presence easy. I liked how their friendship was growing, even if Gilly and Beck's wasn't quite on the uphill. This new routine of all of us eating together brought out a sparkle in me. For so long, I'd dreaded lunchtime conversations and sitting with anyone but Beck. But I had a group now. I fit in. October was already proving to be incredible.

Mrs. Ashley discussed the school events taking place in October. As per usual, I braided Gilly's hair while we listened.

"The sheriff has decided that we will still have all of our festivities this month," Mrs. Ashley announced. "That means the corn maze, trunk-or-treat, chili contest—all of it—is still on."

Gilly leaned back. "I'm great at corn mazes."

"You'll have to prove it," I whispered.

"That being said, there will be more officers stationed around the school at these events," Mrs. Ashley said. "So those of you who partake in 'extracurricular activities' on the school grounds may want to reconsider."

"Guess I'll be kissing you behind the cornstalks," Gilly said.

She brushed her fingertips over mine, electrifying my hand. A second later, she sat forward to pay attention to the lesson while I focused on the tingling feeling left by her fingertips. No matter what, her touch always had that effect on me.

After school ended, Beck and I took the shortcut through the woods to get to Rink's house after school. She convinced Harry the two of us needed to study for a test in the library, and that we planned to walk home from school together. We waited by the bleachers until we didn't see anyone. The police still had the woods taped off. As we walked through them, it was even more eerie than before. Beck armed herself with a pocketknife while I only had a calculator.

It took us a few minutes to see Rink's backyard in our line of sight. I panted, worn out from the exercise. A nap was in my foreseeable future. We crept around the side of the house, making sure there weren't any peeping neighbors or other students returning from school. Rink's car was in the driveway, so we rang the doorbell.

His heavy footsteps approached the door. When he opened it, he looked and smelled awful. Days of smoking weed were masked by his cheap cologne, and his eyes were crusty and bloodshot.

"You look like shit," Beck said.

"I feel like shit," Rink said.

He stepped aside to let us in without an argument. The house was still orderly. Rink led us to his bedroom, and I debated staying in the hallway. Clothes were strewn everywhere, including bags of fast food, some with stale fries peeking out. His room smelled faintly of greasy food, ketchup, and weed.

"Why haven't you been in school?" Beck asked.

"What's the point?" Rink said. "Everyone thinks I'm guilty. Jon Willis is one step away from arresting me. Might as well live out my time in solitude before he gets me."

"Why are you so adamant that he is going to arrest you?" I asked. "Do you not have any faith in yourself?"

"You answer that for me, Quinn," Rink snapped. "Tell me, what do *you* think about everything?"

His accusatory tone made me fall silent. For a split second, I thought I was talking to Christine with her cryptic theories and puzzling remarks.

Beck handled him while I picked up some trash from his room, unable to stand the mess any longer. If he wouldn't help himself, I would at least make his bedroom halfway decent. I nearly jumped when I found a dead fly clinging to a molding french fry.

"Quit pitying yourself and get up," Beck said. "Go to school. Who gives a shit what people say. You never have."

"This is different," Rink said.

"I know that," Beck replied. "But I know you're innocent. I completely believe you. That's one person. All you need is one person."

At that, I glanced over. Just the other day, Beck had claimed she didn't know if she believed him or not. It seemed things had changed. Beck turned to me, waving her hands for backup.

"Two people," I said, shoving some bags in his already overflowing trash can.

I meant to keep my promise to testify in his favor. I really was under no obligation to follow through with it, but if it helped him get out of his literal funk, then so be it. Rink stared at the two of us. I wanted more than anything to flush his eyes out with saline.

"I promise I'll go to school tomorrow," Rink said.

Beck and I held out our pinkies until he connected his with ours. Our fingers wove into a clump, Rink's larger than ours.

"And take a shower, would you?" Beck said. "You smell awful."

Rink drove us both home so we wouldn't have to walk. He yelled at us for going through the woods, but we assured him we were armed. He actually laughed when I pulled out my calculator. It was a good sound, hearty and full. He dropped Beck off first. Harry was in his garage, lifting weights. When he saw Rink's car, he stopped, slowly walking out of the garage. He waved Beck over, and she followed. Harry's look was sharp, threatening to cut into Rink if he got any closer. Guess I knew his stance.

"No way," Rink said. "Are they together?"

"I think it's complicated," I sighed.

I made Rink promise he would go to school tomorrow one last time before I left his car. Mom was on the porch, sipping a cup of coffee. Rink drove off slowly to make sure I made it to the door.

"What were you doing with Rink Matthews?" Mom asked, stern.

"He gave Beck and I a ride home from school," I said.

"I don't want you riding anywhere with him," Mom said. "Do you understand me?"

I rolled my eyes. "Please tell me you aren't feeding into the 'Rink is Guilty' propaganda. They have no evidence. Besides, Sarai was his sister. He didn't hurt her or Marki."

Saying it made me believe in myself more. And Rink. Maybe I was on his side, after all.

"I just want you to be safe," Mom said.

"If someone wanted to kill me, they probably would have done it by now," I muttered, walking into the house.

I closed the door before she could yell at me and ran up the stairs. My hand hovered over the desk drawer where I'd tucked away Christine's address. I, once again, decided against going to her house. But the more I ignored the desk drawer, the closer it seemed to get. Inching closer, until, if I turned in my bed, it would be in my face, the drawer shooting out to hit me. I grabbed my notebook instead, tapping my pencil against my page of evidence. Marki and Christine. Secret cousins? Ex-best friends? A popular girl seeking solace in a loner like Gilly and me?

I could've sworn the drawer moved out an inch.

"I'm not going," I said. "And you can't make me."

Rink surprised us when he showed up at school the next day, hair clean, eyes clear. For once, his clothes didn't have the lingering scent of marijuana. At lunch, he sat at the table next to us so we could talk discreetly. We all ignored the stares and whispers.

"I actually went to all of my classes today," Rink said, forking a mandarin slice.

"That's a first," Beck mused. "Did you have some period of enlightenment that's making you want to clean up your act?"

"If it keeps me out of jail, I will do anything," Rink said.

I looked at Gilly, who swirled her spoon around her pudding cup.

"Well, you got a whole table to back you up," Harry said.

His feelings must have changed since yesterday. Gilly nodded her head, silently agreeing. I knew she was close with her dad, and I wondered if talking about Rink's situation made her feel as if she were betraying him. I nudged her arm with mine, which made her smile. It was a small smile, her lips barely curling upward, but something about it made me feel as though I'd fallen through five floors. I realized then that I was falling in love with Gilly Willis, and I would do anything to keep putting smiles on her face.

I rode my bike home that day. The air was cool enough so I wouldn't break a sweat. I couldn't handle the musty bus anymore. Beck would get her license in a month; she'd promised me. I didn't have much homework, so I decided to prolong my bike ride. I rode around town, catching Harry leaving the store with a bouquet of flowers. I figured they were for Beck. I laughed at the gesture; Beck hated flowers.

The pumpkin patch was already in full swing. Mini jack-o'-lanterns were carved to show how cute the pumpkins would look on Halloween. A few teenagers were there along with some families, already picking out their pumpkins. Children rode in wagons, chubby fingers gripping their pumpkin of choice while their fathers wheeled them around. It got me excited for the pumpkin carving party my family had every year.

I hadn't realized how far I'd biked until I approached the cemetery. Graves were full of fresh flowers, bright and beautiful like the trees above them. I stopped to stare at them for a moment. I spotted Marki and Sarai's graves the easiest; theirs had the most stuff placed by them. Teddy bears, scrunchies, bouquets of flowers bigger than the usual ones. That's when I noticed Christine walking with a singular flower. I couldn't tell what flower it was except that it was bright white with a long stem. She crouched in front of Marki's grave and sat down. Her back was turned to me, but she reached her hand out to touch her headstone. What the hell tied her to Marki?

Before I could bike away, Christine turned and saw me. I debated peddling away, but she held her finger up, signaling she wanted me to wait for her. So, I walked into the cemetery, bike clicking next to me, and met her halfway.

"Spying on me?" she asked.

"No," I said quickly. "I was biking home and saw their graves."

"I come by once a week to leave a fresh flower," Christine said. "They never last long out here."

"What happened between you and Marki?" I asked.

"In order for me to tell you, you'll have to come by my house. I can show you everything."

I rolled my eyes. "Did you two have a secret relationship or something?"

"Come to my house," Christine said again.

"It's a simple yes or no question," I argued.

Christine grabbed my arm to pull me behind a tree. I fought with her, but she put her finger to my lips and pointed back toward Marki and Sarai's graves. Jon Willis approached with two flowers in his hands. He set one on Marki's grave and another on Sarai's. He crouched down to stare at their headstones before continuing to another set of graves. I assumed they were for his wife and son.

"I come every week," Christine said. "And so does he."

# CHAPTER EIGHTEEN

After my brief encounter with Christine at the cemetery, I knew I needed to go to her house. I tried to rationalize why Jon Willis would bring flowers to Marki and Sarai's graves. Town sheriff being the hero, the good guy, bringing flowers to the graves of the dead victims? The two of them were also his daughter's best friends. He practically watched them grow up alongside Gilly, so paying his respects made the most sense. But a piece of me still found the scene weird. I'd watched him bring flowers to their graves instead of his wife and son's.

I called Beck and explained to her what had happened in the cemetery.

"I'm all for skepticism," Beck said over the phone, "but I genuinely believe you're overthinking this one."

"I want to believe you're right," I said. "I think Christine has gotten to me."

"Just stay away from her." Beck cleared her throat. "Not to change the subject, but Harry brought me flowers today."

"That *is* changing the subject," I pointed out, halfway amused. "But I know. I saw him leaving the store with them today."

"And you didn't think to tell me?"

"It was a surprise!"

"You know I hate surprises," Beck sighed.

I flopped down on my bed so I could lay on my stomach.

"What did you think of the flowers?" I asked.

"They were nice," Beck mumbled. "But I still don't know how I feel about him. He's not the type of person I normally go out with."

"That's because you normally go out with assholes," I said. "And Harry isn't an asshole."

Beck sighed. "I have a lot to think about. I'll see you tomorrow."

When Beck hung up, my thoughts turned to Gilly. Should I bring her flowers, or would that be too weird? I didn't want people to stare at us if I showed up to school with a bouquet for her. I vetoed the idea and turned my light off, going to sleep. All I could see as I closed my eyes was Jon Willis and those two flowers in his hands.

Gilly slipped me a note in English class the next day. She folded it up, drawing a small pink heart on the front, addressing it to me. I opened it up quietly so Mrs. Ashley wouldn't see it and held my laughter in as I saw Gilly's curly pink handwriting. *Roses are red, violets are blue, I want to go on a date tonight because I miss you. Check yes or no.* The "yes" had little pink hearts drawn around it along with a smiley face, while the "no" was next to a crying face, pink tears spilling down the page. I checked "yes" with my pencil and slid the note back to Gilly.

She turned around. "Park tonight. Meet me there."

"Will your dad let you?" I asked.

"I'll beg him if I have to," Gilly said. "Or I can just sneak out. It's more fun that way."

I looked forward to our park date the rest of the day. All the paranoia I felt surrounding Christine and Jon had been replaced by butterflies.

Gilly found me in the hall before I took the bus home and kissed me quickly before anyone could see. I swore I floated.

At around seven, I told my mom I was going for a bike ride. I promised I'd be home by ten and left with a picnic blanket sitting on my lap.

I biked down to the gazebo at the park where Gilly and I had our first picnic. She was already there, watching the pond. Her bike was propped against the gazebo, and I figured she had snuck out. When she saw me, she stood up and waved, bouncing slightly on her toes. My stomach flipped.

"I didn't think to bring anything else," I said, blanket in hand.

"I don't care," Gilly said. "I just wanted to see you."

She helped me lay the picnic blanket out next to the pond. We sat, watching the water ripple. When the sky grew darker, we laid on our backs and looked at the sky. The stars shone brightly, and we reached our fingers up to make it seem like we were touching them. Gilly pointed out "the second star to the right," but all I saw were clusters that looked the same, none shining brighter than the other.

"I used to love reading *Peter Pan*," Gilly said. "It was my brother and I's favorite bedtime story when we were little."

"Who read it to you?" I asked.

"Mom did," Gilly said. "She made little notes in it for us to find when we were older. She doodled Tinkerbell on one of the pages. I thought she was as good as Picasso."

"My mom used to read me *The Little Mermaid*," I said. "She claimed I looked like Ariel, but I think it was only because my hair is red."

Gilly sat up on her elbows to look at me. "I'd say you look more like Annie."

"Hey!" I lightly pushed her, but she grabbed my arms so I was looking down at her. She laughed, but the smile faded as her eyes darkened from their normal misty blue-gray. Her eyes matched the blanket of twilight above us. I saw stars swimming in them.

"Have you ever done *it* before?" Gilly asked.

"No," I said, my face burning. "Have you?"

Gilly shook her head no. Her eyes widened as she reached up to touch my cheek, hesitantly. I melted into her touch, butterflies tearing a storm around my stomach. I steadied my breathing. It was only Gilly and me. There wasn't reason for my nerves.

"Do you want to?" she asked.

My heartbeat was all I could hear. I lost my words, so all I did was nod. Gilly sat up and kissed me quickly. The quick kisses turned deeper when Gilly put her hands in my hair, relaxing me. Mine found her arms and squeezed. I pulled away, our chests heaving.

"Gilly, I love you," I blurted.

Her eyes softened. She smiled and kissed me again on my lips, my cheeks, my nose, my forehead.

"I love you, Quinn," she said.

I let out a breath of relief. I'd mentally prepared for the mortification if she didn't say it back to me. After all, I'd never said it to anyone romantically. But Gilly had said. Gilly and I loved one another.

I kissed her again, laying her down gently on the picnic blanket when I heard rustling from behind the trees. We both froze, staring in the direction of the noise. All we saw were trees and darkness, and I had to remind myself we weren't trapped behind the woods at the school. We were in the park. *Our* park.

"Is someone there?" Gilly called.

I looked at her, horrified that she would engage.

"What?" Gilly said. "Some pervert isn't getting a free show from us."

Fearlessly, Gilly stood and walked toward the trees. I followed her, heart beating faster than before. I got in front of her, stopping when we heard another noise.

"What if it's the killer!" I whispered.

My heart leapt to my throat. The rustling noise came again, and Gilly charged into the trees. "We can hear you!" she shouted.

I chased after her, keeping my eye out for whoever was spying on us. The stretch of trees wasn't vast. Whoever was spying on us would be caught. I hoped that when we caught them, they weren't waiting with a hunting knife.

"Gilly!" I called, no longer able to see her.

I whipped around, snagging my sleeve on a branch. I'd barely stopped to inspect the ripped flannel when I heard Gilly scream. I ran toward her scream, only to collide with her. Gilly's eyes were full of terror. Footsteps crashed away from us in the distance. I didn't care enough to catch them. Gilly held her arm, blood running down her fingers in scarlet lines.

"What happened?" I gasped.

"They stabbed my arm," Gilly said, trying to hold in tears.

"We need to leave," I said. "Come on."

Gilly looked down at my torn sleeve, mortified. "Did they stab you too?"

"Tree branch," I explained hastily, "I'm fine, but you're not. We need to get home."

"Your house is closer," Gilly said.

We ditched Gilly's bike. She rode on my handlebars, gripping her arm to try and keep it from bleeding further. She leaned her head back into my shoulder, her tears soaking my flannel. I kept my eye out for anyone who might be running around. My blood boiled, fury replacing fear. I wanted whoever did this to pay.

Mom didn't hesitate to grab her first aid kit when we busted through the door. She kept her head and didn't say anything while she cleaned and bandaged Gilly's arm. I let her squeeze my hand when Mom cleaned the wound with alcohol.

"Gilly," Mom said, "I don't want to alarm you. But you might need stitches. The gash is a little too deep for only a bandage."

"Can you call my dad?" Gilly asked me tearfully.

While Mom did her best to help Gilly for the time being, I dialed Jon Willis. He answered, slightly groggy.

"It's Quinn," I said frantically. "Something happened to Gilly. She's here at my house, but you need to come quickly."

I could've explained it better than I did, but my anger had been replaced with shock, the stages of emotions hitting me in waves. I hated seeing Gilly cringe and cry from the pain in her arm. There was nothing I could do to help her, and that made me feel even worse.

Jon must have sped, because five minutes later, he was there. I let him in. His eyes were bloodshot, and he looked disheveled. When he saw Gilly, she ran to hug him, crying into his chest. He rubbed her back, and Mom stopped focusing on Gilly to examine me.

"I promise I'm fine," I said. "It was a stupid tree branch."

The branch had slightly scratched my arm, but Mom claimed she needed to clean it regardless. I winced at the feeling of cold, burning peroxide seeping into my open scratch.

"We need to get you to the hospital," Jon said. "Maggie, thank you."

"Not a problem," Mom assured. "Please, keep us updated."

"I will," Jon said. "Quinn, thank you for calling me."

I nodded, squeezing Gilly's hand before she left with her dad. When the door closed, I cried and let my mom rub my head.

Everything caught up to me at once. My breath hitched with each inhale, body shaking. I explained what had happened to the best of my ability. My words caught in my throat as I wheezed with tears. Mom rubbed my back to soothe me.

"Someone tried to hurt her, Mom," I sobbed. "Gilly's next."

"Shh," Mom tried to soothe me.

She carried me up the stairs like she used to when I was little. My body slumped in her arms as my tears subsided. She placed me on her bed, the smell comforting me.

"Don't forget to lock the doors," I said before drifting off.

I woke up in my mom's bed. I slept horribly. All I dreamt about was Marki, Sarai, and Gilly, all of them dead and asking for my help. But I was tied up and couldn't move to save any of them.

Mom made me my favorite breakfast: strawberry pancakes. I ate slowly and silently. Owen even let me have the bigger portion of the pancakes.

"Jon Willis called about an hour ago," Mom said. "Gilly is fine. She got her stitches but is still shaken up from last night."

I nodded, chewing my pancakes. Gilly could've died last night, and I would've been the only one to witness it.

"Quinn," Mom said, grabbing my hand. "He wants you to go in for questioning today. He won't keep you long, but for police purposes, he needs you to go tell him everything that happened."

"Will Gilly be there?" I asked.

"Probably not, honey," she said. "Jon said she was really spooked about the whole thing, and he doesn't want her going out for a few days."

I scarfed down the rest of my pancakes and let Mom drive me to the station. We passed the park, and I remembered that Gilly's bike was still there. My heart broke. Our special place had quickly become a sour memory, and I never wanted to set foot there again.

The police station smelled faintly of coffee, newspapers, and cigarettes. Mom came in with me, promising to wait until I was done being questioned. When Jon saw us, he hugged both my mom and I, then led me back into a room for questioning. The room was bare save for a desk and two chairs. The walls seemed to press in on me.

"Take a seat, Quinn," Jon said. His voice was gentle and tired.

"I'm sorry," I said before he sat down, a lump in my throat forming.

"None of this is your fault," Jon assured.

"They wanted to kill her," I breathed. "I just know it. They're targeting all of them."

"I need you to calm down for me, Quinn. Take a few breaths, okay?" Jon demonstrated, filling his lungs with air. "Gilly is safe at home with her uncle."

I took a few breaths, finally calming my shaking legs.

"Now," Jon said, "tell me every detail you can remember about last night."

I told him how we'd been sitting there, talking, when we heard rustling in the trees. How we'd investigated it. How a tree branch had scratched me, after which I'd found Gilly, stabbed.

"And you didn't see who did it?" Jon asked.

I shook my head no. "It was too dark."

Jon wrote down a few notes and closed his notepad. "Thank you, Quinn," he said.

"What happens now?" I asked.

"I'm going to have some people investigate the park," Jon said. "See if anything was left behind that can be used as evidence. Until then, maybe stay home this weekend."

"Do you think I'm a target?" I asked.

"It is a possibility that every teenager at your school is a target," Jon said.

I pulled at my cuticles. "Can I call Gilly?"

"Give her a day to rest," Jon said. "But I think she'd like to hear from you sometime this weekend."

We stood up at the same time. Jon gave me another hug before stepping aside so I could leave the room.

I turned before I left. "Gilly left her bike there."

"I'll be sure to return it to her safe and sound," he said, giving a playful salute.

I chuckled as best I could, but a sinking feeling weighed my stomach down. Jon knew his daughter was a target, and by association, I probably was too.

# CHAPTER NINETEEN

I finally called Gilly on Sunday afternoon. She was groggy when she answered, but her voice brightened when she realized it was me.

"Quinn!" she said. "Hi."

"How are you?" I asked.

"I'm honestly still freaked out," Gilly said. "How about you?"

"Same here," I said.

I tapped my foot against the floor, trying to find the words. I wanted to comfort her, but

when I thought of that night and racing Gilly home on my bike, I froze.

"Do you think you'll be at school tomorrow?" I asked, changing the subject.

"I think I'm going to stay home for a couple of days," Gilly said. "I'll miss you, though."

"I'll miss you too," I sighed. "I'm sorry we got split up. I should have kept a closer eye on you."

"Quinn," Gilly said, "what happened wasn't your fault. I'm still this psycho's target."

"I won't accept that."

"I don't want to either." Gilly shook her head. "But I feel like I have to."

She choked on the last word, and all I wanted to do was hug her. She didn't deserve any of this. My anger came flooding back. I told Gilly I loved her before hanging up the phone. I marched up the stairs to my room and yanked my desk drawer open. The sticky note was the first thing I saw. I unfolded it. Today was the day I'd finally go to Christine's house. I'd had enough of the murders, the killer, Gilly and her friends being targeted. I was fed up and ready for some answers—even if it meant getting help from Christine.

I biked to her house around two and knocked confidently on the door. Christine answered, a smirk spreading across her lips when she saw it was me, like she knew I would come to her eventually. She let me in, and I followed her to her room. Her desk was a mess, covered in papers and notes all having to do with Marki and Sarai's murders. She wasn't lying about the information she had gathered; there was tons of it.

"Why are you here?" Christine asked.

"Gilly and I were attacked in the woods a couple nights ago," I said.

Her face fell. "No shit."

"Someone stabbed Gilly in the arm," I said. "I think they might have tried to . . . kill her, but they missed."

Christine pushed past me and wrote down what I'd said.

"Hey!" I snapped.

"I'm only writing it down to remember," Christine said. "Everything having to do with these murders is a clue. Haven't you ever read any mystery novels?"

I already regretted my choice of coming to her house. Beck's nickname of "Nancy Drew" for me didn't compare to the sleuthing Christine had done. There was a flood of information I was missing.

"This is real life," I said. "My girlfriend and I were attacked, and she got hurt. I'm here to see what information you have that can help me figure out what the hell is going on, so I don't have to keep having nightmares of my girlfriend being murdered!"

Christine looked at me wide-eyed. I didn't feel bad for snapping. I was tired of messing around. She organized her desk as best as she could so all of her papers and notebooks lay flat and visible. I didn't even know where to begin. She picked up a torn envelope and handed it to me. Inside was a letter to Christine, addressed from Marki.

> Xtine! I know you hate when I write your name like that, but it's so Aguilerian. I also do it to annoy you ;). I never thought I'd like writing letters back and forth but here we are. Keeping you as my secret is fun but I hope you know I do care about you. Nobody knows I'm bisexual yet. I know my friends will support me—Jen's bi—but I don't think I'm ready yet. I'm glad you don't push me to come out. It's one of the many things I loooove about you. I'm not much of a writer so I'm not sure what else to say here except I like you, a lot! And I can't wait to see you at our spot.
>
> XOXO, Marki P

I handed the letter back to Christine, my mouth agape. I closed it when I caught her staring. It felt weird holding such a personal letter in my hand, even more so knowing it was written by a dead girl.

"Marki didn't show up to our spot that night like she said she would," Christine said. "I waited over an hour before I left, thinking Marki wanted to get rid of me finally. Little did I know, at that time, she was probably—"

Christine choked on her words, swallowing hard. I didn't let her finish the sentence.

"That's why you haven't gone to the police?"

Christine nodded. "My alibi is that I was waiting for Marki, and she never showed up. Our relationship was a secret—nobody knew about us at all. I buy weed from Rink Matthews nearly once a week. Miss Perfect in a secret relationship with a delinquent who barely shows up to class half the time? What narrative do you think that would've painted for me?"

Christine would've come across just as guilty as—if not more than—Rink in the eye of Jon Willis. Oddly enough, I trusted her. She had genuinely been in the wrong place at the wrong time. Her current "relationship" with one of the most popular girls in school didn't help either.

She handed me a notebook that began with Marki's name. Facts I was already aware of were listed under her name next to dark purple bullet points, including past hookups: Brady and Vance. Sensing that it was time to let everything out in the open, I explained the Brady situation to Christine. She took a red marker and crossed Brady's name out. I moved on to Sarai and noted how Christine had marked down the way Sarai flirted with Jon Willis.

"I noticed that at the football game," I said, pointing to the note. "I saw her talking to him by the fence at concessions."

An image of Sarai twirling her hair as she looked up at Jon filled my mind. It made me quiver with disgust.

"There was this one time it really made me do a double take," Christine said. "It was maybe a few days before she died. I tagged along with her, Alma, Jen, and Gilly into town to walk around, and we bumped into Jon Willis. Sarai became a whole different person when she spoke to him. I don't know if anybody else noticed and decided not to acknowledge it, but it was so blatantly obvious."

"Gross," I said, flipping the page. "You don't think she and him. . . ."

"I hope not," Christine said with a scowl.

I read through the next page on Alma and Jen, trying to get that idea out of my head. The Vance situation was under Alma's name, but there was nothing about the call log. I told Christine about it and watched as she scribbled it under Alma's name.

"She never acknowledged it?" Christine asked.

I shook my head. "Never."

"Maybe I can get Jen to get some information about it," Christine said. "I wonder if she knows?"

"They're twins," I said. "Don't they tell each other everything?"

Christine shook her head. "Not everything. Keep reading."

Jen, for obvious reasons, had the most written under her name. The list was as follows:

- Jealous that Alma spends most of her time with Sarai.
- Gilly and Marki are more the glue of the group, according to Jen.
- Jen caught Alma talking to Vance late a few nights when he was supposedly also seeing Sarai.
- Jen thinks there is competition between Alma and Sarai. They are passive aggressive about it and never speak about how they really feel.

- Jen is too stupid to carry out any kind of murder.
- Alma and Sarai have been dropped off by Jon Willis before from parties Jen never went to (I'm not sure if Gilly or Marki know about this).
- Jen saw Marki make out with Rink Matthews under the bleachers where he gave her a small bag of weed afterward.
- Jen will sometimes talk about Marki and Sarai as if they are still alive.

All the bullet points struck me, but the last one made me curious. To me, it seemed the most suspicious, but clearly Christine found her "too stupid" to murder anyone.

"I need explanations," I said.

"For starters, I don't think Jen killed either of them," Christine said. "She talks too much and has never organized anything in her life. There is no way she did it."

"What do you mean she sometimes still talks about Marki and Sarai like they're still alive?" I asked.

"She tells stories as if they are happening in the present when really they're in the past," Christine said. "She can go a mile a minute when she talks, so it's hard to keep up. When I've asked her things about Marki and Sarai, it's more like: 'Yes, Marki loves doing that on the weekends.' Is it weird? Yes, but not too suspicious. It's quite sad, actually."

Christine took a seat at her desk chair and scooted closer to me so we could look at the notebook together. There were more bullet points under Jen's name, following Sarai's murder:

- Jen says Alma cries like she is faking it.
- Sarai was nervous when she called to let them know she wasn't going with them to the football game.
- Jen thinks Rink is suspicious and doesn't trust him.
- Alma freaked out about Sarai being found with the German candy wrapper.
- Jen thinks a part of Alma is glad that Sarai is dead.

The more I read, the more my suspicions for Alma grew, but I still couldn't shake the feeling that Jen was partly guilty for something as well. I'd never looked twice at the twins, but Christine's list made me want to.

"What do you think about all of this?" I asked Christine.

"Alma is suspicious in her own way," Christine said. "I spend a good amount of time around her since her and Jen are connected at the hip again, but I still haven't figured her out yet."

"And you're positive you don't suspect Jen at all?" I asked.

"Yes," Christine said. "Well, mostly. Sometimes, I'm ten percent unsure. Alma, on the other hand, I don't know."

"Do you really think it's someone who knows them?" I asked. "A student killing another student with a knife seems so barbaric."

"All murder is barbaric," Christine said. "Besides, their murders aren't coincidences. And now that Gilly and you were attacked at the park, I'm even more sure they're being targeted."

I flipped the page again. Gilly's name was written on the page next to mine. Christine wrote down the park incident and how I snapped the night of Sarai's party. The word "innocent" was written in bright red next to my name. Most of the bullet points under Gilly's name had to do with her dad and his interesting relationship with her friends. I turned the page again and found that Jon Willis also had his own column, next to Beck's. Both shared an equal number of bullet points. Numbers were next to their names. Jon Willis with a one and Beck with a two.

"What do these numbers mean?" I asked.

Christine sighed before replying. "They are my top two suspects."

My heart dropped. I had to refrain from throwing the notebook at her. How *dare* she suspect my best friend, who I knew better than anyone in this world.

"Quinn, please, before you get angry, read what I've written," Christine insisted.

"I think I'm done for today," I said, getting up to leave.

"Will you sit down and listen!"

Beck's name in the notebook stared at me. Beck was innocent, that I was sure of, but I had to hear Christine out. I sat back down. She had, after all, given me more to go off of than anything else.

"I'll hear you out," I said. "But I won't believe it."

"That's fine," Christine said. "You can even ignore every other bullet point, but I need you to look at this one. It's the most important."

- Beck's dad had an affair with Gilly's mom.

# CHAPTER TWENTY

Christine gave me a moment to process what I had read. There was a faint buzzing in the room, and I couldn't stand it. The hum of betrayal played out as I read the sentence over and over again.

"How did you find this out?" I asked.

"I loved Marki," Christine said. "So much. I would do anything to figure out what happened to her. It took a lot of digging for me to figure it out. But I won't tell you exactly how."

I turned on her in a rage. "What do you mean you can't tell me? You suspect my best friend, drop this absolute bomb, then won't even tell me how you know it? For all I know, you could be bullshitting me to get inside my head and make me distrust Beck."

"That's not what I'm doing," Christine said calmly. "I can't tell you *everything*, but I will say, Rink told me most of it. It was one of those times we smoked a lot of weed, and she came up in conversation. He told me he had a crazy story about Beck's parents. And there it was. But I have no idea how he knows."

"That doesn't mean anything if it came from Rink in a high stupor," I huffed. "I call bullshit. Besides, Beck would have told me."

Christine groaned. "Rink caught Mr. Wood and Mrs. Willis in the car once by his

house," Christine said. "That's how he knows. And Beck cried to him about it because she knew. She knew while it was happening and didn't know what to do."

"Bullshit!" I yelled.

"I'm sorry you're finding out this way, Quinn, but it's true," Christine said. "If you think I'm lying, then ask her yourself, but I don't know how wise it is to bring it up."

My cheeks were hot, fist clenched while my heart plummeted into the pit of my stomach. I wanted to scream in Christine's face and burst into tears. Surely Beck wouldn't have kept this from me? Even the possibility of that betrayal stung my heart.

I let out quick, deep breaths. I wouldn't let Christine see me upset. I remembered the day Beck came to my house crying because her parents got divorced. I let her stay three nights until she was ready to go back home. Reasoning that it would have been too painful for Beck to reveal something like that to me, I was able to slightly calm down. Still, knowing she confided in *Rink* with this was the biggest blow to my stomach.

Putting Beck aside in my mind, I focused on Jon Willis and the number one beside his name.

"You honestly suspect the sheriff?" I asked, still breathing heavily.

"Do you not find him suspicious?" Christine asked.

"I think you only find him suspicious because of how he treats Rink," I said. "I understand the suspicion, but do you really think a grown man is killing his daughter's best friends?"

"I know how it sounds, but I don't trust him."

"Nobody trusts the police." I shrugged.

"You saw how he was around Sarai," Christine argued.

"It was creepy, yes, but do you really think that makes him a killer? And why would he attack his own daughter?"

Christine thought for a moment. I watched her second-guess herself, and the doubt inside me grew. I was just about to excuse myself to leave when Christine spoke up.

"Maybe he has an accomplice, and there was some misinformation," Christine said. "They could've thought they were attacking you but got confused. It was dark."

"You think they might have been trying to attack me?" I asked, dread filling me.

"You're tied to Gilly now," Christine pointed out. "I don't want to alarm you, but that doesn't exactly make you safe."

My heartbeat sped up. The whole time I had been there, I'd thought Christine might be onto something, but now everything sounded too hard to believe.

I looked through the rest of her notebook, but the pages were blank.

"No Rink?" I asked.

"No," Christine said. "Besides you, he's the only other person I *know* is innocent."

I opened my mouth to argue, but Christine was on her feet before I had the chance. She left to get us some water, and I took the opportunity to look through more of her stuff. She had a few pictures she took at the cemetery. One was of Jon Willis crouched by his wife's grave. It was too much of a personal moment for Christine to have captured. I sifted through more photos. Some were of the woods edge, others beneath the bleachers with graffiti and old pieces of gum. One was tucked under the stack, and I peeled it from beneath the other photos. It was a picture of Christine and Marki beneath the gazebo at the park. Mine and Gilly's park.

Christine returned, two cups in hand, catching me with the photograph.

"That was taken at mine and Marki's spot," she said. "We'd always meet there because nobody ever went."

I suddenly remembered riding my bike in the park and spotting two girls on a date by the gazebo. I hadn't been able to tell who it was back then, but the photograph made it clear. I'd seen them on a date before. I'd been jealous of both of them before. Gilly and I had taken over what had once been Christine and Marki's place. Christine moved to the desk to reorganize it while I chugged my water. I kept my eyes on Christine, adding her to my own list of suspects.

Monday, I skipped first period and lunch at school. I couldn't face Beck, and with Gilly out of school, I ate in the library where no one would find me. There was still a sting in my heart every time I thought about Beck and what she kept from me. I wouldn't have been as hurt if she hadn't confided in Rink about the subject—but she had chosen him over me. We had been friends since we were little girls. She told me almost everything. Sometimes she kept minor details I didn't care about hidden, but the major things were always shared between us. I picked at my food as I figured out how to confront her. Her parents' divorce was always a sensitive subject, but I needed to know why she never told me the reason it happened.

I kept my headphones on in the hallway to avoid everyone. When I saw the back of Christine's head, I turned away. At one point, Harry tried to catch up to me, but I power walked to the girl's bathroom to escape him. I dodged every human interaction successfully up until the very end of the day, when Beck tracked me down.

"Why haven't I seen you?" she asked, arms folded.

I shrugged. "I wanted to be alone today."

"Bullshit," Beck said. "I learned you were attacked in the park and haven't heard from you all weekend, and you want to avoid me? Why didn't you tell me?"

I could've asked her the same thing. People stared at us, so I pushed through a side door leading to the football field.

"I needed time to process what happened," I said over my shoulder. "This isn't helping my stress."

Beck chased after me as I made a b-line for the bleachers. "Don't walk away from me when I'm trying to talk to you!"

"Quit following me!" I demanded.

Beck grabbed my arm, and I yanked it away.

"What the hell is the matter with you?" Beck snapped.

With a breath, I let it rip. "Why did your parents get divorced?"

Beck took a step back, clearly caught off guard by my question. "Why would you even ask me that?"

I could see my own betrayal mirrored in her eyes for bringing up the one thing that most hurt her. "I need to know," I said. "Because apparently Rink Matthews does, but not your own best friend."

Beck rubbed her temples. "I was too embarrassed to tell you."

"Embarrassed?" I said, my voice softening. "Beck, why would you be embarrassed to tell me *anything*? We tell each other everything."

She shrugged. "It was easier to tell Rink because I thought he would forget about it. He smokes so much he tends to forget things. I guess he didn't. . . . Wait, did he tell you?"

"Yes," I said, easing into the lie. "I ran into him this weekend, and we talked for a little bit. He was rambling about a bunch of different things."

I felt icky lying to Beck, but telling her I learned the information from Christine would have caused more trouble than it was worth.

"Oh," Beck said. "I'm sorry I didn't tell you. It's a sensitive subject."

"I know you hate talking about it," I said. "And I'm sorry for not calling you about the attack. It really scared me."

We walked over to the bleachers and took a seat.

"Rink wasn't the only person I saw this weekend," I said. "I went by Christine's house."

"What for?" Beck asked.

"To talk to her about the murders," I said. "She's compiled a lot of information about it."

I told Beck everything about my trip to Christine's house, except for a few key things, like everything relating to her. Hell, I didn't tell her anyone was a suspect, only that Christine had information on all of us.

"How do you know Christine isn't trying to manipulate you?" Beck asked.

"I honestly can't answer any more questions right now; my brain is overloaded," I said. "I don't know what to believe anymore."

Beck and I sat together silently for a while. The buses left, meaning we would have to walk home, but neither of us cared enough to move.

She held out her pinkie for me. "Promise me we'll always believe in each other, even if we can't believe in anyone else during all of this."

I connected our pinkies, but I couldn't stop the image of her name in Christine's notebook from popping into my head. We turned toward the field, gray clouds eating up the bright colors of the grass and muting them to murk.

"Is Gilly doing okay?" Beck asked.

"I don't think so," I said. "She won't be at school this week. It really did a number on her, and I feel horrible about it."

"She was targeted," Beck said. "There's no way she wasn't. We have to realize that whoever killed Marki and Sarai wants to kill the other three, maybe even you, and maybe even me by association."

Christine had basically told me the same thing. I masked my fear with dark humor, something I was best at.

"They could get us right now," I said. "We're out here all alone."

Beck screamed. "You want to kill me, you bastard? Kill me!"

"Come kill us!" I screamed alongside her.

Our words turned to incoherent screeches as we got rid of all the shit we had bottled up. When we were done screaming, we laughed and began our walk to my house. Careful to make sure Beck wasn't paying any attention, I threw glances behind us.

I spent my nights talking to Gilly on the phone. I did my best to make her laugh and forget about what happened in the park. The stitches on her arm were healing well, but she had to be careful not to tear them.

"Dad is oddly calm," Gilly said over the phone. "I'm waiting for him to lose his shit any time now."

I laid in my bed, feet against my headboard. "What do you think will happen when he does?" I asked.

"World War III," Gilly huffed. "Or maybe I'll go full Rapunzel and be locked away for the rest of my life."

"Well, start working on growing your hair out so I can climb it."

Gilly laughed, making me smile.

The police didn't have any more leads into the murders, nor mine and Gilly's attack. Everything felt clueless, hopeless. Gilly told me they'd talked about canceling all the fall events, but that parents and kids alike had fought against it.

"I miss you," I told Gilly.

"I miss you too," Gilly said, sighing. "Alma and Jen came by today with my favorite cupcakes. I honestly can't recall the last time I truly spoke to either of them. They think they're next, but I told them they can't live with that mindset."

Hearing their names pricked my concern, especially with everything I'd learned from Christine. I couldn't let myself fall into the spiral of suspecting anyone, especially Alma or Jen.

"What kind of cupcakes?" I asked, changing the subject.

"Strawberry with buttercream frosting."

"I'll remember that."

"Do you have any favorite sweets?" Gilly asked.

"Butter pecan ice cream," I said.

Gilly laughed. "That's such an old person flavor."

"It's the best, and I will die on that hill," I said.

Instantly, I regretted my choice of words. We both fell silent over the phone.

"I'm going to come to school tomorrow," Gilly said. "I can't stand being in this house anymore."

"I'll see you tomorrow, then," I said. "I love you."

"I love you too."

Gilly hung up with a click, and I listened for the buzz of the dial tone before hanging up myself.

## CHAPTER TWENTY-ONE

With Gilly back at school, everything felt better. Our lunch table was back to normal with Beck and Harry sitting across from us. Sometimes, Harry would sneakily put his hand on Beck's knee or try to grab her hand under the table. According to Beck, things were still complicated between the two of them, and I wished they would finally make things official and save us all the headache.

Before English class, Gilly pulled me into a side hallway next to a huge vending machine. We stood beside it, out of view from the rest of our classmates, so we could kiss. I remembered walking down the hallway, catching Marki with Brady in the same spot. Was it during the time of her and Christine's secret relationship? Did Christine feel a certain way about Marki being with other people?

"I can tell your mind is elsewhere," Gilly said, pulling away.

"Sorry," I sighed. "Long day. I feel like having algebra first always fries my brain."

Gilly stood with her hands locked behind my neck, gazing at me. It was like she wanted to study my face—remember it, even.

She pulled away, taking out some quarters from the pocket of her bookbag.

"What are you doing?" I asked.

"Probably the most cliché thing I've ever done," she said. "Don't look."

I hid beside the vending machine with my eyes closed while Gilly pushed its buttons. I heard the treat fall, along with Gilly rummaging to get it.

"Keep your eyes closed," Gilly said. "I'll tell you when to open."

She pulled open the package of whatever she got, shoving the wrapper into her pocket. I felt her in front of me but kept my eyes closed.

"Open," Gilly said.

She was on one knee with a cherry ring pop in her hand. I covered my mouth, acting surprised but trying to hold in my laughter.

Gilly giggled. "Quinn, with this ring pop, do you accept my proposal of a fake engagement?"

I jumped up and down. "Yes! A thousand times, yes!"

Gilly slid the ring pop onto my ring finger. We kissed one another, pulling away to laugh at ourselves, not really caring how ridiculous it all was.

"Now we can say we were engaged once," Gilly said. "Even if it was with a ring pop."

She threw her arm around me, and we turned away from the vending machine. Christine was on the other side, as if she had been waiting for us. She quickly brushed past us, keeping her head down low. Gilly looked back at her to wave, but she didn't look at us.

"That was weird," Gilly said. "Jen said they're still together, so I don't know why she wouldn't say hi."

"Maybe she felt awkward because she watched us get engaged," I suggested.

"It was purely romantic!" Gilly mock-gasped. "How could one ever feel awkward about such romance?"

We laughed, barely making it to Mrs. Ashley's class on time. As soon as we took a seat and Gilly turned away from me, my face fell. I wished for naivete. I didn't want to look at this as a huge murder case that would keep growing, but I couldn't help it. I felt it then, like a hollow, dark energy around all of us. Someone we knew was the murderer. Call it intuition or being realistic based on the facts I knew—someone was after all of us, and I couldn't shake the feeling that Gilly was the next target.

I found Beck at the end of the day and dragged her out to the bleachers with me. It was the only place I could think of where we could speak freely without the fear of someone eavesdropping. It's ironic how the most "safe" place was across from the woods where Marki and Sarai were found.

Beck stared at my half-eaten ring pop. "Reverting back to childhood?"

I gave her a confused look until she pointed at my finger. "Gilly proposed to me," I explained as we kept walking.

"Is this why you're dragging me out here when we could go home?" Beck asked.

"No. We need to talk about some things."

I would make Beck take this seriously with me. It would be us against Christine in cracking this case. I had information on everyone, including Christine, all thanks to her sleuthing.

"I want us to figure this out," I said. "I know you already told me to leave it to the police, but I know way too much to do that."

Beck didn't answer right away. Instead, she stared at the caution tape billowing in the distance. It was torn, either from the weather or by some teenagers who'd decided to go into the woods like we had.

"So, what do we do?" Beck asked.

"I'm going to write down everything I found out from Christine," I said. "Then we go from there."

Christine came out from underneath the bleachers along with Rink. I hadn't even noticed them when we got out there.

"I heard my name," Christine said. "What's going on?"

"We were leaving," Beck said, grabbing my wrist.

"Tell me why you were talking about me," Christine pressed.

"It's none of your business." Beck scowled.

"Feels like it." Christine cocked her head to the side. "What, you got as much dirt on me as I do you?"

Beck tensed. Christine had set her off; a fight brewed, and Beck never backed down from a fight. I had relied on this fact as Christine and I thought up our plan.

"Let's go, Beck." I attempted to pull her away.

Christine looked down at my ring pop, still half-eaten, and I wanted to hide it from her.

"From the vending machine, right?" Christine said. "Marki and I did that once. Except we both got each other rings."

"Are you jealous or something?" I asked. My plan was in motion even.

"Christine," Rink warned. "Give it a rest."

"No, I'm not jealous," Christine said bitterly. "How could I be?"

"Because I don't have to keep my relationship a secret with Gilly the way you had to with Marki," I shot back. I wondered if this dig was too personal, but it needed to feel real.

Christine got up in my face, but I didn't falter. I let my bookbag slip from my shoulders.

"Be careful what you say," Christine said.

Before I could react, Beck pushed Christine away from me. Rink tried his best to hold Beck and Christine away from one another, but they pushed past him, then at each other. Christine fell to the ground. Beck backed up slightly as she got back up.

"I don't mind fighting you," Beck said.

"As if that'll make you look good," Christine huffed.

"What's that supposed to mean?"

"Ask your father."

Beck lunged for her, taking her to the ground. Christine fell back, her head smacking the earth, and Beck took that chance to land the first punch. She hit Christine's mouth, and I thought I heard a crack.

"Quinn, help me!" Rink said, trying to pull Beck off of Christine.

I moved to help him, dragging Beck away from Christine. She thrashed, cursing us. Christine stood, wiping blood from her mouth.

"Say one more thing about my father!" Beck yelled. "I dare you!'

"What the hell is going on here?" I heard Jon Willis shout as he and two other deputies jogged over to us.

The distraction allowed Beck to escape our arms and go for Christine again. I tried to pull her back, but her arm collided with my stomach. I fell to the ground, my ring pop landing candy-side-down. When I sat up, it was covered in dirt and grass.

"Fuck, Quinn," Beck said, ignoring Christine. "I'm sorry."

Jon Willis helped me up while the other deputies shielded Beck from Christine.

"Anyone care to explain this?" Jon asked.

"Why don't you ask the busybody over there?" Beck said. "Huh? Want to tell him what you *suspect*?"

"Quit talking," I hissed under my breath.

Rink was off to the side, avoiding Jon's eye.

Jon Willis sighed when he looked at him. "Why am I not surprised to see you here?"

"Why do you always think I'm the cause?" Rink said, anger flushing his face. His hands clenched into fists at his side.

"Watch it," Jon warned. "You don't want to dig your grave even deeper."

Christine looked up at me, and I shook my head, signaling for her to leave it alone. Everything had already escalated enough; it was time to get out of here.

"Go home," Jon said to all of us.

Christine and Rink walked off before Beck and I did. Jon and the other two deputies headed for the woods, probably to examine the caution tape and put a new one up. Beck's breathing was heavy, her knuckles red from where she'd punched Christine. We didn't say a word to each other as we walked home, not even when we parted ways.

I threw my bookbag on the couch once I got inside my house and ran my ring pop under some water. Even though I'd cleaned it, I didn't have an appetite for it anymore. I took a pair of scissors and lightly beat the rest of the candy off the ring until it was clean and not sticky. The only good thing to come out of today was my "engagement" to Gilly. I placed the ring on my nightstand so I could always look at it.

After dinner, I called Christine.

"What the hell was that?" I asked the second she picked up.

"You told me to start a fight," she said.

"A small one," I deadpanned. "With me. That was taken way too far."

A couple of days after I confronted Beck about the affair, I'd called Christine. Granted, Christine was still on my own radar, but I'd needed her. She had far too much information on everyone for me to pass up the opportunity to keep working with her. Just like she'd used Jen for her own personal gain, I used her. I didn't suspect Beck, but I feared that if she knew about Christine and I partially sleuthing together, things would go south.

"The less people that suspect we are figuring this out together, the better," I said on what was now my second phone call to Christine. "I told Beck I want to dig into this deeper with her, so that throws her off. A subtle fight would've also thrown her off. It didn't need to become what it did."

"You're right," Christine said. "I'm sorry."

"I'm going to try and do some sleuthing with Beck," I said. "Only little things, so it doesn't paint a bigger target on either of us. We can only do this sparingly. It doesn't need to get around how much we know."

"I agree," Christine said. "What did Gilly say when I didn't say hi to you guys?"

"She thought it was weird, but I told her you probably felt awkward seeing us kiss," I said.

"Good," Christine said. "It was the only thing I could think of that might logically make you want to start a fight."

"It was good," I said. "But for now, we still need to avoid each other."

"You're right." Christine made a clicking noise with her tongue. "Well, I'll see you around. Call me if you notice anything."

I hung up and pulled out my own notebook, one I had only recently started. I wrote down what Jon Willis said to Rink and put question marks around it. I also wrote down what I had seen in Christine during the fight. What was supposed to be a small fight had escalated, and when I'd asked Christine if she was jealous, her eyes had grown dark, full of hate. Thinking about it still gave me a chill. Either she was a great actor, or she genuinely felt jealousy toward Gilly and me. I wrote her name down again, putting a number one next to it.

# CHAPTER TWENTY-TWO

I woke up on Saturday excited. Not only was I sleeping over at Gilly's, I had a plan to do a little more digging on Jon Willis as well. How would he act toward me when we were alone in his house? Would it help me see him in a new way? The way Sarai twirled her hair for him made me think he had to feed into her flirting, but did he ever start it? And was there anything more to it? I needed to know.

I flipped a coin back and forth in my mind, wondering if I should tell Gilly *some* things. It would either make it easier to keep her safe, or it could, once again, place her on the radar as a target. I hated making decisions.

Mom decided to drop me off at Gilly's house instead of letting me bike there. She was hesitant about letting me go, and I wondered if she felt the lingering weight of death around us, waiting. After the incident in the park, she kept a closer eye on me, asking me to assist her with random chores in the house just so I'd stay home with her and Owen more. She didn't ask much about Gilly. She never turned her nose up at the mention of her name the way she did with some of my ex-friends, but the silence made me wonder if there was a growing distaste for Gilly. I wanted to ask but was afraid of the answer.

"I'll pick you up before lunch tomorrow," Mom said.

I nodded. "See you tomorrow."

"Hey." Mom stopped me, her hand on my wrist. "You and Gilly stay here tonight. It'll be a cold night, so you shouldn't go out."

"We weren't planning to," I assured her. "Bye, Mom."

Mom waited until I was safely inside Gilly's house before driving away. She didn't want us to go out because of what happened—that much was obvious. What she probably didn't realize was that I wasn't too keen on going out myself.

Gilly's dad ordered pizza, and we ate it in her bedroom. I leaned against her dresser while she sat in her usual nook at the window. It was pineapple and pepperoni pizza—Gilly's favorite. I had never thought to add pineapple to a pepperoni pizza, but I was hooked after taking one bite.

"I have a surprise for you after dinner," Gilly said.

"What is it?" I asked, standing up straighter.

"I'm not one to spoil surprises," Gilly said. "You'll have to see."

I impatiently ate another slice of pizza, too eager for the surprise Gilly had. She laughed at me as I paced around her room, looking at every trinket I could while I waited on her to finish her last slice of pizza. She seemed to drag out the waiting, taking her bites slowly. Whenever someone told me there was a surprise waiting, I couldn't sit still.

"I don't think I've ever seen you so eager for something," Gilly said.

"I get antsy when it comes to surprises," I admitted. "I don't like not knowing what is coming next."

Gilly ate the last of her crust and grabbed my plate to take downstairs. I followed her into the kitchen. She put the plates in the dishwasher, grabbing a glass of water and sipping it slowly.

"Gilly!" I whined. "The surprise?"

Gilly reached into her silverware drawer and pulled out two spoons. She handed one to me before reaching into the freezer.

"Ta-da," Gilly said, presenting me with a carton of butter pecan ice cream.

"I thought this was an old person flavor," I mocked, taking the carton.

"I'll give it a try just for you," Gilly said.

I made sure Jon wasn't around before I kissed her. It was a quick kiss, but something felt different about it. My feelings for Gilly hadn't changed, but something weary seemed to surface after we kissed. I wanted more than anything for things to go back to normal between us. The attack had shaken us both, but I was ready to put it behind us. Gilly, on the other hand, didn't seem to reciprocate the feeling. She smiled at me best she could, but it felt forced.

"Thank you," I said.

"Anything for you," Gilly said.

I followed behind as she led us back to her room, the spoons clinking in her hand. I almost asked if she wanted to talk about what happened but thought better of it. How much talking could we actually do? It wouldn't change the fact that Gilly still had a bright, red target on her back.

We listened to music in her room while sharing the ice cream. It was the best butter pecan ice cream I'd ever had.

"You won me over," Gilly said to the carton.

"See!" I exclaimed. "And to think you doubted me."

"I promise not to ever doubt you again."

Gilly put the lid back on the carton and shoved it onto her nightstand so she could kiss me. Her lips tasted like butter pecan, and I made a mental note to never eat it again unless it was with her. The sweetness lingered when her hand found my hair, and she scooted closer to me. If we got any closer, we would mold together. I accidentally brushed her arm where her stitches had been. There was a rough patch of skin left, and I ran my thumb along it.

"We need to find a new place to make ours," I said in between kisses.

"Behind the vending machine seems like a good idea," Gilly said. "It's where we got engaged, after all."

I smiled. "I meant like the park. Where we can go alone."

Gilly pulled away. "Any ideas?"

"Are there any places you like to go to clear your head?" I asked.

Gilly thought for a moment. "There's this greenhouse I used to go to when I was little. It's been closed down for a while, but it's somewhere quiet, where nobody goes."

"An abandoned greenhouse," I said. "Sounds very apocalyptic."

"It's the only place I could think of," Gilly pouted.

I smirked. "Let's go sometime."

Gilly agreed and kissed me again. We'd found an almost perfect rhythm when the phone in Gilly's room rang. She rolled her eyes as she answered with a monotone, "Hello."

I could faintly hear crying on the other end, and Gilly furrowed her brow. "You broke up?" she said.

I gave her a confused look, and she mouthed "Jen." Jen? Why would Christine break up with her mid-sleuth?

"I know," Gilly said. "That isn't a good reason. You're right. I'm so sorry, Jen."

Jen continued to cry on the other end of the line. Perhaps it was time to make a quick exit.

"I'm going to get water," I whispered.

Gilly nodded before reassuring Jen that everything would be okay. I grabbed the carton of ice cream, spoons, and pizza box to bring back down.

I carefully walked down the stairs, not wanting to make a lot of noise. Just my luck; Jon Willis was in the kitchen, packing up leftovers of his own pizza.

"Quinn, thank you for bringing that down," he said, grabbing the pizza box from me.

I ruffled my hair a little and immediately felt stupid for doing so. He packed up the rest of mine and Gilly's pizza while I put the ice cream back in the fridge.

"I'll take those," Jon said, grabbing the spoons from me.

He stuck them in the dishwasher. While he rummaged for the detergent, I grabbed a cup from the cupboard next to him. He didn't seem to take notice of me. I moved slowly, filling my cup of water halfway. He still was too involved with the dishwasher. I rolled my eyes, already feeling the embarrassment creep into my cheeks as I tried to start a conversation with him.

"Do you think you'll have deputies stationed at the fall events this year?" I asked. "I know the corn maze is next weekend."

Jon turned the dishwasher on, then stood to face me, leaning back against the counter.

"At least two," he said. "Don't worry. It'll be completely safe."

I sipped my water. "Will you let Gilly go?"

Jon smiled. "All she has talked about every year since she was little is that damn corn maze. I don't want to take that away from her. I assume you'll be going together?"

"Probably," I said. "We haven't talked about it yet. But if we do, we'll go with Beck and Harry, so it'll be a group of us."

"Beck Wood?" Jon asked.

I nodded. He had to know about the affair, right?

"She's been my best friend since I was little," I said.

Jon began putting away some dishes from the sink. I couldn't tell if I should keep the conversation going or walk away from the dead end I was hitting.

"She hangs out with Rink Matthews, right?" he said.

"Sometimes," I admitted. "I don't know if I'd even classify them as friends."

"Keep your eye on her," Jon said. "I'm sure my distaste for Rink Matthews isn't a secret."

Bingo. I'd wondered how much I could get him to admit to me.

"Is he really that bad?" I asked. "I've seen him around school, and I know he was Sarai's stepbrother. But I don't know too much else."

"He's gotten into trouble far too many times," Jon said. "I don't trust that kid."

I was about to ask more when Gilly walked into the kitchen.

"What am I missing?" she asked.

"We got to talking about the corn maze next weekend," Jon said. "Quinn wanted to know if you were going."

"I really want to." Gilly's eyes sparkled as she looked at me. "Are we going?"

"Yeah," I said. "I thought we could go with Beck and Harry."

"Sounds like a plan." Gilly walked over to Jon and pecked his cheek.

"Goodnight, Dad," she said.

"Night, kiddo," he said.

Before I turned to follow Gilly back to her room, Jon smiled at me and winked. I didn't know what to make of it. He hadn't told Gilly about us talking about Rink, so maybe it was for that. Gilly didn't seem to know she'd walked in on us in conversation about him. I didn't like sharing a secret with Jon Willis. It felt wrong.

As Gilly laid on my chest that night, I considered asking her what Jon had mentioned about Rink. If he'd freely given me his opinion just now, it made me question how much Gilly actually knew about everything concerning Marki and Sarai's murders—but I didn't press her on it.

"I'm glad you get to go to the corn maze," I murmured.

Gilly turned to look up at me. She shared Jon's smile. "Me too. We have to get candy apples when we go. This one lady, Suzanne, volunteers every year and makes the best ones."

"I'll buy you a candy apple to return the ring pop favor," I said.

"It can be my engagement gift from you," Gilly laughed.

She settled back in on my chest. I looked down at her eyelashes, then her back as her chest heaved up and down. I always let her fall asleep first.

Christine didn't answer any of my calls for days following my weekend with Gilly. Every time I called, the line was either busy or nobody picked up. I left her two voicemails, explaining I needed to speak with her about homework and going to the corn maze on Friday. "Homework" was our codeword for when we needed to talk about the murders.

I looked for Christine every day at school. I lingered in places I'd seen her before and even went back to the vending machine, but I never saw her. It was like she'd disappeared. Dread seeped into my stomach. No, Christine didn't go out past dusk, and if she did, it was always with her parents. She was fine.

At lunch on Thursday, my eyes scanned the cafeteria for her. Alma and Jen sat in a two-seater together. Jen picked at her lunch, barely eating anything. I almost asked if we should move to a bigger table so they could sit with us. They looked lonely by themselves, two distraught twins. But I didn't. Gilly didn't say anything about it either.

"Who are you looking for?" Gilly whispered.

"Hm?" I blinked. "Oh, nobody. I'm feeling antsy today."

"Did someone mention they have a surprise for you?" Gilly asked, smirking.

I smiled at her joke but continued to look around. Beck and Harry were in their own world talking about Halloween costumes. I hadn't even thought about Halloween plans yet.

"Are we all still good for the corn maze this weekend?" Gilly asked.

"Sure," Beck said.

"I'll drive us," Harry offered. "I suck at corn mazes, though."

"Gilly's really good at them," I said, still looking around.

A girl with blue hair walked by, but it wasn't Christine. Beck snapped her fingers in front of my face.

"What are you on?" she asked.

"Lack of sleep," I replied. "I'm going to go splash some water on my face to see if it helps."

"Lunch ends in like ten minutes," Beck said. "If you wait, I'll go with you."

"It's okay," I said. "I'll get the head start to class. See you later."

I gathered my things and went out into the hall. I passed two guys arguing about Pokémon cards and another trying to do pull ups on the door frame. Still, no Christine.

I walked past the bathroom and out the side door of the school to go to the bleachers. I could already smell the pot as I approached them. Underneath, I found Rink and the two other guys that were there the last time I went with Beck.

"Hey," I said.

Rink took a hit of a joint and passed it to his friend, who stared at me.

"There's no way you came to smoke so what do you want?" Rink asked, blowing it sideways so it wouldn't hit me in the face.

"Do you know where Christine is?" I asked.

"Why do you need to see her?" Rink asked.

"I don't think that's your business," I said.

His friends made an "ooh" sound, and I rolled my eyes. I didn't come here to argue.

"I need to see her," I said.

"The other day wasn't cool." Rink frowned. "None of you should've gone at each other like that."

I shrugged. "Things escalated. But it happened, and it's done now. Do you know where she is or not?"

Rink shrugged. "Maybe she's at home trying to figure out another way to start a fake fight with you."

I paused. Surely, I hadn't heard him right, but the smirk on his face told me otherwise. I tugged on his wrist, pulling him out from under the bleachers so we could talk without meathead one and two listening.

"How much do you know?" I asked.

I knew he had been interrogated enough, but now it was my turn. Rink laughed as if I wasn't serious.

"I know you and Christine are trying to solve this without help from anyone except each other," Rink said. "I honestly find it stupid that you're both doing this."

"Why is helping prove your innocence stupid?" I asked.

"Because it has nothing to do with me," Rink said. "You're obviously doing it for Gilly, and she is doing it for Marki."

"So then what do you think?" I asked. "Who killed Marki and Sarai?"

Rink stared at me with his arms crossed before he shrugged. "Someone really sick in the head."

He walked off before I could ask him anything else.

## CHAPTER TWENTY-THREE

I threw on a multicolor scarf before leaving the house Saturday night. The air was cold, and I could see my breath when I spoke. Harry's high beams were on, blinding me as I walked to his car. Beck was already in the front seat, hands stuffed in her pockets to keep warm.

"Do you not believe in heat?" I asked as I crawled in the back seat.

"It takes her a while," Harry said, patting his dashboard. "But she'll get there."

"I think you need to buy a new car," Beck grumbled. "You told me you have a ton of savings."

"I will never get rid of Shayla." Harry crossed his arms. "I've known her for years."

"It's time for her to retire," Beck said, shifting to sit with her knees up to keep warm.

We picked up Gilly last. She walked out in a pink coat, white gloves on her hands. Mine were ice-cold in my own jacket pockets. Jon Willis waved at us from the doorway, then disappeared inside.

"Is he going tonight?" I asked Gilly when she got in the car.

"Eventually," Gilly said. "Two other deputies will also be there, so I think that's why he's not racing behind us."

Gilly snuggled close to me in the backseat of Harry's car. Shayla slowly began to blow hot air but not nearly enough to warm us. The first thing we did when we arrived at the school was get hot chocolate. The Styrofoam cup was warm, the hot chocolate scalding as I took a sip. I didn't care that I burnt my tongue; I was still cold. Somehow, it was warmer outside of Harry's car than it was inside.

After my interaction with Rink, I had given up on searching for Christine. I stopped calling, not that she'd ever returned my calls. Harry stood with his arm around Beck's waist while they drank their hot chocolate. His tall frame contrasted her short one. She caught me staring, and I made a kissy face at her.

"They aren't doing the hayride this year," Gilly said, observing the lay of the festival.

I blinked. "I didn't know they did hayrides."

"I guess they can't because the woods are blocked off," Gilly sighed. "The driver would go into the woods, and sometimes people would jump out and scare riders."

She looked bummed as she sipped the rest of her hot chocolate. I finished mine and left the group for a moment to find the lady who sold candy apples. Her cart was red and wooden, matching the fall theme. She had a bright smile on her face as I walked up.

"One candy apple please," I said.

"Sure thing, dear," she said.

I handed her my money and waited for her to grab the candy apple. It was plump and red, sparking under the stadium lights. I held it behind my back as I walked back up to Gilly.

"Close your eyes, "I said, echoing her words the day she gave me my ring pop.

She closed her eyes, trying to fight back a smile. I took one of her hands and placed the stick of the candy apple in it.

"Open," I said.

The second Gilly opened her eyes, she took a massive bite. The red candy cracked, and I was tempted to buy one for myself.

"Everyone!" Mr. Leland said from a megaphone. "A reminder the corn maze will become a haunted corn maze in an hour. If you don't want to be spooked, get in line to head through now."

"Want to wait for the haunted one?" Beck asked.

"I wouldn't mind going twice," I said.

"I can walk and eat," Gilly said through mouthfuls of apple.

Harry led the way to the line for the corn maze. It wasn't too long, and we got in pretty quickly. A map was provided in case we got lost, but Gilly promised we wouldn't need it. Her and I took over the front while Beck and Harry stayed behind us. Gilly, deep in the candy apple, still kept her focus on getting us through the corn maze.

"This way," she said, taking a right while a couple of other people went left.

I trusted her instincts and followed, reaching out to touch the fake corn that felt too much like paper. There was one other couple in front of us as we approached what seemed to be the middle of the corn maze. There were four different paths to take. Gilly thought for a moment before going left.

"Are you some sort of corn maze compass?" Harry asked.

"I've come to the corn maze ever since I was little," Gilly explained.

"So you've memorized it?" Harry looked around, seemingly impressed.

"I've memorized the *strategy*," Gilly corrected. "They change the layout of the maze every year."

Soon enough, we found the end of the corn maze. Because we completed the maze, we each got a corn sticker. Beck placed hers on Harry's cheek, and it seemed that was where it would stay the rest of the night.

"How many of these have you gotten?" I asked.

"Too many," Gilly chuckled. "If I had saved them all I could probably cover my bedroom walls with them."

We found a trash can for Gilly to throw the remainder of her apple away. Beck wanted a funnel cake, so she and Harry went to find one. I spotted two deputies walking around before Jon Willis appeared behind them. Gilly waved at her dad but didn't make any effort to go speak with him.

"I'm assuming you've done the haunted corn maze before," I said to Gilly.

"This is actually the first year they're doing it," Gilly said. "Probably because they aren't doing the haunted hayride."

We found a bench to sit on while we waited for them to set up the haunted corn maze, and so Beck could finish her funnel cake. It was smothered in powdered sugar and chocolate, making my mouth water. Beck handed me a decently sized piece, and I ate it slowly, savoring it. My hands were sticky after. Of course Beck forgot to get napkins.

"I'm going to wash my hands," I said, getting up from the picnic table.

The bathrooms were near the bleachers. I passed the candy apple lady, who smiled at me again, and this time I returned it. There were people getting dressed in costumes in the bathroom. I assumed they would be stationed in the haunted corn maze. They ignored me while I washed my hands. As soon as I left the bathroom, I stopped dead in my tracks. Christine was at the bottom of the steps, looking at me. I ran down to her, checking to make sure nobody noticed us.

"Why the hell haven't you called me back?" I whispered.

Before she could answer, Mr. Leland came through on his megaphone again.

"Alright folks, the corn maze will now shut down so we can set up for our haunted one!"

"Because I needed to get my head on straight before I talked to you," Christine said. "I figured everything out."

My breath hitched. I almost didn't believe her.

"How do you know?" I asked.

"I just know, okay?" Christine snapped. "Listen. I'll call you tomorrow. I'm checking on something tonight to confirm everything, but I promise I'll call."

She got to her feet, seemingly about to leave, so I stood in front of her.

"Is that all you're going to say to me?" I asked. "What happened to figuring it out together?"

"That involves too much!" Christine pinched the bridge of her nose. "I can't drop that bomb on you in the middle of a public event without any concrete evidence. I promise to call you tomorrow."

She kept trying to walk away, but I wouldn't let her.

"Quinn!" she snapped. "Give it a rest tonight. And go straight home after this."

I paused. Why did she need me to go straight home? Blood boiling, I followed after her again.

"Did you only come here to tell me that?" I asked. "And why did you break up with Jen? Why haven't you been at school?"

She marched closer to me, and I had to scoot back so her body didn't collide with mine.

"Stop asking me so many questions right now!" Christine all but hissed.

Red-hot anger welled up in my chest. How dare she not share what she found. We'd had a plan, and even though I'd strayed from it, I didn't like that she was doing it too.

"Fine," I said.

Christine stopped me before I could walk away.

"Be very careful," she said. "I'm pretty sure whoever killed Marki and Sarai is here tonight."

"They have to be," I said. "Nearly everyone in town is here."

I walked away, but my heart was pounding. I didn't need Christine to see me falter from worry. I hadn't thought about the possibility of the killer being there until she mentioned it. When I saw Gilly at the bench, laughing with Beck and Harry, I wanted to grab her and get out of there. Then I saw Jon Willis standing nearby, eagle-eyed. No, Gilly would be safer here in the eyes of everyone, including her dad, than at home by herself.

"Want to go get in line?" Gilly asked when I came back.

"Sounds like a plan," I said, trying to smooth out my expression.

Beck noticed. I could feel her questioning me with her gaze, but I couldn't explain my run-in with Christine in front of Gilly and Harry. I let Gilly lead the way to the line, which had already formed. Christine was with Rink toward the front. I needed to speak with both of them. It would be too suspicious if I skipped all the way to the front, but I was itching to. I had to know what was going on.

Jon Willis and the deputies walked down the line, greeting people and checking to see who was there. When Jon saw Rink, the two held eye contact, both full of resentment.

"Have fun, honey," Jon said to Gilly when he passed by us.

Another deputy walked around the corn maze to stand by the exit.

"Thank you everyone for coming out!" Mr. Leland said through his megaphone. "This is the first year we have done a haunted corn maze to replace our haunted hayride, and I think it might beat out our normal event. Everybody, have fun! If you get lost, tell one of our ghouls within, and they can help guide you. The corn maze is now open!"

The field lights shut off, leaving only the snack carts lit. From the outside, the corn was lit up with black lights every few feet to offer a bit of illumination. The line moved quickly but not fast enough. When we entered, I couldn't find Christine or Rink.

"Hey, you guys!" I heard Alma say from behind us.

The twins walked over to Gilly, hugging her, causing a few people behind us to get mad.

"Keep it moving!" some guy yelled.

Beck and Harry were in front of me. Someone dressed like a decaying scarecrow jumped out, and Beck screamed, making Harry laugh. Another girl in a white dress with a pale face ran her long nails against the corn and hissed at Harry. He leaned in toward Beck, and she pushed him off of her, returning the laugh. Gilly was too busy talking in between Alma and Jen, so I made my escape. I turned left while everyone else went right. The sea of people covered my mistake, and nobody called out for me.

I heard a haunting laugh, followed by the sound of a chainsaw revving up in the distant maze. There were fake body parts on the ground, and I nearly tripped over a severed foot. I heard a crow caw, followed by the sound of someone dragging a machete on the ground. I turned the corner and found the source. A guy. He didn't look up at me but continued dragging the machete back and forth in front of him. I tried sneaking past, but his head shot up, and he blocked my path, which turned out to be a dead end anyway.

"Where do you think you're going?" he asked.

I backed up slowly, nearly tripping again, and ran. I passed a few people going the same way I had tried. They asked if it was a dead end, but I ignored them. Regret ran at my heels; I shouldn't have split from my friends. Walking faster, I turned several times and jumped from the people lurking in the corners ready to scare everyone. To me, this was the perfect place for a killer to be. All the weapons looked far too real to be fake, making my heart beat faster.

I nearly gave up until I took a right in the center of the maze and was led straight to Christine and Rink. They disappeared behind some stalks, and I ran to them.

"Christine!" I called.

I turned the way they had gone but didn't find them. I took another left and saw them again. They both turned to look at me. Rink paused; Christine grabbed his arm and dragged him with her. There was no way she was going to tell him who she thought the killer was before she told me. I caught up to them in a part of the maze that was covered so corn hung down from the top.

"Quinn," Rink said. "Where did you come from?"

"Did you tell him?" I asked Christine, ignoring Rink.

"No," Christine said through gritted teeth. "I wasn't planning on it either."

"Tell me what?" Rink asked.

"That Quinn is going to get herself killed if she doesn't stop opening her big mouth," Christine seethed.

She held up a piece of corn dangling near my face and let it go. It hit me in the eye, and by the time shock of it left me, they were gone.

"You bitch!" I yelled, gripping my eye.

"Christine, what the hell?" I heard Rink's voice trail off as Christine pulled him away from me.

I didn't know what the hell her problem was. I blinked a few times. My eye was watery, my vision blurred. I kept my palm pressed against it. I could barely see anything with my one good eye as I pushed through the corn and found another forked path to choose from. I vowed to never do another corn maze again.

I found a girl sitting with her back up against the corn, unmoving.

"I need help getting out," I said to her.

Without getting up from her spot, she pointed to her left. I walked over her feet and went straight for a while until I finally found my friends.

"Where the hell did you go?" Beck asked.

"I took a wrong turn by accident," I said. "There were too many people, and I couldn't find you guys."

"What happened to your eye?" Gilly asked.

"I ran into a piece of corn," I said.

"I think we're almost out of here," Gilly said. "We can get you a wet paper towel from the bathroom."

"Awesome," I sighed.

She grabbed my hand. Jen took the lead, swearing she knew where to go. We went down a dark path lit up by strobing lights. Exactly what my one good eye needed. The chainsaw sound I heard earlier revved up, and a man in a mask approached us, chainsaw lifted in the air. Alma and Jen screamed, running. He chased them, which gave us the opportunity to power walk out of the maze. I looked around for Christine and Rink but didn't see them.

"Let's go get you that paper towel," Gilly said.

Gilly led me to the bathroom where she ran a paper towel under the sink water. The coolness made my eye feel better, but my vision was still slightly blurry. Before we left, we got more hot chocolate to warm us back up. I sipped mine slowly, the chocolate sinking to the pit of my stomach, mixing with the anger I felt against Christine and the need to know what it was she discovered. My friends tried to talk to me, but I was too dejected to engage.

I kept the paper towel on my eye the whole car ride home until the blurriness was gone. The next time I saw Christine, she would be in for a rude awakening.

# CHAPTER TWENTY-FOUR

I didn't want to admit that I waited by the phone the majority of my Saturday. As furious as I was with Christine, I still wanted to know who she believed the killer to be. It was odd that she and Rink had been casually at the corn maze together. Neither piqued me as people who enjoyed community events.

"Whose call are you waiting for?" Mom asked me.

"Gilly's," I lied.

"Let's all watch a Halloween movie together while you wait," Mom said. "I can assure you that you'll hear the phone if it rings during the movie."

"Fine," I said, needing the distraction.

Mom forced Owen out of his room to join us on the couch. She chose *The Addams Family* and made a bucket of popcorn mixed with candy corn. She poured three orange sodas in glasses with jack-o'-lantern faces on them, topping them with whipped cream and green sprinkles just as she had when we were younger. I used to love our movie days as a kid and all the funky ways Mom incorporated Halloween treats into them. But it didn't feel as fun this year.

At least Mom's popcorn was good. I loved salty and sweet things mixed together, and it didn't disappoint. The candy corn got softer from the warm popcorn, making it delectable. Mom had a smile on her face the whole movie. She mixed the whipped cream in with her orange soda, turning it pastel.

"Try it," Mom said, taking a sip. "It's delicious."

It tasted like a Creamsicle. I tried my best to keep my attention on the movie, but every now and then, my eyes trailed to the phone, as if I could magically make Christine call me.

"I was thinking of baking this year for the trick-or-treaters as well," Mom said. "Maybe cupcakes?"

"Great idea," I said quickly.

Mom didn't notice my lack of enthusiasm and kept her attention on the movie. Owen was already asleep, his hand in the small bowl of popcorn Mom had poured for him. I nudged Mom and pointed at Owen. She threw popcorn at him, which woke him up. We both laughed, and I was finally back in the present.

When the phone finally rang, I flew from the couch to answer it. I picked up with a desperate, "Hello?" On the other end of the line, Gilly breathed shakily.

"Quinn. . . ." she started, words full of terror.

My heart dropped. "What's wrong?"

I didn't even care that it wasn't Christine's call. I could tell Gilly didn't have good news for me. Had Alma or Jen been murdered?

"Dad said he had to go to the station today," Gilly said. "A body was found in the park."

"*Our* park?" I whispered, my heart beating faster.

"Yes," Gilly said. "I don't know who it is yet, but Dad left about thirty minutes ago. I locked all the doors, but I'm scared, Quinn."

"It'll be okay," I whispered so Mom and Owen wouldn't hear. "It's daylight. And I'm sure your dad wouldn't have left you home alone if he didn't think you'd be completely safe. Have you called anyone else?"

"I called Alma and Jen first," Gilly said. "They're fine."

Relief filled me, only for panic to set in moments later. If it wasn't Alma and Jen in the park, then who could it be? My stomach recoiled as I thought of Beck and how I hadn't heard from her today.

"I don't want to hang up on you, but I feel like I need to check on Beck," I said.

"I understand," Gilly said. "I'll call you back later when Dad gets home."

After I hung up, I frantically dialed Beck's number. The phone rang and rang until, finally, it clicked on the other end.

"Hello?" Beck said.

"Thank God," I whispered. "You're safe."

"What are you talking about?"

I peered at Mom and Owen to make sure they weren't eavesdropping on me.

"Gilly told me Jon Willis got a call about a body being found in the park," I said. "It's not Alma or Jen. so I thought. . . ."

I couldn't finish the sentence.

"Shit," Beck said. "Another body?"

"They haven't released who it is yet," I whispered.

"We were all at the corn maze," Beck said. "Maybe it's someone random."

"Maybe," I said. "I'll call you back later if I find out anything."

I joined Mom back on the couch and slowly sat down, trying not to let my demeanor give away my worry. Maybe Beck was right, and it was a random person, unrelated to Marki and Sarai's murder. If the pattern had continued, it would've been Alma, Gilly, or Jen found in the park, and each of them was safe.

I steadied my breathing again, sipping my soda slowly, but the sweet flavor was gone.

The rest of the day was spent in my room, waiting, once again, for the phone to ring. Part of me took it as a good sign it wasn't ringing, but it also meant Jon Willis might not have returned home yet. As dusk fell, I grew more anxious and hugged my pillow tightly so I couldn't feel the nerves fluttering in my stomach. I accidentally fell asleep and woke up with a start from the shrill ringing of the phone. It stopped short, and I figured Mom had answered it.

I carefully walked downstairs quietly, listening to Mom. She mumbled, and I couldn't pick up on anything until the very end, when she said, "Okay, I will tell her."

She hung up and gripped the table beneath the phone, looking down.

"Mom?" I said. "What's wrong?"

"That was Jon Willis," Mom said. "He is going to need you to come in for questioning tomorrow."

"What for?" I asked.

"Another girl has been found dead. In the park this time," Mom said glumly. "He said you knew the victim, and that he saw you talking with her last night at the corn maze."

I already knew, but I asked anyway. "Who was it?"

"Christine Gateman," Mom said.

I was the only one waiting to be questioned the next morning. Mom drove me, again, and waited until I was called back by Jon Willis. My stomach was twisted in knots. Had the police found all of Christine's evidence? If so, they could investigate whatever she'd found that she never got to tell me—or, they would see how set she was on Jon Willis as a suspect. Would that lead to them figuring out our plan to work together? I looked around for a trash can, feeling the urge to vomit. The smell of coffee and warm printer paper drifted by with every cop. It reminded me of the front office at school, only more dreadful. Nobody seemed to pay me any mind, even as I gripped my leg to stop it from shaking. For all they knew, *I* could be the killer. Yet they didn't even bat an eyelash.

"Quinn," Jon said, startling me as he approached. "Follow me."

I followed him slowly, attempting to steady my breathing even as my heart threatened to burst through my chest. The déjà vu I got from walking to the back room with Jon was repugnant. I could tell he was fed up with doing this as well. Defeated even. His skin looked paler, eyes bloodshot and exhausted. His hair even looked greasy. I took my seat across from him at the table. I had to be careful about what I told him.

"How well did you know Christine Gateman?" Jon asked.

"I met her at Sarai's party," I said. "The one you busted before she died. She was close with Jen, and since I'm close with Gilly, we saw a lot of one another more recently."

"I saw the two of you speaking by the corn maze on Friday night," Jon said. "How close did you two become after you met?"

My palms went clammy.

"She was asking me if I was going into the haunted corn maze," I said. "Every interaction I've had with her has been pretty casual. I'd say we were acquainted but not quite friends."

Jon nodded and wrote down what I said on a yellow notepad.

"This is the same Christine I saw you with that day on the football field, correct? Where I broke up that fight between her and Beck Wood."

Shit. "Yes."

"Tell me about that," Jon said.

"Beck and Christine said some things to each other, and it went south," I said. "It really wasn't anything serious. Beck can be a hothead sometimes."

"What was said?" Jon asked.

I couldn't think of a lie on the spot. I looked into his eyes and felt he was peeling me back like frayed wallpaper. He could sense my lies and knew what I truly wanted to say. I couldn't tell him the truth, about Beck and I knowing of the affair.

"I don't exactly remember," I said. "It was probably something stupid."

He wrote more down, and I could feel myself growing hotter.

"Rink Matthews was there, too, correct?" Jon asked.

I nodded. "He was also at the corn maze last night. We were all there."

"What time did you get home last night?" Jon asked.

"Around eleven," I said. "Harry dropped me off right after we took Gilly home."

Jon nodded. "Did you leave your house after that?"

I furrowed my brow. I couldn't hide my emotions; they always came across on my face.

"No. . . ." I said.

Was he insinuating I left my house and killed Christine? There was no way he would suspect me, right?

"I'm trying to get a clear understanding here," Jon said. "It seemed to me there were some problems with Christine between other people. Quinn, I really need your help here to tell me everything you can so we can find out who killed this girl."

"I don't think I have enough information to give you," I said. "I'm sorry."

Jon sighed but wrote that down anyway. Ratting out Christine's sleuthing would come back to bite me in the ass. I had to look out for myself.

"Thanks for the help," Jon said. "Come on; I'll walk you out."

He let me walk ahead of him, and as I did, he placed his hand on my back. I jumped.

"My fault," Jon said. "Wanted to make sure you went the right way."

I turned to him, and he forced a small smile before motioning me forward. I left the station as quickly as I could.

There was tension when I got in the car with Mom. Her hands stayed high on the steering wheel, knuckles white. My back hummed from where Jon's hand had been. I wanted to get home as fast as we could so I could change.

"Is something wrong?" I asked Mom, needing a conversation to get my mind off of the interaction.

"Why is it that you are being questioned so often?" Mom asked. "I don't like that."

"I don't like it either, Mom," I said, defensively. "But I can't help that people I go to school with are being murdered. Of course if I know them I'm going to get questioned. That's how investigations work."

Mom's mouth moved into a tight line, and I knew she was holding back from arguing with me.

"Ever since you started hanging out with your new group of friends you've been sucked into this," Mom said. "You have no business being in that station questioned by the police."

Heat rushed up my face, and I didn't hold back.

"You mean Gilly," I said. "Ever since I've been hanging out with Gilly. Her dad is the sheriff. I see him when I go to her house all the time. My questioning doesn't even feel official."

"How did you meet that Christine girl?" Mom asked. "Through Gilly?"

"Mom, stop!" I yelled. "You're taking this way too far."

"You're staying under my watch for a long while," Mom said. "School and that's it."

"Why?" I asked.

Mom didn't answer me and continued driving home, speeding. I repeated the question, yelling as loud as I could, but she still didn't answer.

"What?" I snapped. "Do you think I killed them?"

Mom slammed on her brakes, throwing my head forward. The seatbelt sliced into my neck.

"Don't you ever say that again!" Mom shouted. "Of *course* I don't think you killed those girls."

There was pure fury in her eyes. I turned away from her and sat forward. The rest of the drive home was silent. Once we made it home, Mom slammed the front door, and I slammed my room door. The phone rang once, and I reached over to lift it off the machine and setting it aside, silencing it. I wasn't in the mood to speak to anyone.

## CHAPTER TWENTY-FIVE

Mom hadn't been kidding when she said I would only be going to school. She changed her work schedule just so she could drop me off and pick me up. I felt like a kid again, needing my mommy to drive me to and from school. We hadn't talked since the car ride yesterday, and something told me it would be that way for a while.

In the halls, I passed by so many people talking about Christine.

"She was hanging around with Jen," someone said. "That group's curse must have latched onto her."

Other people talked about how the girls of the town were now cursed because of Gilly's friend group. Marki's name, for the first time in weeks, was said again. She was blamed for starting the "murder trend." It was horrid hearing people turn on the dead girls.

"We're fine, bro," a football player said, giving his friend a fist bump. "Only girls are being killed."

Maybe they were right. Maybe all the girls in this town were cursed, and we had to wait our turn for the curse to hit us. For some, it came as a bad breakout before prom, for others it meant never seeing prom because they were found dead in the woods. Our own *Blair Witch Project* woods.

I went to the bathroom before class and found Jen crying, wiping her tears on a thin, brown paper towel. Polka dots of her tears soaked through it.

"Jen, are you okay?" I asked.

Her dark eyes were the saddest I'd ever seen them. "I think I might have loved Christine."

My heart sank. Not because she lost someone she loved, but because Christine had used her from the second they started hanging out—not to mention completely invaded her privacy by writing all those things about her in that journal. Unease took over me at the thought of it. Was the journal still in Christine's room, hidden away?

"I'm really sorry about Christine," I said, because I didn't know of any other way to console her.

"I'm really sick of losing people, Quinn," Jen sighed. "I haven't even turned seventeen yet, and I've already lost three people. All I have left are Alma and Gilly."

It wasn't like me to do it, but I hugged her. Her bookbag prevented me from rubbing her back, but I think she still appreciated the hug anyway. She cried harder, letting her head fall onto my shoulder. I forgot about the fact that I never got to hear about what Christine had found out. Instead of wanting to read them, I wanted to find the journal and all of her notes and burn them up. This was bigger than the both of us. *Murder* cases were bigger than the both of us. Hugging Jen in the bathroom changed my entire perspective, for good. I was done trying to catch a murderer. That was the job of Jon and his deputies.

At lunch, the four of us sat more huddled than normal. I think we all felt like Jen. We all had the same question: How much time did we *really* have left with one another?

"Rink found me in the hall earlier," Beck said. "Quinn, he wants you to meet him under the bleachers after school today."

"Did he say why?" I asked.

"He said it wasn't anything too serious," Beck said. "He figured it was easier for me to pass the message along."

"Sure," I said. "I ran into Jen today in the bathroom. She was really upset."

Gilly turned around to look at the table where Alma and Jen sat. Jen wasn't eating; instead she was staring at the table while Alma chewed slowly.

"I think I'm going to go sit with them today," Gilly said. "Is that cool?"

"Of course it is," I said. "Jen needs you."

Gilly squeezed my hand before grabbing her lunch to join her friends. She sat at the table across from the twins, back to us so she could talk with them. Jen smiled slightly when she saw Gilly and even kept her head up. Alma talked more, from what I saw. Gilly really was their glue.

I watched the clock the rest of the day until the bell rang to signal the end of school. I theorized all day about why Rink needed to meet me. Did he only tell Beck it wasn't that important so she wouldn't snoop? That had to be it. Maybe he did hear about Christine's findings, or maybe he knew who killed her.

I jogged over to the bleachers and found Rink sitting on them, the stack of Christine's notes in his lap. The notebook was closed, and I itched to open it up.

"Beck said you wanted to see me," I began. "I'm assuming it's because of all that."

"Christine gave me everything the night of the corn maze," Rink said.

"Before or after?" I asked.

"Before," Rink said. "I swear to you, after the corn maze I dropped her off at home and went back to mine."

"I wasn't accusing you."

I tried to motion for Rink to hand me Christine's things, but he wouldn't budge. I didn't want to take them from his lap, so I sat next to him instead.

Before I could stop the question from leaving my mouth, I was pulled right back into the case. "What did Christine find out?"

"I honestly don't know," Rink said. "I promised her I wouldn't read anything. She left it solely for you."

My heart skipped a beat with eagerness. All my doubt fled. I wanted to tear the pages open and finally figure out what was going on, but as I reached for the notebook, Rink pulled it away from me.

"No," Rink said, head down. "I want to burn everything."

I looked at him, appalled. "Christine spent weeks on all of this, though. She knows who did it. Besides, she left it to me."

I went to grab the notebook again, but Rink pulled away.

"She *thought* she knew who did it," Rink said. "And that's what got her killed. I'm as tired of being around death as anyone. So, I'm burning it, right here, right now. You can help me, or you can walk away. I'm sorry, Quinn. You're not getting this notebook."

The key to everything rested in Rink's lap. I stared at the notebook, his fingers tightly wound around it. What good would knowing actually do? Rink watched me carefully, face blank. I exhaled, long and slow.

"Do you have a lighter?" I asked.

There were old barrels in the storage closet by the bleachers. I helped Rink drag one out of the closet and away from the building. He let me hold Christine's notes one last time before I dropped them into the barrel. He dumped half a bottle of vodka in the barrel, then threw in an old Zippo lighter. As the flames licked

Christine's notebook, I nearly dove my hand in to fish it out. My curiosity burned like the pages. As much good as her findings could be, they'd also caused damage and doubt. Besides, what if she had been wrong?

"Rink," I said. "Honestly answer this for me. Did you have anything at all to do with the deaths of Marki, Sarai, or Christine?"

He sighed. "No, Quinn. I swear I didn't."

Once the fire ate up the notes and died, we left the barrel there before walking away from the stadium. Three cop cars, lights strobing, sped into the parking lot. The asphalt crunched under their tires. Both Rink and I froze, unsure of what to do. Jon Willis was the first to exit his car, along with the two deputies that had been at the corn maze.

"Rink Matthews," Jon said. "You are under arrest for the murder of Christine Gateman. You have the right to remain silent."

Rink looked as confused as I felt, but he didn't try to fight. A look of defeat and betrayal saddled its way onto him, and I was left defenseless. My ears rang at the click of handcuffs sliding into place. Jon Willis didn't look me in the eye until Rink was in the back of a cop car. He looked pitiful, small, in the window behind the deputy taking him away.

"Would you like a ride home, Quinn?" Jon asked.

"No thanks," I said, far away from myself. "I think I'll walk instead."

But I didn't walk home. I walked into town, footsteps on autopilot and muscle memory the only things moving me forward. Rink had been arrested right in front of me, and I'd done nothing. But what *could* I have done? Argued with the police and potentially found myself next to Rink, unable to help us both? Rink Matthews wasn't a killer; he was a grieving brother who didn't deserve to be behind bars. This time, I finally, truly believed that.

I walked into Karson's. Nobody was in there except the store clerk, who was listening to music on their headphones. The news played on the TV.

"Can you turn it up?" I said, tapping on the counter.

The clerk grabbed the remote. As the volume increased, a reporter spoke, unseen. Instead, the images on the screen were of the park, caution tape wound around the trees.

"A keychain belonging to the suspect was found this morning," the reporter said.

My eyes moved back and forth as a picture of the keychain flashed on the screen. I recognized the skull with the cigarette in its mouth. The keychain I'd noticed on Rink's bag the day the police had questioned him at school. My heart fell to the pit of my stomach. Why had his keychain been there in the park?

I resumed my walk home shortly thereafter. Numb, I only looked up as a car came to a violent stop next to me. Owen peered at me through the passenger side, eyes warning me to run. Shit. Mom was supposed to pick me up from school today. I opened the car and braced myself for the screaming that would surely ensue.

"Did you have fun on your little adventure?" Mom asked.

"I'm sorry," I said.

"You're sorry?" Mom echoed, voice rising.

I drowned out her lecture as she screamed above the music in the car, barely reacting when she turned the radio completely off. I let her yell at me without fighting back. When she finally went silent, we pulled into the driveway.

"Rink Matthews was arrested in front of me today," I said, but neither her nor Owen responded.

# CHAPTER TWENTY-SIX

The seriousness of this questioning with Jon Willis was unlike any before. This time, he had a convict, ready to sentence to life in prison for murder now that Rink was eighteen. It was far too hot in the tiny room. Jon didn't feel like my girlfriend's dad anymore. He was a cop ready for justice. Yet, I still thought Rink was innocent. The keychain in the park could have meant anything. I clenched my hands at the scratchy sound of Jon's notebook flipping over to a new page. The hum of the white fluorescents above gave me a headache. When would it end?

"Quinn," Jon said far too formally, "will you tell me about your relationship with Rink Matthews?"

"I met him the night of Sarai's party," I said. "Until then I only knew of him from Beck."

He scratched his pen on the paper, and I wanted to grab it from his hands and throw it at the wall.

"Do you recognize this keychain?" Jon asked, sliding a plastic bag in front of me.

Rink's keychain was in the bag, slightly dirty from where it had been found in the park. As I looked closer, I swore I saw the rusted brown residue of blood.

"Yes," I said, swallowing. "That's Rink Matthews's keychain."

"Do you have any suspicions regarding Rink Matthews or know why this keychain may have been found in the same place we found Miss Gateman's body?" Jon asked.

I shook my head no.

"I need a verbal answer," Jon said.

"No," I said. "Nothing Rink has said or done has led me to be suspicious of him. I'm not sure why his keychain was left in the park."

"Going back to the night you and Abigail Willis were attacked," he began, and I shivered at the formality of him using his daughter's full name, "do you think you may have seen Rink Matthews?"

"I don't know," I said. "It was dark, and I was focused on getting to Gilly."

"Is there any other useful information that might be able to help further this case?" Jon asked.

I chewed my lip. Do I send him on a wild goose chase to look for Christine's notes and find them gone? Or do I leave it at that and go home?

"Christine Gateman told me she was looking into the case herself," I said, my mouth making the decision for me. "Apparently, she had a notebook where she wrote down every suspect she personally had. After hearing about what happened to her, I believe that might be the reason she was murdered."

Jon nodded and scribbled in his notebook. "Christine's home has already been inspected for anything unusual. Is there anywhere else this notebook could be?"

"I'm not sure," I said. "In fact, I'm not even sure if it exists. Christine could've easily made it up."

I tapped my foot, trying not to seem nervous as Jon seemingly wrapped up his notes.

"Thank you for your time," Jon said.

I let out a large breath when I finally got out of the station. I ducked into Mom's car; she didn't say anything as we drove back home. I didn't like the silence, but lately, anything I said seemed to get twisted into an argument.

That night, while mom and Owen slept, I snuck out with my bike. The cold air hit my lungs like shards of glass, and I tried my best to make my breathing shallow. Nerves jittered my legs as I rode. In my heart, I knew Rink was innocent, so there was still a killer out there. I had to cover my tracks.

When I reached the school, I made sure nobody lurked around. The yellow streetlights made the place eerie, and my skin crawled as I walked toward the stadium. I felt a thousand eyes watch me from the woods. What lurked in the dark taunted me, and I wanted to teleport myself back home immediately. Being out here was a stupid idea.

I shut down my fears when I saw the barrel was still where Rink and I had left it. Nobody had bothered to move it even an inch away from the spot we'd burned all of Christine's notes. I walked up to the barrel, hands in my pockets. Inside, everything had been burned except for a fresh piece of paper, folded up that hadn't been there before. I reached into the barrel and pulled it out, unfolding it. *Keep digging and end up like Christine.*

Shuddering, I whipped around to see if I could catch anyone lurking in the dark. I stuffed the note in my pocket and worked with all my strength to tilt the barrel over and clean it out. The wind took most of the debris with it. If the police inspected it for some reason, it would look like it simply hadn't been cleaned in a year.

I pulled the barrel back into the closet and positioned it the same way Rink and I had found it. When the job was done, I sprinted to my bike and took off home. The amount of fear in my body made my heart race to the point that darkness started to splotch my vision. Whoever had killed Christine had left me a note. Whoever had killed Christine knew I also had my own suspicions, and it looked like I was the next target.

Beck, Gilly, and I sat on a red bench outside of Martha's Grab and Go. I got onion rings with a chocolate milkshake and let Beck dip her fries in it. My appetite was barely there. Ever since I'd found the warning note, I hadn't wanted to eat anything. I still got chills thinking about it.

"I never want to be questioned again," I said. "I feel like I've been at that stupid station more than my own house this last month."

"It wasn't too bad," Beck said. "I told them Rink was my dealer, and they warned me about the weed, but other than that, I was in and out pretty quickly."

"It's more nerve-wracking than anything," Gilly said. "I wish Dad would ask me things at home, but he's afraid if he gives me special treatment, then the other guys will get onto him about it. He has to 'set an example as sheriff' or something."

I passed the rest of my milkshake to Beck. I finished off the crumbs of my onion rings and went to throw the trash away. A few tables whispered about Rink and his arrest.

"What happens to Rink now?" Beck asked when I sat back down.

"He'll go to trial," Gilly said. "And they'll either find him guilty or not."

"Do you think we will be witnesses?" Beck asked.

Gilly shook her head. "I doubt it. If you didn't give Dad much information, then he probably won't call on you."

I thought back to when I'd promised Rink I would testify for him. Even though the promise hadn't been rock-solid, after finding the note, it didn't seem like a good idea anymore even if I wanted to. Even now, I wanted us to drop the conversation in case the killer could somehow hear us.

After Martha's Grab and Go, Beck came over so we could do our algebra homework together. Mom smiled but didn't say anything when we saw her. We still barely spoke. I lingered to see if Mom would ask about my day or give me *something* other than silence. But, like me, she could be petty when she was mad.

"What is with the hostility?" Beck asked, emptying her bookbag on my bed.

"Everything is going to shit," I said. "I've never fought this much with Mom before."

"It happens," Beck said, shrugging.

"It's not normal for us," I said. "Mom's mad at me for everything that's going on. She thinks I'm too involved."

Beck went silent and pulled out her algebra worksheet, writing her name in the top-right corner.

"Do you also think I'm too involved or something?" I asked.

"Yes," Beck admitted. "I don't want you to end up like Christine if you keep digging into everything."

I froze and registered what she'd said. The barrel. The note *in* the barrel. Had Beck left it for me?

"You left me that note in the barrel," I breathed.

"What?" Beck said. "What note?"

"Don't lie to me, Beck," I snapped.

"I'm not lying to you!" Beck snapped back. "I don't appreciate you accusing me of something I didn't do."

"You're the only other person who hangs around the bleachers!" I shook my head in disbelief. "Did you see Rink and I burn Christine's things? And how did you know I'd go back that night?"

Beck threw her pencil down, standing up. "What are you even talking about? What did you burn?"

Her eyes were full of concern, and I realized I had screwed up. It didn't make Rink nor I look good admitting we burned Christine's things. When I couldn't find a valid response, Beck gathered her things to leave. My hands went clammy. First Mom and now my best friend . . . when would I stop screwing up?

"Beck, wait," I said.

"Sounds like *you're* the one hiding things from me," Beck said sourly, slamming my bedroom door on her way out.

I sat in silence for a few minutes after Beck left, then pulled the note out of my desk drawer and read it again. *Keep digging and end up like Christine.* I could no longer tell if it was a threat or a warning. I ripped it into tiny pieces and threw it into my wastebasket.

## CHAPTER TWENTY-SEVEN

Five days. That's how long it had been since Beck and I said a word to each other. We didn't talk in algebra, and she stopped showing up to lunch. Gilly and Harry didn't ask questions, but I could see their concern in the way they stared at her empty spot. Small talk filled our table, and I barely contributed. I too stared at the spot where Beck used to sit. I missed my best friend. Five days of not speaking felt like an eternity, but we were both too stubborn to break the silence.

Gilly went ahead of Harry and me when we left the cafeteria so she could use the bathroom before class.

"Is Beck okay?" Harry asked when Gilly was gone. "She's barely talked to me all week."

Beck gave everyone the silent treatment when she was mad or felt betrayed. I knew Harry wouldn't be immune to it. She liked her walls up so she could deal with things on her own.

"She needs space," I said. "Give her a few more days; she'll come around."

"Was it something I did?" Harry asked.

"No, it was something *I* did," I said. "But it doesn't even matter. It was a stupid best friend fight."

"Can I help fix it?" Harry asked.

I shook my head no. "I'll see you later," I said, getting up to leave the lunchroom.

I figured Beck was hiding out, smoking under the bleachers. Without ringleader Rink, I had no clue where she was going to get weed from. I could casually go to the bleachers and "run into her" but knowing Beck, she would simply acknowledge my presence and walk away so she wouldn't have to deal with me. I hated when she gave me the silent treatment.

When I got home, I stared at the phone, wondering if it was worth anything to call her.

"Quinn?" Mom said, lightly knocking on my door.

"Hm?" I answered.

"I want to carve pumpkins tomorrow evening," Mom said. "Before dinner. Try to be home at a good time."

"Can Gilly carve pumpkins with us?" I asked.

Mom hesitated. "Sure. I'll pick up the pumpkins tomorrow."

She walked away from my room, and I smiled. Maybe things would finally get better between Mom and me. I started to dial Beck's number by accident. I quickly hung up and called Gilly instead. She was ecstatic to carve pumpkins with us, saying she really hadn't done it since her mom and brother died.

I was relieved Mom said she could join us, but a piece of me felt sad. Beck normally carved them with us, but it didn't look like that would happen this year. My mind went back to all the time we'd spent picking out the perfect pumpkins, almost always identical in size so they could match, even if our designs were different. For nearly a decade, Beck had been a part of the pumpkin carving party, but now Gilly was taking her spot. Guilt settled in my stomach. I hoped Beck never found out.

—

The worst part about carving pumpkins was scooping out the guts. The stringy, wet parts got lodged under my nails, and I couldn't stand it. Owen didn't care. He always tried to throw pumpkin guts at me, but Mom would yell at him to stop. Gilly used a ladle to get the guts out of her pumpkin, but the flimsy handle caused some bits to fling up and smack her in the face. She had pumpkin guts in her hair, and I couldn't help but laugh.

"What are you going to carve?" I asked Gilly.

"Probably a cat," she said. "I'm not artistic enough to be fancy. What about you?"

"Ghostface," I said, showing Gilly the outline I'd printed out.

"Quinn's got a talent for pumpkin carving," Mom said. "She gets it from me."

Mom would attempt to carve a haunted house into her huge pumpkin this year.

"I'm going to carve a scared face," Owen said. "I have a fake ax I'm going to put on the top to make it look like it was stabbed."

"You are so morbid," I said, beginning my first cut into the pumpkin.

Gilly held the knife in a fist, carving sporadically.

"Try holding it with your fingers," I said. "And be gentle with it."

"This is how Dad taught me to do it," Gilly said. "He's probably worse at carving than I am."

Gilly tried to carve a cat sitting with its back to those who would see it. She wanted to do a thin, curly tail, and I knew it would be a disaster when she reached that point.

"Let me know if I can help," I said, trying to hold in my laugh.

She was too focused to talk. Owen finished first, keeping the carving portion basic so the emphasis would be on the fake ax he lodged into the top of the pumpkin. Even though it was simple, the design was still awesome. He left his pumpkin on its newspaper and went inside.

My Ghostface was coming along. I carved slowly, trying not to get too ahead of myself and mess up the way Gilly had. The sides of the cat were jagged angles where the knife had cut too hard. She tried only using her fingers to hold the knife, but it didn't work out for her. Mom's pumpkin looked the best out of all of us. Her haunted house looked as if it belonged in a competition.

"Mom, are there any places that do a pumpkin-carving contest?" I asked.

"I'm not sure," she said, dusting some guts off the face of the pumpkin. "Why?"

"You should enter yours in one," I said. "It looks great."

"Thanks, Quinnie," she said, not taking her eye off the pumpkin.

Gilly finished next. I could tell the creature on her pumpkin was a cat, but like I predicted, the tail was nearly botched. It zigzagged more than it swirled.

"Maybe it will look better when it's dark," Gilly said.

"Gilly, honey," Mom said. "Could you go grab a bowl for the pumpkin seeds."

Gilly wiped her hands on a rag and went in to fetch a bowl. Mom loved roasting the seeds when we carved pumpkins. "Do you still have the good seasoning?" I asked.

"I have a ton leftover from last year," Mom said. "Apple pie, right?"

I nodded vigorously, feeling like a child about to receive a bucket full of candy. Mom always made a big batch of roasted seeds with an apple pie seasoning mix. It was my favorite of all of the flavors in our spice cabinet. After Mom and I finished up, we summoned Owen to bring us some tea light candles. We lit the candles and placed them in the pumpkins. Owen closed the garage so we could see what they truly looked like in the dark. Gilly was right; her pumpkin looked way better with only the candlelight illuminating it. My Ghostface was nearly perfect, and Mom's haunted house would surely be a showstopper on our porch this year.

Gilly and I washed off the pumpkin seeds and set them out to dry some before sprinkling the apple pie seasoning over them. Once they began roasting in the oven, the whole house smelled like fall. It reminded me of my childhood: the smell of cinnamon and apples. The nostalgia hit me hard.

"I remember when I dressed you and Owen as Sally and Conrad," Mom said, stirring the pasta she'd decided to make for dinner.

"Horrible idea," I said. "It's the first costume I actually remember wearing, and I hated the dress."

"So much so that you stuck a piece of chewed-up candy to it," Mom sighed. "Forty bucks down the drain."

"It was a nightmare," I said.

"Tell me about it," Mom mumbled.

Gilly smiled. "The first costume I remember was a unicorn. My mom made the horn out of clay and right before we left the house, it snapped. I was left with a nub for a horn."

The kitchen fell silent but not with sadness. I noticed how Gilly's eyes sparkled when she thought of the happy memory she had of her mom.

After we ate our pasta for dinner, the oven timer went off: the pumpkin seeds were ready. Gilly and I filled a bowl with some and went up to my room while we waited for Jon to come pick her up.

"These are the best I've ever eaten," Gilly said. "We never even thought to roast our pumpkin seeds because we hated how slimy they were."

"I'm sure Mom won't mind sending you home with some," I said. "That's if Owen doesn't try to eat them all."

I rubbed Gilly's back while she wrapped around my body. I couldn't recall the last time we got to do this—simply exist with one another. I picked a dried piece of pumpkin out of her hair, and we laughed.

"The first thing I'm doing when I get home is showering," Gilly said. "Sorry if you find any stray pieces of pumpkin lying around later."

"Most girls leave bobby pins around," I said. "You leave pumpkin guts."

Gilly pushed my shoulder lightly then kissed me. Her lips were warm and tasted like cinnamon and nutmeg. It was at that moment I started associating Gilly with fall. The smell of apple candles would always remind me of her. We no longer had a spot together, now that the park was a tarnished memory for both of us, but we did have a season.

"Do you want to do a couple's costume with me for Halloween?" Gilly asked.

I hadn't thought about it until then. "Sure. Any ideas?"

"How about Chucky and Tiffany?" she suggested.

I stared at her. "You're only suggesting that because I would have to be Chucky."

"Hey, it's not my fault you're both gingers," Gilly said, laughing as I started tickling her.

"Veto," I said. "Next."

"There's not a lot of gingers I can think of," Gilly said.

"I can wear a wig!" I protested.

"No," Gilly said, running her fingers through my hair. "I like your hair too much."

I thought for a moment. "Harley Quinn and Poison Ivy?"

"For a couple's costume?" Gilly asked.

"They're totally banging," I said. "I have a whole theory that Harley is seeing Ivy behind Joker's back."

Gilly smiled as I went on and on about Harley Quinn and Poison Ivy. "Alright, you've sold me with your fanfiction."

"It's not fanfiction!" I insisted.

"Whatever you say," Gilly said, pulling me into a kiss. "We can be Harley and Ivy."

We kissed for a while until the door opened downstairs, signaling Jon was there to pick Gilly up. I gave her a few more quick kisses before we both went downstairs. Mom had packed a bag of pumpkin seeds for Gilly and Jon. Gilly gladly took the bag and said her thanks before leaving with her dad.

"I think I'm going to be Poison Ivy for Halloween this year," I said. "Will you help me with my costume?"

"Sure," Mom said. "I'll need to find lots of fake leaves at the craft store, but it's doable."

We sat at the table, planning out my costume. Owen joined us, stealing some more pumpkin seeds as he explained how he wanted to be a "cereal killer" for Halloween. Mom and I both thought it was insensitive, but he promised he only wanted to do it to make other people less scared. Speaking to Mom again made me feel better. We were back to discussing Halloween costume plans excitedly. Everything felt normal again.

## CHAPTER TWENTY-EIGHT

I almost thought Beck was going to talk to me when she saw me in the bathroom, but she decided not to. She caught my eye for a split second before bolting. My brain screamed at her, trying to telepathically communicate that I missed her and wanted to talk. I swallowed my pride and followed her.

"Beck!" I said, finding her in the hallway.

She had headphones on and couldn't hear me. Annoyed, I put my own on and continued

to class. At lunch, Harry looked as if he were going to explode.

"I can't do this anymore," Harry said. "You and Beck need to make up."

"I tried talking to her earlier," I said. "But she didn't hear me call her name."

"So call her."

"She won't pick up." I gave a sigh. "Believe me. I know Beck more than anyone."

Harry bounced his leg, making the table vibrate. Gilly tried sharing some of her chocolate muffins to distract him, but he refused to eat.

"I don't understand how I'm wrapped into this," Harry said.

"I honestly don't know why she isn't speaking to you," I said.

"She is speaking to me," Harry said. "She's just full of attitude every time she responds."

I felt bad for Harry. I didn't want Beck to ruin something good she had going with him. I nearly left the lunch table to confront her at the bleachers but realized that probably wasn't the best place to do it. I didn't even want to be out there. Not after I'd seen Rink get arrested right in front of me and found that note left in the barrel.

"Do you want me to see if she will talk to me?" Gilly asked.

"I don't want you getting involved," I said. "Beck can be a grouch."

"If I bump into her, I'll ask her something stupid—like for lip gloss—and see if I can keep a conversation going," Gilly said.

"Careful when poking a bear," I warned.

When lunch ended, I walked with Gilly to English class. Mrs. Ashley made it a tradition to wear something spooky every day during the month of October. Today, she had on dancing skeleton earrings and a spiderweb dress. I tried to put on a smile when she played "Monster Mash" and passed out candy, but fighting with Beck always made me feel hollow. There was no fight that was as bad as one with a best friend.

I threw my headphones on after class and walked to the bus alone. Mom had finally let up about taking me to and from school. I almost wished she hadn't changed her mind about it, though, having grown fond of not taking the musty bus smell home with me. One of the buses hissed, and I rolled my eyes.

Before I got on my bus, I noticed Beck and Harry standing by his car. She was halfway in the passenger's side as Harry held the door open so she couldn't slam it. Beck rolled her eyes, and Harry threw up his hands. Anger spread across her face as she spoke to him. When Harry finally released the car door, she slammed it, immediately turning toward the window to ignore Harry. Harry ran his hands through his hair. Not caring what Beck would have to say about it, I jogged toward them.

"Harry!" I called.

Beck scowled when Harry met me halfway to his car but didn't try to stop us.

"What?" he said, defeated.

"What just happened with Beck?" I asked.

"I confronted her for avoiding me, and she told me I was being dramatic," Harry said. "She needs space right now, or whatever."

"I'm sorry," I said. "I'll call her tonight."

I peeked over Harry's shoulder to get a glance at his car. Beck folded her arms and turned away from us.

"No point," Harry said. "Apparently, she's going to some party with Rink's friends. 'Strictly for the stoners,' she said, meaning I'm not allowed to go with her."

Most of the time, Beck only hung out with them at school. Sometimes on the weekends, but she mostly hated going to parties alone, especially if Rink wasn't there.

"Why are they having a party when their friend was just arrested?" I said aloud, wishing I would have contained the thought in my head.

Harry shrugged. "In his honor, I guess."

"I don't understand what's going on with her," I said.

"How bad was the fight?" Harry asked.

"Not bad enough to cause this." I paused. "Can I ride home with you?"

Harry looked between me and his car. Beck still wouldn't look at me.

"Promise you two won't cause me to crash my car?" he asked.

I held out my pinkie. "Promise."

Beck furiously shook her head every step I took toward Harry's car. She mouthed "no" repeatedly until I opened the door, letting out her loud words.

"Absolutely not," Beck said, unbuckling. "I won't ride home with her."

"It's just a ride," I said. "Relax. My bus is late."

"Not my fucking problem," Beck said.

"Hey!" Harry said, raising his voice. "It's my fucking car, and I'm giving you both a ride. Now suck it up."

Like children, we both crossed our arms and turned toward our respective windows. Harry turned the music on low to cut through our silence. When we were nearly at my house, I finally decided to speak.

"I'm sorry about our fight," I said.

She whipped around in her seat, arms still folded, eyes blazing with anger. "You're sorry about the fight?"

I nodded, which made her chuckle bitterly. She turned back around, ignoring me.

"Will you please talk to me?" I said.

"No," Beck said. "I am not talking to you until all of this murder bullshit is figured out. You *burned* evidence, Quinn. Not only that, you thought I left you some stupid note? I would tell you to your face if I think you're being stupid, and you are."

Harry met my eye in the rearview mirror.

"You burned evidence?"

"Stay out of it!" Beck and I both said.

"I haven't looked into anything since then," I said. "Besides, it was Rink's idea to burn her things."

"Like that makes it any better," Beck said. "He was arrested. I don't want to believe he killed Marki, Sarai, and Christine, but his keychain was found where Christine's body was! He never took that thing off his bag."

I didn't have the energy or the words to argue with her further. I sulked until we pulled into my driveway. Neither of them said goodbye to me, so I silently slipped from the car. Harry was still gracious enough to wait for me to get in the door, but part of me wondered if his perception of me had been spoiled by Beck airing out the fact that I burned evidence with Rink Matthews.

A mug of apple cider waited for me on the kitchen table. I took a sip, but it didn't taste as sweet as it normally did. I poured the rest down the sink and stared as the liquid swirled down the drain.

"Look what I got," Mom said, bursting into the kitchen.

I turned to see a big, clear bag full of green items, including fake ivy.

"My Halloween costume?" I asked.

"Well, pieces of it," Mom said. "I was thinking we could spend tonight making some of it. Maybe put on a Halloween movie, eat junk food. Want to?"

I walked over to my mom and hugged her. She squeezed me back as tight as she could; sometimes she knew exactly what I needed. I breathed in and out, inhaling the laundry detergent scent of her cardigan to calm me down.

"I would love that," I said, my hands wrapped behind her back.

Her hugs were healing. I could tell by the way she rubbed my back that she knew something was wrong, but she didn't press me to tell her. Some things were better kept to myself. Especially when it dealt with the murder cases.

I called Gilly to talk to her about my shitty day before my plans with Mom, but Jon answered and told me she went out for coffee with Alma and Jen. Radio silence was all I got that afternoon from all of my friends. Even Owen went to spend the night at a friend's house, leaving only Mom and me.

Mom ordered takeout from my favorite Chinese restaurant. As per usual, we got two orders of crab rangoons so we could each have our own. She set up a bowl of candy corn, as well as more mugs of apple cider.

"Owen's really missing out," Mom said.

"I'm glad he's not here," I said. "He'd eat all of our crab rangoons."

Mom laughed before taking a crunchy bite. Having a peaceful meal without the inhaler there threatening to eat everything gave me time to eat more slowly. I savored the food, its warmth making my eyes grow heavy with sleep.

"Don't fall asleep on me now," Mom said. "We have work to do."

We watched *Goosebumps* episodes instead of a movie while we ate our food. Every year, we binged-watched the series to get our spooky fix. Only one episode ever scared me: "Cry of the Cat." The first time I'd seen the lady slowly turn into a cat, I screamed and locked myself in my bedroom until Mom finally coaxed me out with a chocolate bar. I had nightmares thinking I would turn into a demonic cat. Now, it was one of my favorite episodes.

When we finished our main meal, Mom handed me a fortune cookie. On the count of three, we broke them open.

Mom laughed out loud. "Mine says: 'It's about time I got out of that cookie.'"

I chuckled, even though I wasn't feeling inclined to find my fortune amusing.

"What does your fortune say?" Mom asked.

"'You think it's a secret, but they know,'" I said.

"How spooky." Mom playfully wiggled her fingers at me. "Perfect timing getting that one for Halloween."

I laughed it off but couldn't help thinking about the note I'd found in the barrel. I tried to tell myself it was only a coincidence that I'd pulled that fortune, but the murders had proven nothing was a coincidence. This fortune was a warning from the universe.

Someone knew fully about what Christine discovered. They also clearly knew that I knew more than I let on.

I jumped when Mom tore open one of those skillet popcorn makers. I hadn't even noticed she got up from the couch.

"I figured we could watch *Scream* while we work on your costume," Mom said. "And eat like Casey Becker."

"Sounds like a plan," I said, although I wasn't in the mood to watch a bunch of murder.

Mom slid the skillet back and forth on the burner as the kernels began to pop. I crumbled up my fortune and shoved the tiny ball of paper into the takeout bag.

It took Mom and I a while to actually start on my costume. We were too interested in the movie. Every time the knife popped up, I squirmed. All the girls in town had been killed with a knife. Were their final moments similar to the victims in *Scream*?

When we finally decided to stop procrastinating, I plugged in the hot glue gun and waited for it to heat up. Mom had bought green jeans as well as a green long-sleeved top. The goal was to glue on as much fake ivy as we could. I sat with my back facing the TV. I couldn't take any more gore.

"I also thought I could do some hot glue designs and put green glitter over it," Mom said, pulling a pouch of glitter from her bag.

"Whatever your heart desires, Mom."

This costume was different from what I normally dressed up as. Last year, I wore a yellow raincoat and carried around a paper sailboat. I went out with Beck and dealt with stupid boys saying "Hi, Georgie," everywhere we went.

As expected, the glitter got everywhere. Mom tried to blow it onto the ground, and we laughed as it rained down on us.

"At least you'll have a cute costume," Mom said. "What are your plans?"

"Gilly's going to be Harley Quinn," I said. "Other than that, I don't know what we are going to do."

"So, a duo costume?" Mom asked with a small smirk.

"We figured we both have their hair colors, so it would work," I said, my face growing warm.

Mom smiled and continued to make swirly designs with the hot glue gun.

"Gilly and I are dating," I blurted.

My ears grew hot, and I wanted to run upstairs. Mom didn't stop her gluing process to even look at me.

"I know," Mom said. "I've been waiting for you to tell me."

"What?" I balked. "How do you know?"

"Please, Quinnie, you hang out with her more than Beck," Mom said.

Hearing Beck's name stung my heart, but a feeling of relief also washed over me. It was exhausting hiding the nature of mine and Gilly's relationship from my mom. After all Gilly and I had been through recently, I was scared there would be a lack of approval. But Mom didn't mention anything about the attack in the park, or Jon Willis constantly questioning me. She just kept glittering my costume until she was satisfied with the sparkles.

"I better clean some of this glitter up before we glue on those leaves," Mom said.

She got up and headed to the kitchen pantry to grab our broom. The rest of the night consisted of us gluing leaves to the items of clothing, then leaving them on the table to dry. We listened to a Halloween playlist and allowed ourselves a few dance breaks in between.

It was a little after midnight when Mom kissed me on the head and went up to her bedroom to sleep. We'd gotten most of my costume done. Mom wanted to fix a few sparse areas before I actually wore it, but beyond that, it was perfect. I flipped through some channels, not quite tired yet and far too lazy to head upstairs myself. After about an hour, I drifted off but was woken up by a light, frantic knocking at the front door. I abruptly sat up, thinking I had imagined it until I heard it again. I checked the clock: 2:04 a.m.

I stood up, wrapping the couch blanket around my shoulders. The only person that could possibly be at the door at this hour was Owen. The knock came again.

"Coming," I said groggily.

I yawned as I opened the door. Harry stood on my doorstep, tears pooling in his eyes. He looked wilted in his gray sweatshirt.

"Harry? What's wrong?" I said.

"It's Beck," he said. "The police found her in the woods."

# CHAPTER TWENTY-NINE

A ringing rose into my ears as I blinked the sleep from my eyes. There was no way I'd heard him correctly. No . . . I must have heard him wrong.

"What?" I said, my eyebrows furrowing together.

"The police found Beck in the woods," Harry said. "She was taken to the hospital."

He choked on the last part of the sentence, words nearly failing him. He squeezed his eyes shut as tears made tracks down his olive-toned cheeks. I collapsed in the doorway, sinking to the hardwood floor with the blanket still wrapped around me. I kept shaking my head, not believing any of it.

"Is she dead?" I asked, the words coming out thickly.

"No," Harry said. "But she's in really bad shape."

I could breathe easier, but knowing Beck had been attacked made me feel sick. How had this happened? Guilt sucker punched me. For over a week, Beck and I fought, wasting our time together stupidly. Now Beck was in the hospital, nearly dead. What if I never got to speak to her again? I choked out a sob, but contained myself. I couldn't be a prisoner to my emotions just yet.

"Okay," I croaked, collecting my thoughts. "We have to go to her. I'm assuming she's in the emergency room. I know exactly where it is. We can go, and when she wakes up, we will figure out what happened."

I tossed my blanket to the side and shoved my feet into my shoes, not bothering to lace them.

"Quinn," Harry said. "Quinn, there's no way they will let us see her tonight."

"We have to try!" I cried. "She's my best friend. We're practically sisters. I'll riot if I have to."

"Quinn, what on earth is going on?" Mom asked, coming down the stairs with her own blanket wrapped around her shoulders.

She saw Harry and his tear-streaked face, then me, ready to go with my shoes already on.

"Beck's in the hospital," I rasped. "We have to go to her."

"Slow down," Mom said. "What happened?"

"The police found her in the woods," Harry said, like a recording on repeat. "She's in the hospital in really bad shape."

"Okay," Mom said. "Go get in the car."

Mom grabbed the car keys while Harry and I bolted for the car. Harry rode with us, biting his nails at every red light we hit. Mom kept calm as she drove, but I knew worry leaked off me and filled the entire car like smog. We all felt the nerves as we pulled into the hospital. Harry was a wreck in the back seat. His hair stood in different directions from where he'd run his hands through it.

I flew into the hospital, Mom and Harry right behind me. I expected the emergency room to be bustling with people, but it wasn't. Nobody was in the lobby. Mom spoke with the lady at the front desk, who took far too long to tell us where Beck was.

"Can you please hurry?" I yelled far louder than I meant to.

The lady's eyes grew wide as she filed through a drawer of documents. Mom tapped her fingers against the desk, impatient.

While we waited, Jon Willis walked out from another door.

"Quinn?" he said.

"Let me see Beck," I said immediately. "Please."

"They can come back with me," Jon said to the lady at the desk.

"Thank you, Jon," Mom said, squeezing his arm.

I plowed in front of him to reach Beck quicker. "Where is she?" I asked, searching the closed doors and curtains.

"Quinn?"

I recognized that voice. Beck's mom, Cami, pulled back a curtain to my right. Her eyes were red and puffy. She buckled into Mom's arms when she opened them for a hug. Mom stroked Cami's hair while she cried in her arms. Beck's Dad, Eric, came and placed a hand on his ex-wife's shoulder. She didn't move away from the touch. Eric and Jon made eye contact, but only briefly.

". . . lost a lot of blood," Cami muttered into my mom's shoulder.

"Where is she?" I asked Jon.

"She's in surgery right now," Jon said. "It shouldn't be too long."

"Where?" I said. I needed to see Beck.

"Quinn," Jon sighed. "You won't be able to go in there while she's being worked on."

*Worked on.* As if she was an object that needed to be fixed.

"When will we be able to see her?" Harry asked.

"I'm not sure," Jon said. "That will be the doctor's call once she regains consciousness."

"Regains consciousness?" I said, nearly sick.

Jon breathed out deeply before placing a hand on my shoulder. My bones recoiled beneath his touch.

"She was found unconscious," he said. "But that's not always a bad thing. She probably won't even remember the attack."

But the thing was, I needed her to remember. If she did, then maybe this could all *finally* come to an end.

"Go find a seat and get some rest," Jon said, patting my shoulder.

My legs couldn't hold me up anymore. Harry took a seat next to me. We both stared at the floor, neither of us speaking. I closed my eyes and tried sending Beck a telepathic message. We used to claim we had "best friend telepathy," but I needed it to truly work this time.

*Beck, wake up. I need you.*

Mom tended to Cami while Eric spoke with the police. I tried not to listen. There was no part of me that needed to imagine what had happened to Beck.

"I shouldn't have let her go to that party," Harry said.

I turned to him. He'd started crying again. I reached out and held his hand; it was warm, something whole to ground me there in the blinding light of the emergency room.

"You don't even know if she actually went to the party," I said softly.

"Do you think she went into the woods?" Harry asked. "Alone?"

I shook my head. "She's smarter than that. Something happened. I don't know what, but I do know Beck. She wouldn't go into those woods without us."

". . . alcohol levels are high," a doctor said to Cami who burst into tears again.

I looked at Harry. It was all the confirmation we needed to know that Beck had in fact gone to the party. But it still didn't make any sense. Beck preferred smoking to drinking. Even if she'd been in a mood and gone alone, the most she would've had was two drinks.

Jon Willis walked back over to us.

"I won't ask the two of you tonight," he said, "unless you're up for it, but I will need to question you soon, since you are close to Miss Wood."

Neither of us were up for questioning. When Cami calmed down enough, Mom asked if we could leave. My stomach twisted at the thought of leaving and waking up to bad news about Beck.

"I want to stay," I said.

"I'll stay too," Harry said.

"I need to get home so I can get some sleep before I pick up Owen," Mom said. "I'll come back to get you two mid-morning."

Harry and I pushed a couple chairs together so we could sit with our feet up. I was half-asleep the rest of the night, occasionally jumping awake when I realized where I was. Sleeping in hospital chairs was the most uncomfortable thing I ever experienced. Harry snored, drooling slightly onto his shoulder. I could almost hear Beck making fun of the sight of him, and it made me smile. The cops waded in and out of the hospital. Cami didn't sleep at all. She drank five cups of coffee until Eric cut her off. She wouldn't stop shaking. I left a sleeping Harry and sat with Cami.

"Quinnie," she said, pulling me into a hug.

Her hands shook against my back.

"Did the doctors say anything while I was asleep?" I asked.

"They finished stitching her up," Cami said, trying not to cry. "She's . . . alive, but still unconscious."

"I want her to be okay," I whispered.

"I know, honey," Cami said. "I do too."

I sat with Cami for a while until Harry woke up, disoriented. He went to hunt down coffee for the two of us. A doctor came out, and Cami and Eric immediately stood, asking about Beck. I held my breath while they spoke.

"She's completely unresponsive," the doctor said.

The words hummed in my mind, and I only caught the last word of the next sentence: ". . . comatose."

Cami's shriek ripped through the emergency room. Eric caught her before she could fall on the floor. Harry approached us, two coffees in his hand. I couldn't get the words out to tell him that Beck was in a coma.

When I woke up Monday morning, life didn't feel real anymore. I'd spent the weekend at the emergency room with Harry, waiting to see if Beck would wake up. She didn't. Mom made me go to school in order to distract myself with my routine. I stared at Beck's spot in algebra. I waited for Beck to walk through the door, late as always, but she never did. I walked alone in the hallway. Sometimes Harry walked next to me, but neither of us said anything. We had spent the weekend together in that desolate place; nerves jittered in my stomach as I remembered each and every beep of the machine Beck had been hooked into. She'd been breathing, but it'd felt as if she could die any second. I hadn't been able to sleep out of fear my mom would wake up and tell me Beck hadn't survived. Three sleeping pills had done the trick for me to actually get a semblance of rest.

Harry decided to skip lunch, leaving only Gilly and me. I hadn't spoken to her the entire weekend, and I felt guilty for not keeping her in the know.

"Hi," Gilly said, picking her grapes off their stems.

"Hi," I said, taking a seat across from her. "I'm sorry I didn't call you this weekend."

"Dad told me about Beck," Gilly said, reaching for my hand. "Quinn, I'm so sorry."

"Did he tell you she's in a coma?" I said.

Gilly nodded. "I was going to call you this weekend, but he told me you were probably going to be at the hospital every day."

"I was."

Despite myself, a sort of bitterness rose into my throat. It wasn't Gilly's fault; she wanted to be there for me. But I shimmied my hand out from under hers all the same and opened up my lunch. If anything, I'd eat the applesauce in the bag, but not much else. Gilly noticed my demeanor and quickly ate her grapes, probably trying to keep her mouth busy. There wasn't any room for conversation between us. I didn't want her to feel that she had crossed a line because she hadn't. I simply knew that if we talked about Beck, I wouldn't be able to hold it together.

"Why don't we have a movie weekend?" Gilly suggested. "We can rent a movie from Karson's and eat a ton of butter pecan ice cream."

"Sure," I said, knowing I sounded distant. "Yes, I would love that. I need a distraction from everything."

Gilly seemed to lighten up. "Great! We can go pick out the movie together."

Part of my bitterness melted. Spending a night with Gilly sounded like just what I needed.

After school, I met Harry by his car. We'd made a pact to go to the hospital every day until Beck woke up. We didn't care how long it took, but we wanted to see how she was with our own two eyes. The nurses knew who we were and, by Cami's orders, let us go back to see Beck. Cami was there, reading a book while Beck laid in her hospital bed. The machines were loud, the beeps sounding like a countdown of how much time Beck had left.

"Harry, Quinn," Cami said, greeting us both with hugs.

"Any updates?" Harry asked hopefully.

"I'm afraid not," Cami said. "Do you mind if I run to grab a coffee? Do you want anything?"

"I'm okay," I said.

"Same here," Harry said.

I stood next to Beck's bed, too afraid to sit anywhere and get comfortable. Her hair was pulled back in a bun, and I reached down to loosen it. I didn't want her to wake up with a headache from her hair being pulled back too tightly. Harry grabbed her hand and ran his thumb along her fingernails. Her blue-chipped polish was still on.

"Should I bring some nail polish remover next time?" I asked Harry.

"It's a very Beck thing to have chipped nail polish, so no. I think we should leave it as is," Harry said.

She was still Beck. I had to keep telling myself that as I stared at her closed eyes. She could have easily been the next murder victim. People would've turned her into another "dead girl." Now, she was the girl in the coma. Her hospital gown covered where she had been stabbed, just below her left breast. I gripped my side, as if I could feel the phantom pain of where the knife had pierced her.

## CHAPTER THIRTY

I invited Gilly over to my house for our movie night. She'd been perfectly fine with coming over, but I hadn't told her the reason for it: that her dad reminded me of Harry and I's interrogation the second day we were at the hospital. He'd kept the questions short, and none of them had sounded accusatory. He'd probably tried to keep it easy since the both of us were hurting. Maybe. A part of me hoped he had a good heart.

Mom had gotten Gilly and I a carton of butter pecan ice cream. She left a sticky note threatening to ground Owen for life if he took any without asking me first, then drove Gilly and I to Karson's. She waited for us in the car while we went inside. The bell above the door to the rental shop rang. The clerk waved but continued shelving movies.

"Any ideas?" Gilly asked, picking random movies off the shelves to inspect.

"Maybe a scary movie," I said. "A classic slasher?"

"Are you sure?" Gilly asked.

"How about *Halloween*?" I suggested.

Gilly nodded in agreement, but I noticed a hesitance on her face as I picked the movie from the shelf.

"I think I'll also go pick one out in case we want to watch two," Gilly said, wandering away.

I went up to the register and set the movie down. The clerk came from the aisle, a stack of movies in his hand.

"Is this all?" he asked.

"One more," I said, pointing toward the back where Gilly was.

"You're Quinn, right?" he asked.

I nodded. "Yeah, why?"

"I heard about your friend, Beck," he said. "I'm really sorry. I know it's probably tough."

"She's in a coma," I said, as if the whole town didn't know.

"I—I know," he stuttered. "It still sucks."

He typed into the cash register, not meeting my eye anymore. My heart sank and I wondered how many more times I'd have to repeat that Beck was in a coma. Gilly approached and set a movie on the counter.

"*Halloween*," the cashier said, "and *The Princess Bride*. Great choices."

I rolled my eyes at Gilly's choice. Before I could hand the cashier my money, Gilly shoved her own cash into his hand. He gave her change, and we left.

"I could've gotten the movies," I said.

"Don't worry about it," Gilly said. "My treat."

She kissed me on the cheek before we got back in the car. Was this the treatment I would receive for the remainder of Beck's coma? I didn't want to be coddled or looked-out for. It made everything feel abnormal and reminded me of pity.

Mom ordered us a pepperoni and pineapple pizza when we got home. It felt as if everything was coming full circle from the night we ate the same pizza in Gilly's bedroom; the night I tried to see if Jon Willis would act suspicious around me. It made me think of Beck. Any appetite I had vanished.

"Want to start with *Halloween*?" Gilly asked.

"Sure," I said.

I put the movie in while Gilly grabbed the box of pizza for us. I ate slowly while the movie began. My grumbling stomach was the only thing that kept me eating. I didn't want to pass out. The pizza was delicious, but I felt guilty for enjoying it when Beck couldn't.

Gilly sat close to me during the movie. We brushed elbows as we took bites of our pizza slices. The theme song for Michael Myers always made the hair on my arms stand up. It was so eerie, but I couldn't help but love it.

"This music has always terrified me," Gilly said, eating her pizza slices more quickly.

"That's why it's brilliant," I said.

We kept only the light above the kitchen sink on so the living room was dark. I had seen *Halloween* countless times, but it felt like I was watching it for the first time again.

"Want me to grab us some ice cream?" Gilly offered.

"Not yet," I said in a trance.

I watched Michael spy on Laurie, quietly stalking his prey. My heart sped up. Gilly braced herself for his first kill, and when it happened, cold rushed all over my body. My hands shook. It became hard for me to breathe. A weight crushed my lungs. My breath quickened. The room felt hot and cold all at once as I stared at the body of the first victim.

"Quinn," Gilly said, grabbing my shaking hands. "Quinn!"

I stood up, shaking my hands to get the feeling of pins and needles to stop. Was I having a heart attack? I gripped my chest, trying to breathe.

"I need my mom," I said.

Gilly ran up the stairs as fast as she could to retrieve my mom. They both ran back down the stairs, but as they approached me, my panic worsened. They were crowding me. The walls were crowding me. I pushed my Mom's arms away and ran out of the house and down the street until was alone—alone enough to breathe. The cold air was cleansing. It freed me from the heat and constraint within the house. I folded over, placing my hands on my knees. My relief slowly melted into fear took as I realized where I was. Alone. In the dark. The killer could be in the shadows the way Michael had been as he'd stalked Laurie's house. A new wave of panic overtook me—until Mom and Gilly ran up to me. My mom hugged me while I cried. Gilly kept her hand on my arm. I was safe. I was with two people I loved, and they would keep me safe, but could I keep them safe when I had failed Beck?

Three days passed since I'd last seen Gilly. She'd ended up staying the night after my panic attack, holding me the way I always held her. I didn't understand how strong she could be after the deaths of her two best friends. Beck wasn't even dead, but I was still losing it. We didn't talk about what had happened in the morning before she left. I hadn't called her since.

Harry and I were at the hospital with Beck after school on Tuesday. Cami had taken Beck's hair down and brushed it after I expressed my concerns about the bun. Her hair lay down by her shoulders. I moved some stray pieces from her neck in case they tickled her. It was only Harry and me today; Cami had finally decided to go back to work a couple days a week. I sat down, picking my cuticles.

"I've been doing a lot of thinking," I said.

"About what?" Harry took a seat next to me.

"We have to figure this out," I said. "I don't think there's any other way around it."

"Quinn—"

“I know what you’re going to say,” I said. “But I want to. We need to find out everything the police don’t know. They are asking the wrong questions to the wrong people. Nothing is ever going to be solved unless we dig for the answers ourselves.”

“Does this have anything to do with what you burned of Christine’s?” Harry asked.

“It has everything to do with that,” I said.

Harry grew quiet and stared at Beck. He tapped his foot, and I crossed my fingers, hoping he would agree to help me. Even if he wasn’t on board, I would do it myself. I needed to find answers, for Beck’s sake.

“I’m in,” Harry said. “But you can’t keep anything from me.”

I held up my pinkie finger. “Deal.”

We both watched Beck’s chest move slowly up and down. Whatever came of Harry and me working together, it would all be for Beck. I mentally took an oath to find whoever tried to kill her, even if it meant putting myself back in danger. *Keep digging and end up like Christine.* Then so be it.

## CHAPTER THIRTY-ONE

Gilly invited me to a sleepover with her and the twins. Alma and Jen's house looked like it belonged in a catalog for southern living. The yard was clean cut with a cardinal flag waving around in the breeze. The only un-perfect thing in the yard was the sun-bleached, small American flag stuck in the ground, which I inferred was left over from Fourth of July. Why had I agreed to this?

The inside was more lived-in than the outside. Potholders with wacky patterns were strewn about, some with strawberries, others with chickens. How had Christine been able to stand being here when she dated Jen?

"Hey guys!" Jen squealed when she saw us. "Mom is making chicken and dumplings for dinner."

I wondered if I should fake food poisoning.

"Anne makes the best chicken and dumplings," Gilly said to me.

In the kitchen, their mother was stirring a large pot. She had on a frilly red apron, which matched her red glasses.

"You must be Quinn!" she said. "I'm Anne. It's so lovely to meet you."

Her southern drawl was heavy. My name sounded more like "queen" falling off her lips.

"Nice to meet you," I said.

"Bowls are already on the table," she said. "You girls take a seat wherever you like."

I sat next to Gilly. The bowls were primary colors, and I got a yellow one.

"Jen," Anne said. "Get everyone something to drink, would you?"

"Is peach tea alright?" Jen asked.

Gilly and I nodded, but Alma went to the fridge and popped open a Coke.

"Alma, be careful drinking all those sodas," Anne said, pinching Alma's stomach.

Alma rolled her eyes and put the Coke back in the fridge, grabbing a bottle of water. There it was. The crack in their relationship. Alma touched her stomach when she sat down, shooting daggers at her mother with her eyes.

Anne scooped each of us a heaping spoonful of chicken and dumplings. They smelled amazing. The dumplings were thick, the chicken finely shredded. I took a bite and worried my eyes would roll back into my head.

"These are delicious," I said.

"Well, thank you, Quinn," Anne said, getting her own bowl.

She joined us at the table in between Alma and Jen. Alma scooted away from her, but Jen barely took notice of her mother's presence. Anne asked Gilly about her father and school. Small talk—a southern specialty.

"How is school for you, Quinn?" Anne asked.

"Great," I said.

"Mom, nobody wants to talk about school," Alma said, picking at the dumplings.

Anne pursed her lips but didn't banter with Alma. The rest of the meal was statically silent. As soon as Jen took her last bite of dumpling, we rushed upstairs to hang out in their bonus room. It was filled with scrapbooks and novels; there was a desk covered in paper, pencils, and scissors.

"Welcome to our escape," Alma said.

I walked around and looked at everything. Their mom must have kept books up here as well because there was a whole shelf dedicated to ones with shirtless men on the front. Alma started venting about some guy she had been seeing. I didn't know him. Jen pretended to listen while she flipped through the TV to find something to put on. Gilly offered some input, but it was mainly Alma complaining how he hadn't called her in two days. When I got to the desk, I could barely see anything through the mess. While nobody paid me any mind, I pushed a few things around until I saw a magazine. I opened it and found that some of the pages had been cut around, more specifically, letters. Bingo. Clue number one.

"Whose craft station?" I asked.

"Alma's," Jen said, distracted by the TV still. "She spends all her time up here so she doesn't have to deal with Mom."

"I either craft or I kill Mom, take your pick," Alma said.

The comment threw me, but only slightly. While Alma continued to talk, I looked through the magazine to see if I could pin together any words she might have made, but there were too many missing. When Alma's phone rang, I jumped.

"It's Christopher!" Alma said. "Hello?"

Her voice rose to a higher pitch as she talked to him. The conversation consisted of Alma saying "yeah" and "sure" breathlessly. I rolled my eyes.

"He asked me to dinner tomorrow!" Alma said. "Gilly, you have to help me pick out an outfit."

She grabbed Gilly's wrist and dragged her out of the room, leaving Jen and me. I took a seat on the couch while Jen finally decided on a TV channel where music videos played constantly.

"How is it going?" I said.

I cringed at myself. I was horrible at small talk.

"A lot better," Jen said. "I'm assuming you mean with Christine?"

"Yeah," I said. "Sorry to bring it up."

"It's okay," Jen said. "And how are you? I know Beck is still in the hospital."

"I'm managing," I said.

Jen turned to me. She'd never looked more serious.

"What do you think happens now?" she asked. "If Rink was the one committing the murders, then who attacked Beck? Does this mean Rink is innocent now?"

I hadn't even given it any thought. My focus had been on Beck; I'd all but forgotten Rink was still locked up. Jen was right. Whoever had attacked Beck had killed Marki, Sarai, *and* Christine. It was a feeling I couldn't shake.

"I honestly haven't thought about that," I admitted.

"I've been thinking about it a lot," Jen said. "Especially since Christine died. You know, she used to write in this pocket notebook every time she was over. It was constant. She never let me see what it was, though. Said she was writing poems I couldn't see until she was finished or something."

I paused. "A notebook?" I asked, lifting my tone to show my curiosity.

"Yeah," Jen said. "About the size of my palm. I have no idea how she even wrote in it; the thing was so tiny. And trust me, her handwriting was sloppy."

I hadn't seen any small notebooks with Christine. I wanted to believe it was probably nothing, but Christine had gotten so wrapped up in the murders, I knew it had to be a copy of the larger notebook she kept at her desk. How else would she remember everything that was in the bigger notebook? But most importantly, where was the notebook now?

"Did they take it in as evidence?" I asked.

"I went by her house to ask her mom about it," Jen said. "But she said she wasn't found with a notebook."

I didn't say anything else. Somehow, I knew I needed to get back to Christine's house. Between Alma's crafts and Jen dropping the bomb about the small notebook, I should have been spending more time here with them. They seemed to know a lot—maybe *too* much. Alma and Gilly returned, giggling about the boy who'd called Alma. She couldn't stop talking about their next date. I pretended to be interested, but I needed to talk to Harry.

Our night consisted of face masks, gossip, and silly games from the hoard of magazines Alma had. As much as I loved being with Gilly, this wasn't my scene. It made me miss Beck tenfold. I excused myself at one point to sit in the bathroom, trying not to cry. None of them came to check on me, but I didn't care. When I returned to their bonus room, they had moved on to their next activity without me. Gilly snuck smiles at me and brushed her arm against mine, but it still felt like I was imposing on her friend group. I was the first to crawl into my sleeping bag, but the last to fall asleep.

The next day, Mom picked me up early from Alma and Jen's. I quickly said goodbye before walking out to the car. Gilly decided to spend the day with them, which gave me the space I needed.

I immediately called Harry when I got home. Without giving him any time to say "hello," I dove into what I learned at Alma and Jen's.

"We need to find that notebook," I said. "There's no telling what all she has in it. It could lead us straight to the killer! This could be the key we need."

"Where would it even be?" Harry asked. "She wasn't found with it."

"It could be hidden in her room," I said. "Or someone stole it."

We were silent as we mulled over the worst-case scenario.

"It doesn't sound promising, Quinn," Harry said. "How do we get into her bedroom? And if someone stole it, how do we find it? For all we know the killer could have it."

I rolled my eyes even though he couldn't see me.

"We can easily get to her bedroom. We go talk to her mom and say we were friends of Christine's, and we want to see her bedroom one last time. If the notebook isn't there and someone took it, then we're screwed."

"When do you want to go?" Harry asked.

"Tomorrow," I said. "After school. I'll meet you at your car."

# CHAPTER THIRTY-TWO

Christine's house was a dull yellow with one car parked in the driveway. A cross sat in the front yard circled by lilies and forget-me-nots—the family's memorial for their daughter. Harry parked on the side of the house and awkwardly followed me to the front door. I knocked instead of ringing the doorbell. Christine's mom answered, roots growing out gray in her hair, eyes with purple rings around them as if she hadn't slept in weeks.

"Hi," I said when she frowned at us. "My name is Quinn, and this is Harry. We were friends with Christine."

She forced a smile. "She mentioned Quinn at one point, but I'm not sure I've heard the name Harry."

"We were more acquainted," he said. "Quinn was closer with her."

"Why don't the two of you come in?" she said, stepping aside.

She spoke like she was far away, and I felt a twinge of guilt for manipulating her, but to avenge her daughter, it had to be done. My heart beat fast as we crossed the threshold into the house. As torn up as her mother seemed, the house was still livable with no mess. Not even old cups littered the tables. I took a seat on the couch, and Harry did the same.

"Do the two of you want anything to drink?" Christine's mom offered.

"No thanks," Harry and I said.

We looked at one another, then turned our attention back to Christine's mom.

"What brings you here today?" her mom asked.

"I've been very sad about her this week," I said. "I thought coming here and seeing you might help me with some closure. I feel like I never got any."

Tears welled in her mom's eyes, and my stomach turned at the fact that I was faking my sadness when clearly her mom was still smothered by her own grief. Harry shifted uncomfortably next to me.

"Some days are harder than others," her mom said. "I don't think I'll find closure until they figure out who actually killed her."

She grabbed a tissue to wipe her nose and eyes.

"Rink was arrested," I said. "That's a lead."

"Call me conspiratorial, but that boy didn't kill my baby," she said. "It might be mother's intuition, but I believe he was framed. I've known that boy for a while now, and he wouldn't dare hurt her."

I couldn't believe I was having this conversation with Christine's mom. She stood up to retrieve something from a shelved book. She opened it up about halfway and pulled out a note.

"I tried showing this to the police, but they didn't believe it," Christine's mom said. "They said anybody could have forged a note."

She handed me the note, and my blood ran cold. *It wasn't Rink Matthews*. I knew that handwriting. I'd stared at the note with this very address on it enough times to know it was Christine's handiwork. Her "sloppy" handwriting, as Jen called it.

"The police didn't accept this?" I said. "How? That is clearly her handwriting. What about fingerprints?"

Christine's mom shrugged. "I begged Jon Willis to run it as evidence, but he wouldn't."

I nearly got sick right there in her living room. Everything seemed to come right back to Jon Willis.

I handed her the note and let out a breath. "Wow."

"I hate to put this on you," her mom said. "But I feel like I'm going crazy. Nobody will listen to me."

I regretted burning all of Christine's evidence with Rink. I needed to find that small notebook and give it back to Christine's mom.

"We're listening," Harry piped up. "And we believe you."

Those words alone seemed to release a pound off her shoulders as she exhaled.

"Before we go," I said. "Could we possibly see her bedroom again? It might help with how I'm feeling."

"Of course," her mom said. "If you see anything you'd like to keep, take it. I don't have the heart to go through it all."

The stairs seemed bigger as Harry and I climbed them. The door to Christine's room was closed. Opening it felt like opening a tomb. Her mom had barely touched a thing. The only thing neat was her desk, which had been cleared of all the evidence she had compiled.

"Is there anything specific we should look for?" Harry asked.

"Anything that can be a clue," I said.

We quietly searched through her things so her mom wouldn't get suspicious. I checked around her desk for any loose pieces of evidence that may have been left behind. Harry found an old yearbook along with some dried-up mascara tubes—none of which provided clues. It wasn't until I stepped on a weak spot in the floor, noting how it creaked, that we found anything worthwhile.

I moved my foot back and forth. I knelt down on my knees and found the spot. The wood was loose.

"Harry, help me," I said.

We carefully pulled the loose plank from the floor. Harry shone a light down into the hole. There wasn't a pocket-sized notebook, but there was a rolled-up piece of paper tied with a rubber band. I pulled it out and unraveled it.

"Holy shit," I said.

"What is it?" Harry asked.

"It's a map of everyone's house that leads into the woods," I said. "Marki, Sarai, the twins, and Gilly's. They all have direct access to the woods."

"Which means . . . ?"

"I think Christine and Beck were red herrings to throw any suspicions off the original plan to kill Gilly and her friends."

"Why does Christine have this map?" Harry asked.

I bit my lip. "I don't know."

I kept the map in my desk drawer and occasionally pulled it out to stare at it. Alma and Jen's house was the farthest in the woods from the others, but still close enough in proximity that if they walked through the woods, they could get to each other's houses quicker. Gilly's led to a random back road, and obviously, Marki and Sarai's led to the school.

My thoughts turned to Jon Willis yet again. How convenient was it that Jon lived by the woods? Why had he brushed off Christine's mom's evidence and arrested Rink anyway? The missing pocket notebook. How easy would it be as a cop to steal evidence from a crime scene? I didn't have solid proof, but my suspicions of him grew. There was no way Jon Willis *didn't* have something to do with the murders. I had only one more place to search for evidence, and I hoped it would lead me where I needed to go.

Goose and PJ, the two boys Rink and Beck always smoked with, were under the bleachers as normal after school. I had finally learned their names after asking around for half the school day. If anyone knew anything random, it would be the two of them. They were everywhere—well, except class. Harry waited for me in the parking lot while I went to ask them about the party Beck had attended. The two were smoking and jumped when they saw me.

"You're Beck's friend," PJ said, grabbing his chest.

"Quinn," I introduced myself for the millionth time to them.

"What brings you to the fortress?" Goose asked.

"I need the two of you to be serious for like five minutes," I said. "I need you to tell me everything about the party Beck went to the night she was attacked."

They finished off their joint before throwing it on the ground. Like two heads sharing the same brain, they looked at each other, faces settling on sadness. At least they were compassionate idiots.

"Are you cracking the case now?" Goose asked.

"Considering nothing is being done to figure out who tried to kill Beck, yes. I am," I said. "Now will you please help me?"

"What do you need to know?" PJ asked.

I sat down on one of the buckets they had placed in a circle. "Tell me every detail from that night that you can remember."

"Well, I picked up Beck around eight and brought her to Goose's house," PJ said. "She seemed pissy, so we let her smoke with us for free. She kept to herself most of the night, but we kept an eye on her, especially when she started drinking."

"Beck rarely drinks," I said.

PJ shrugged. "She downed about four cans of beer within the first hour of being there."

I wished I had been there for her; it felt like my fault.

"Continue," I said.

"It was like any other house party," Goose said. "Except way more laid-back since it was all of our friends. We played beer pong, smoked, sat around, smoked some more. Then the party got busted a little after midnight."

"Busted by who?" I asked.

"Jon Willis and his two minions that are always following him around," Goose said. "He let everyone go without handing out tickets, though."

"So when did you take Beck home?" I asked PJ.

"Oh, I didn't," he said. "About halfway through the party, she went out to get some air. When we asked her to come back in, she started bitching at us. She's probably the reason the cops were called."

"Then what happened to Beck?" I asked.

"She got a ride home from Jon Willis," PJ said. "He wouldn't let us drive her since we were 'under the influence.'"

My heart stopped. That meant the last person to have seen Beck that night was Jon Willis—the same one who brought her into the hospital.

"Thanks," I said. "I have to go."

I ran back to Harry's car, trying my best not to cry, but I was freaking out. Jon had been there at the hospital with Beck's parents when Harry and I arrived. Jon had politely questioned us so he wouldn't upset us any further about Beck. Jon was my girlfriend's dad. Jon was the town's fucking sheriff.

But Jon was also the one who had put his hand on my back. Jon had been the one to flirt with Sarai at the football game. Jon was inappropriate with his daughter's friends, and now I truly believed Jon was also a murderer.

# CHAPTER THIRTY-THREE

October 30th.

The day before Halloween. It was supposed to be the day before we all went trick-or-treating one last time, knowing the neighbors would start rejecting us the following years. My costume was ready. Gilly's was too. Today would be Halloween-eve, celebrated much like Christmas-eve here at my house, but Harry and I hadn't slept at all, and Beck was still in the hospital. We'd been up all night with my pile of evidence trying to figure out a way to concretely go to the police with it. All signs pointed to Jon Willis being guilty.

"They're still holding Rink in jail," Harry said. "He would be our ticket for this."

"I don't see how he could help us," I said. "There's no evidence that truly supports Rink. Even Christine's handwritten letter is a bust."

Harry tapped his finger against his cheek while he thought. "What if Beck left something in Jon's car?"

"I'm sure if she did, he would have gotten rid of it by now," I said.

"But what if she left something in there on purpose, somewhere he couldn't find it?"

"Beck's clever. . . ." I shook my head. "But she was drunk, remember? Even if she did miraculously leave something, how would we get into his car?"

"Gilly," Harry said.

"'Hey, Gilly, I think your dad killed your friends and tried to kill mine. Can I snoop in his car to see if I can find anything?'" I said, holding my hand to my ear like a phone.

"You're smart, make something up," Harry said. "Unless you want to actually break into his car."

I didn't like the fact that I had to use Gilly to gain evidence, but I agreed to it anyway. I called her while Harry stayed quiet.

"Hey!" I said.

"Hi," Gilly said back. "Not that I'm not excited to hear your voice, but why are you calling?"

"I know we will be with each other tomorrow night," I said. "But I really want to see you. I haven't had the best couple of days."

"Do you want to stay the night?" Gilly asked. "We could make our own caramel apples and watch a silly Halloween movie."

"I'd love that," I said.

"Great," Gilly said. "Come over in an hour?"

"I'll be there."

When we hung up, a chill of guilt settled in my stomach. The reason I was actually going there had nothing to do with Gilly. In fact, I didn't want to see her at all. Facing her meant knowing things she didn't. It meant knowing her father was a killer, and once the police found out, her life would turn upside down once again. He was all she had left, and I would be the one responsible for taking that away from her.

"I'll head over there in about an hour," I said to Harry. "If I find something, I'll try my best to call you."

"Be careful," Harry said.

"Always am," I said.

I biked to Gilly's house an hour later. She had two granny smith apples out along with heavy cream and chewy caramels. Jon Willis was home, but apparently, he had locked himself in his room to work on something. I itched to know what he was doing.

"I was thinking we should cut them into slices and dip them in," Gilly said. "I feel like that'll be easier than trying to coat a whole apple."

"That's a great idea," I said cheerily.

Gilly glanced at me strangely before cutting the apples. "You must really love Halloween. I don't think I've ever seen you this excited for anything."

I kissed her cheek. "You're who excites me."

Gilly giggled while I heated up our caramel mixture. When it was soft and gooey, we put the apple slices on skewers and dipped them in. We made sure each slice had a massive amount of caramel on it. Gilly had lined a baking sheet with tin foil; we set them on it to solidify.

"Should we add toppings?" Gilly wondered out loud.

She grabbed some peanuts from the pantry, along with an assortment of Halloween sprinkles. We left some apples plain but added toppings to most of them. I watched her shake sprinkles onto one of the apple slices. She was smiling and looked so utterly happy. I didn't want to ruin her life, but I had to get justice for Beck. Now was my only chance.

"Have you ever been inside your dad's cop car?" I asked.

"A few times," Gilly said. "Daddy and I used to ride around in it. We would stick Justin in the back whenever we caught him stealing anything from me. It's really fun. Have you ever been in one?"

"All the time," I said. "They take me in at least three times a week."

Gilly nudged me and laughed. I faked mine.

"Do you want to go sit in Dad's?" Gilly asked. "We can't drive it obviously, but it's still cool just to sit in."

"Won't he get mad?" I asked.

"He's going to be in his room all night," Gilly said. "He won't even realize we went outside."

My heart skipped a beat at the thought of being stuck in Jon's cop car. Had Beck felt that way when he offered her a ride home from the party? As uneasy as it made me feel, the cop car felt like the one place I would find something to prove Jon was guilty.

"Let's do it," I said. "After we finish decorating our apples, of course."

I decorated mine slowly so I wouldn't seem too eager to get into Jon's car. All my focus went to my apple slices as I listened intently for any movement from Jon upstairs. Any ounce of trust I had toward him was gone.

I put the apple slices in the fridge while Gilly slid Jon's keys carefully off their key holder. They jingled slightly, but not enough that it would alert Jon. Gilly opened the door, hinges creaking as she did so.

"Go," she whispered, while she kept watch.

The night air soothed my nerves and calmed me down. I felt suffocated in Gilly's house, being in the presence of who I believed was the killer. But the night air made me feel invincible, like I could escape at any moment. Gilly carefully shut the door behind her. She unlocked Jon's car door and quietly snuck in. She reached across the passenger seat to unlock my side so I was able to get in. We made sure not to slam the doors, leaving them slightly open just in case. It felt too easy. There were random things in Jon's car. He had an old coffee tumbler, along with Tootsie Roll wrappers he'd thrown on the ground. I looked around, pretending to be intrigued, but didn't catch anything that looked like Beck's.

I pulled at the loose beaded bracelet on my wrist. Nerves punched my stomach.

"Have you ever kissed anyone in a cop car before?" I asked Gilly, hoping she didn't hear the way my voice grew higher.

She smiled. "No. Guess that's something I'll have to do someday."

I pretended to look offended, which made her giggle some more. She leaned in closer to kiss me. I put my left hand in her hair to deepen the kiss. I placed my right hand on the seat and shook the bracelet off until it fell between the crack of the seat and the door.

"My bracelet fell off," I said between kisses.

"We will find it before we go back in," Gilly said.

We kissed for a little while longer before deciding not to test our luck anymore. Jon would kill us if he found out we'd been in his car. Probably literally in my case. I stepped out first, kneeling to look for my bracelet. It nearly fell out of the car, but I shoved it under the seat before Gilly could see. I looked and felt around.

"It's dark," I said. "Do you have a flashlight?"

"I'll go get one really quickly," Gilly said.

I had a few seconds alone to find something. I pulled back the baseboards and felt around. It was hard to see, but my hand found something small and hard. I made sure Gilly was still inside and pulled it from beneath the baseboard. Sweat beaded on the back of my neck. It felt like a thousand eyes were on me as I looked down at what I'd found. I knew it was Beck's immediately. In my hand was a teal *B* earring. A single one from the set I had given her as a gift on her thirteenth birthday, when she got her ears pierced. I almost cried. She'd worn the earrings *I* had gotten her the night she was attacked.

Gilly snuck back out the door quietly with the flashlight.

"Got one," she whisper-yelled.

I moved the baseboard back in place and noticed some crumbs on my hands. But they weren't crumbs; they were pieces of navy-blue nail polish. An image of Beck's chipped nails rose into my mind. Had she also left the flakes as a clue?

"Here," Gilly said, handing me the flashlight.

I shone it and saw my bracelet sparkling under the seat. I grabbed it and slipped it back on my wrist.

"I don't think I've ever seen you wear any kind of jewelry," Gilly said.

"I thought I'd try something new," I said. "I liked messing with Alma's at our sleepover."

"Ha!" Gilly said, like she caught me. "I knew you enjoyed it."

I laughed, my heart weak from the amount of skipping it had done in the past few minutes.

We closed the doors to Jon's police car, and Gilly locked it. Inside, in case Jon grew suspicious of the slam and came down, we positioned ourselves at the kitchen table with the apples to make it look as if we had been there the whole time. Thankfully, he didn't come down.

"I think I'm going to shower while these solidify some more," Gilly said. "Baking and being in that car made me feel gross."

"I'll just hang out in your room," I said.

We went upstairs. As I crossed to Gilly's room, I stared at Jon's door. Light seeped from the bottom of it. Inside Gilly's room, I flopped on the bed casually.

"You should let me paint your nails," Gilly said. "Something other than clear."

"How about green?" I suggested. "For my costume."

Her smile widened as she fought with her dresser drawer. "I should have green somewhere." She wiggled the drawer some more. "This damn drawer always gets stuck."

It rattled the carousel piggy bank on her desk, a clinking sound coming from inside it. When the drawer cooperated, she finally went into her bathroom and closed her bedroom door behind her. I waited for her to turn the shower on before I went over to the carousel. Maybe I was just being paranoid. I was in a house, near the woods, with a man I believed to be a murderer. Still, something inside me screamed to look inside the carousel. I picked it up.

On the bottom was a circular spot that opened to reveal its contents. I opened it carefully. Every clink of whatever was inside made me freeze. But the shower didn't shut off. I hoped for pennies to fall from the silly thing, but inside, there was no money. The first thing I pulled out was a tiny photograph of Alma, Jen, Marki, Sarai, and Gilly when they were little girls. Marki and Sarai's faces had been scratched. When I picked the carousel back up, it made the clinking sound again. I reached inside and nearly fainted. The last thing I pulled out was a small, dirty hunting knife. I flipped the blade out. Bits of what looked like dried blood coated the steel.

I almost collapsed, growing dizzy from what I'd found. A voice in my head screamed at me to get out of there, but my legs stayed locked on the floor. I noticed the jammed drawer of Gilly's, open slightly from where it wouldn't close all the way. Slowly, I pried it open, trying not to make any more noise. When the hole was big enough, I reached my hand into the drawer, the wood cutting the top of my wrist. I had to keep snooping. As much as the voice was telling me to get out of there, it also told me to go further. I stretched my arm as far as it would go in the drawer before my fingers found something small and sleek. I wiggled it out of the drawer, sweating and breathing heavily. I pulled out a pocket-sized notebook. I opened it and nearly choked. Christine's name was on the first page.

Pages of poetry filled the notebook, but each felt like a cryptic message. I didn't have time to decipher any of it, so I quickly threw the notebook in my bag, moving my clothes around so it stayed hidden.

I put everything back into the carousel, listening for the shower, my heart furiously beating in my ears. Just as Gilly turned off the water, I put the carousel back into place. I flew onto her bed and grabbed the magazine off her nightstand. I flipped to a random page in the middle and pretended to read. My mind felt fuzzy, mouth dry with the taste of iron. Fear choked me. It hurt to breathe. What the hell had I just discovered?

Gilly stepped into her room smelling like warm berries with her hair dripping wet. My stomach lurched.

"Are you okay?" Gilly asked. "You look like you're going to be sick."

"I think I'm hungry," I said faintly.

"Let me brush my hair, and then we can eat the apples," Gilly said.

She walked to her dresser, grabbing the hairbrush next to the carousel piggy bank. She stared at it for a moment before gliding the bristles through her wet hair. I met her gaze in the mirror. Her hair was darker when it was wet. It made her eyes look darker as well—or maybe they had always been that way, and I'd been too busy with my infatuation to notice. She looked concerned, and I almost reassured her I was fine, but my eyes betrayed me. They fell directly to the drawer in front of her. The one I'd forgotten to try and shut.

My breathing deepened. In Gilly's eyes, I saw how she felt about me at that moment. She looked at me with nothing but love. I was going crazy. I had to be going crazy.

"I need some water," I said.

I flew out of her room and down the stairs to the nearest phone I could find. I dialed Harry's number with shaky fingers.

"Please, please, please pick up," I whispered.

"Quinn, what's going on?" Gilly said, chasing me down the stairs. "What happened?"

There was a click on the other end of the line.

"Harry—"

I was cut off by a sharp pain against the back of my head. The room went black.

## CHAPTER THIRTY-FOUR

"Fingerprints . . . the knife . . . frame . . . original plan!" a fuzzy voice said.

"No!" another hissed.

"Rink Matthews," the first voice said. "Always . . . bury the knife . . . backyard."

The words didn't piece together in my broken mind. My head lolled as I came to, a steady pounding ruminating at the base of my skull. My eyes didn't want to open, but I forced them to. My vision blurred. I noticed the silhouettes of Jon and Gilly talking in front of me. Gilly was crying and throwing her hands around while Jon tried to calm her. There was a slight ringing in my ears, impairing my hearing.

"Her fingerprints are on the knife," I heard Jon say. "Credible evidence."

"We're not framing Quinn!" Gilly cried.

I shut my eyes again before they could notice.

"You wanted to frame her from the start," Jon said. "Someone who is a loner at school, not many friends, probably a reason to hate you and your friends. Horror-lover. Easy. Knew how killers worked. What changed?"

"I love her!"

The high-pitched scream pierced me, waking me up immediately. I jumped. Jon rubbed his hands down his face while Gilly turned toward me.

"Gilly?" I said, but my voice sounded far away.

Gilly came over and cupped my face, checking my eyes. Jon quickly grabbed an ice pack from the freezer to press against the back of my head. The frost stung me, so I pulled away.

"What happened?" I asked.

"You fell down the stairs," Gilly said, tears in her eyes. "I heard you hit your head."

But I knew I hadn't fallen down the stairs. My arms and legs didn't hurt, only my head did. One of them had hit me in the back of the head. I remembered the evidence in Gilly's room and how I had almost gotten Harry on the phone. I knew better than to reveal that to them.

"How long have I been like this?" I asked.

"About an hour," Jon said. "I already called your mom and told her what happened. She should be on her way soon."

He hadn't called my mom, unless he'd waited a whole hour for me to wake up. But how would he explain the gash I could feel heating up the back of my head?

"I want to try to stand," I said.

"Of course," Jon said.

He and Gilly helped me out of the seat I was in. I was surprised they didn't try to tie me up. I walked to the kitchen, gripping my pounding head. I saw their knife set in my periphery. On instinct, I lunged forward, grabbing the biggest blade I could. When I turned, both of them had their hands up, tears still flowing from Gilly's blue-gray eyes.

"What the hell were you two just talking about," I rasped, flashing the knife between Gilly and her dad.

I mainly kept the knife pointed at Jon. Neither made any moves to take it from me.

"Quinn," Gilly said faintly, heartbreak in her voice.

"Tell me I heard you wrong," I said, my own voice breaking.

"Quinn, listen to me," Jon said. "I will explain it all to you if you sit and calm down."

"Don't try and sweet-talk me like you did Sarai," I said. "That's how you did it, isn't it? How you got her to trust you before you murdered her!"

Gilly and Jon looked at one another before turning their attention back to me.

"And you?" I said to Gilly, my voice hoarse. "You knew? And you hid stuff for him?"

"Quinn, I—"

"What do you mean you wanted to frame me?"

The blood in Gilly's face drained. I kept my eye on her, with the knife pointed in Jon's direction.

"Look, that was a mistake," Gilly said. "It happened so fast, you know. Marki was dead, and I needed someone else to take the blame, and you didn't talk to anyone, and you wear those horror movie graphic tees, so I thought why not blame the person who would know how to kill someone—but that was before us! Quinn, believe me. It wasn't going to be you. And after I killed Sarai, it—"

Gilly stopped before she could finish the sentence. She covered her mouth with her hand, staring at me with her wide, blue-gray eyes.

"What?" I said, dropping the knife. The Freudian slip. I latched onto it. I shook my head. No, she didn't mean it. Gilly wouldn't—

"Gilly," Jon said calmly.

"What the fuck did you just say?" My voice didn't quiver, even though my tongue felt like goo.

"I will explain everything to you," Gilly said. "Just give me a chance."

Gilly took one step toward me, but I lunged past her, pushing her out of my way. I ran like hell out of their house. My legs burned as I tore through the woods. Jon and Gilly called out to me, but I didn't stop running. I gripped my throbbing head. It felt like my brain was jumping around, ready to burst through my skull. I grew dizzy again from the blood loss, and the trees multiplied. My legs slowed down and it felt like I was running in a dream. I cursed myself for dropping the knife.

"Quinn!" Gilly called, closer now than before. "Please come back. Where are you?"

Gilly gaslit me this whole time. She wanted to frame me for Marki's murder, a murder she committed. Not her father. It was never Jon Willis; it had been Gilly this entire time. Of *course* it'd been weird for evidence to be in her bedroom, but the part of me that was in love with Gilly Willis had told me she'd had no clue that was where her father had chosen to hide it. But no, she'd chosen to hide it there because she'd murdered her friends, Christine, and . . . almost Beck. Gilly, the girl I swore up and down that I loved—the girl I wanted to protect—had tried to kill my best friend. None of it made any sense.

I tried my best to keep running but fell onto my hands. Twigs scraped my palms, but I pushed myself up to keep going. When I tried to rush forward again, I knelt over and threw up. Maybe the swelling in my brain would kill me. I made myself keep moving. All I had to do was get to the road that I found on Christine's map. When I saw it, I slowed down, but that was a mistake. Gilly came up behind me and tackled me to the ground. I screamed, but she covered my mouth.

"Shh," she said. "Quinn, I need you to listen to me."

I bit her hand, making her yelp.

"Help!" I screamed.

A rustling behind us stole our attention, but it was only Jon. I noticed he now had a gun sticking out of his jeans.

"Daddy, she's over here!" Gilly called.

"Thank God," Jon said. "We need to get her back to the house. She needs a doctor."

Gilly looked me in the eyes, her tears welling again. "We can't."

"Gilly," Jon said. "She needs medical attention."

"She hit her head and grew so confused she ran out into the woods where we found her dead," Gilly said. "Nobody attacked her because the murderer is behind bars. Rink Matthews killed Marki, Sarai, and Christine. Whoever attacked Beck probably lived in the woods and thought she was trespassing. Quinn's death was an unfortunate accident."

She spoke the words through sobs, staring at me with waves of hurt floating in her blue-gray eyes. I swore they grew grayer. A crack tore through my heart. All the love Gilly had promised me slipped through my fingers and onto the cold, dead earth.

"Gilly," I said, my own tears forming.

"I meant it when I said I love you," Gilly whispered. "But I can't break my family even more."

Gilly choked on a sob. I stopped moving, my eyes meeting hers. The eyes I'd once found beautiful were now the most dangerous things I had ever seen. Her hand moved to my throat, ever slightly. She pushed in, and I realized then how strong she was.

"Stop it!" Jon said. "I'm not going to cover this one up for you."

He scolded Gilly as if she had simply broken a vase. But it worked, because Gilly released me. I crawled away from her, coughing.

"What do I do?" Gilly asked her dad.

I studied the two of them, both broken from their familial tragedy. I was right about one thing: Jon Willis had always had something to do with the murders. He was responsible for covering up the mistakes of his only living kid.

"It'll be alright," Jon said.

He pulled Gilly into his arms to hug her. I stayed low on the ground, watching the two of them embrace. Jon kept his eyes closed, breathing in and out while Gilly sobbed. I didn't risk running away again—not when he had his gun with him. As the two of them pulled away, Gilly grabbed Jon's gun, but she didn't point it at me. It shook in her hands as she pointed the barrel directly at her dad's chest.

"Gilly, put the gun down," Jon said.

"No," she said, shaking.

"Gilly—"

"No!" she screamed. "You did this to me! You made me this way! It's all your fault!"

I saw it in Jon's eyes that he took the blame. The longer the cases had gone on, I'd assumed he'd grown tired of the late nights trying to figure it out, but it was really because he'd worked his ass off to keep Gilly safe and away from suspicion.

"Honey, put the gun down." Jon put his hands out placatingly. "Let's talk."

"I'm done talking," Gilly said. "All I do is talk and talk and talk. When Mama and Justin died, we talked; when I caught you and Marki in your car we talked; when I caught you and Sarai in the kitchen, we talked. I am done talking."

Jon took a step toward Gilly, and she took a step back. I still refused to move, especially since Gilly had the gun.

"Gilly," I said shakily. "What do you mean?"

She turned to me tearfully, the gun following her. I held my breath. "I didn't mean for any of it to get this bad," she whimpered. "Our family was already broken, and then he broke it more by coming onto my friends!"

I felt sick again.

"Gilly," Jon said.

"No!" Gilly yelled. "I'm tired of hiding everything from her."

She turned back to me, gun at the ready.

"I caught my dad and Marki kissing in his car the night I killed her," Gilly cried. "With Sarai, it was the kitchen. I didn't want our family to be split up because of *them*."

I was crying too. "What about Christine? Beck?"

"Christine figured out it was me," Gilly said. "I met up with her after the corn maze and saw all her evidence. So, I confessed. But then I killed her too."

"She figured it out," I said to myself, wondering how I could've been so oblivious.

"I'm sorry about Beck," Gilly said. "But she was kissing Daddy in the car like Marki, except she ran away. I knew then that she would tell someone. I did what I had to do to keep my family together."

Gilly kept the gun pointed on me, but she didn't make any moves to use it. Before me was a broken girl, fucked in the head by tragedy and scum for a father. My anger boiled over at Jon Willis, who refused to look me in the eye.

"You watched how destroyed I was about Beck," I said to him. "You *questioned* me about her, even when you knew the truth."

"I did what I had to do for my daughter," Jon muttered.

"Quinn, I'm so sorry," Gilly said. "I never wanted to hurt you. You were always safe to me."

"Safe?" I said, appalled, turning my attention to her. "You're a murderer, Gilly. I'm not going to sit here and be grateful I wasn't on your radar. Oh, but I was on your radar, right? When you pointed me out in a crowd to frame me. Was that what our first time hanging out was about?"

"Yes, but it was a mistake," Gilly protested. "I didn't think I'd fall for you."

I ignored what appeared to be an attempt at assurance. "What about the threat you left me in the barrel, huh? That doesn't feel very 'safe' to me."

"It was so we wouldn't end up like this," Gilly said.

She pointed the gun at herself, then at me. I looked at Jon Willis, who slowly approached Gilly from behind. He stopped when she turned back around.

"Why did you have to ruin my life?" Gilly said to her father.

"You're right," he said. "It was always my fault. It was never your friends."

"Look who's being the preacher now," Gilly laughed bitterly. "You didn't sound like this when I first told you what I'd done, and you meticulously planned everything so your only living child wouldn't be convicted."

Jon sighed and ran his hands over his face. This would end badly for the both of them. Gilly was in no headspace to be reasoned with.

I thought of Rink and how alone he probably felt. "How could you do this to Rink? Your best friend's brother?"

"We needed someone to frame," Gilly said. "I hate that it was him. It would've been Christine, had she not gone snooping and figured everything out."

So that was why Christine hadn't told me. She knew I wouldn't have been able to hide it from Gilly, even if she'd been wrong about who the killer was. I wished she had told me that night, because maybe then she would still have been alive. And I wouldn't have been face-to-face with my murderer-girlfriend with a gun in her hand.

Jon stepped closer to Gilly, but she was off in another world. Her eyes stayed glued to the ground while the gun swayed lazily at her side. I was trying to piece everything together in my head.

"Then who attacked us in the park?" I asked.

"Nobody," Gilly said. "Well, technically. Turns out Christine was spying on us, but I stabbed myself. I needed to look like a victim. Daddy came up with that one."

My mind spun again. I couldn't believe it. Gilly, the girl who I was in love with, was the killer. The girl who bought me butter pecan ice cream because she knew it was my favorite. I needed to wake up from the nightmare. Somehow, still, all my rage and fury went to Jon Willis.

I mustered all the strength I could to stand and lunge at Gilly. The gun flew from her hand when I took her down with me. I scrambled away from Gilly and grabbed the gun. Without forethought, I closed my eyes and pulled the trigger. The vibration shot up my arm, the gunshot piercing. Gilly and I both screamed as Jon Willis fell to the ground, blood carving an ever-growing spot in the center of his chest.

"Daddy!" Gilly shrieked, falling on her knees next to him.

I dropped the gun, my hand shaking. Gilly took her jacket off and pressed it against Jon's wound. He groaned through his teeth.

"Daddy, I'm sorry," Gilly sobbed.

"It's okay, sweetheart," he said. "I'm sorry too. About all of this. This was all my fault, honey. Remember that."

Jon's breath grew ragged. I didn't say anything. He turned his head slightly to look at me. When his eyes met mine, all I saw were those of a cold-hearted, gross monster.

"Quinn," he said.

Him using my name made me want to hurl a rock at his head.

"Please, do me this one favor," he begged. "It was all me. I am the one who killed those girls. Gilly never had anything to do with it. She didn't know."

A breeze passed through the trees, angrily, like they were warning me not to go through with what he asked of me. I shivered.

My nose wrinkled: the smell of earth mixed with the sour scent of iron as more blood poured from Jon's gunshot wound.

"Daddy, please," Gilly said. "You have to stay with me. I don't have anybody else. We have to figure this out together."

"Frame me and let her go," Jon said, turning his head to his daughter. "It's the least I can do."

Jon took his last breath and died in Gilly's arms. She let out a horrible, grieving scream. It was loud enough to knock the leaves from the trees. I almost felt bad for her, until I realized she would probably kill me now.

"You killed my dad," Gilly whispered, standing to look at me.

I dove for the gun, but Gilly was faster. She stomped on my wrist, and I screamed. Gilly snatched up the gun and wiped her tears away. I grabbed my wrist, sitting on the ground while Gilly held the gun at her side. Defeat settled into her face as she watched me.

"I am really sorry, Quinn," Gilly said. "I really do love you."

I pushed myself off the ground to face her. "Gilly, let me go."

Gilly shook her head. "I can't."

"Yes, you can."

"I don't have anybody anymore because of you." Gilly blinked. "How could you do that to me?"

"I could ask you the same thing," I said.

Gilly lifted the gun shakily. I took off running across the barren road. She fired one shot but missed. I ran in a zigzag until I was on the other side of the woods. I ducked behind a tree to hide from her. I watched her stalk toward the road, gun ready.

"I don't want to do this, but I have to," Gilly said. "I have no other choice."

"Your dad's last words were to let me go," I called out. "Are you really going to go against him?"

A fury I didn't recognize took over as she walked faster. "Don't you dare use my dad against me!"

I peeked from behind the tree. Gilly was in the middle of the road, but before she could take another step, the skidding of tires broke the silence and the brightness of headlights glossed over Gilly. She held up her hand to shield her eyes, but that didn't stop the velocity of the car that surged toward her. One moment, she stood; the next, she was gone. Her body hit the road in a bone-crunching thud. I gasped, stepping back and nearly collapsing. The gun flew out of her bloody hand. Harry stepped out of his car, panic pulling his face into a shocked expression. I stepped out from the trees and slowly approached him.

"Quinn?" he said. "What did I just do?"

I ran over and hugged him, letting out a breath I had been holding into his chest. I forced myself to turn to look at Gilly's body.

"You saved my life," I breathed.

"I came as fast as I could, but you weren't at Gilly's," Harry rasped. "I thought you were dead. . . ."

"You found me just in time," I said.

We both looked at Jon Willis lying dead in the grass on the other side of the road.

"We need to call the police," I said.

"That is the police," Harry replied, bewildered at the sight.

He didn't move a muscle, so I reached into the pocket of his letterman and found his cell phone. He didn't even flinch. I dialed 9-1-1, swallowing all the bile that rose in my throat as I was finally connected to someone.

"I need help," I said. "I'm on Tucker, at the tree line. There's been an accident."

We stood in silence until the police arrived. Blue and red lights flashed around us, giving me far too graphic views of Jon and

Gilly's body. Everything moved in slow motion as I was wrapped in a blanket by a female officer.

"Needs her head checked," I heard her say, but it sounded like an echo.

Harry stayed by my side, trying his best to keep out of the way as my head was checked out.

"What happened here, Miss Levi?" a policeman asked as a light shined in my left eye.

I opened my mouth to answer him, but no words came out.

"I found Quinn here," Harry said. "She was on the ground with a gash in her head, over there by Jon Willis. Gilly had a gun in her hand. I think she saw my car coming because she ran out in front of it, and. . . ."

"Thank you, Mr. Newman," the officer said. "We will still need to get a statement from Miss Levi later."

He left us to zip up Jon and Gilly's bodies. One policeman picked the gun off the ground where it had been next to Gilly's hand. He sealed it in a bag for evidence.

"The paramedics want to get you to the hospital to be thoroughly checked," a policeman said.

Dazed, I nodded and crawled back into the ambulance with Harry. He rode next to me, not leaving my side.

My mom and Owen ran into my hospital room when we got there. They hugged me, even as the doctor checked me out. Neither them nor Harry left my side the entire time.

"My parents are on their way," Harry said.

"I'm going to wait with Harry," I told Mom.

"I'll go pull the car around." Mom kissed my head before heading off with Owen.

Harry and I sat next to each other in the waiting room chairs. I could tell he was also trying to process what had just happened. My mind and body felt disconnected.

I looked up at the clock as it struck 12:01 a.m. A tear fell down my cheek. It was Halloween now. My Poison Ivy costume would stay in the closet after all the work Mom and I had put into it. I wouldn't get to celebrate with my best friend or my girlfriend. It was another day that I lived, while Gilly wouldn't.

"Do you resent me for killing Gilly?" Harry asked, finally speaking up.

I turned to find tears in his eyes.

"No," I answered honestly. "She ran out in front of your car. There was no way you could swerve in time."

Harry stared at me, but I didn't look back at him. We would lie our way through this.

"Thank you," Harry said.

"Shayla saved the day, didn't she?" I said, trying to lighten the mood.

Harry grabbed my hand and pulled me out of the chair.

"Let's go tell Beck," Harry said.

The second we made it into Beck's room, I grabbed her hand and cried.

"I'm sorry I didn't see it," I whispered, hoping somewhere deep in her mind she heard me.

Harry grabbed Beck's other hand. Nobody bothered us. It was just my best friend, Harry, and me, having a moment of peace together. Carefully, I lifted Beck's shirt to find where she was stabbed.

"What are you doing?" Harry asked.

"Looking at her wound," I said. "It's healing."

It was healing as nicely as it could, but it would leave a scar. The place where she was stabbed was jagged, the same way Gilly had carved her pumpkins.

## CHAPTER THIRTY-FIVE

November 13, 2004

"It was Jon Willis," I told the investigator.

The investigator nodded and stared down at his notes.

"So, Jon Willis killed Marki Pickett, Sarai Matthews, Christine Gateman, and attempted to murder Rebekah Wood?" the investigator asked. "You confirm this with the evidence at hand?"

"Yes," I said. "He also framed Rink Matthews for the murders. I have proof."

The investigator sat back in his chair and sighed. I wondered how much he could see through me.

"Run me through the night of October 30th one more time," he said.

I straightened up and took a sip of the water he had offered me. "I went over to Abigail Willis's house that night, where I found a hunting knife with dried blood on it under the baseboard of Jon Willis's police car. I went to call the police when he hit me on the back of my head. I don't know what he hit me with, but it was something hard enough to knock me out. I was unconscious, and he told Gilly—sorry, Abigail—that I had fallen down the stairs. I ran out in the woods to escape, but he followed me, leading Abigail to follow him. He attacked both of us. I was barely conscious when he tried to attack me again, so Abigail shot him. It was out of self-defense. She then jumped out in front of Harry Newman's car and took her own life. He didn't have time to swerve. It all happened so fast."

I had rehearsed what I was going to tell the investigator in the mirror. I kept it calculated, but still slipped up on Gilly's real name to show him how human the statement was. He checked his notes while I talked; I could tell he hadn't found a single flaw in my story.

He closed his notepad and stood up. I followed him. He shook my hand at the door.

"Thank you for all the help with this, Miss Levi," he said.

"The pleasure is mine," I said.

Mom and Owen waited for me in the lobby. Mom hugged me when I got out, then shook the investigator's hand.

"Your daughter has been a tremendous help in this case," he said.

"I'm glad she could help," Mom replied.

The investigator waved us out. "If we need to do some further questioning, we will give you a call."

As we drove, I noticed we weren't turning down the road to get to our house.

"Mom?" I asked.

"We are going to the hospital," Mom said. "Beck woke up."

My heart fluttered at the news. "Well, drive faster!"

Excitement fizzled in me. I watched as the trees passed until we pulled into the hospital. I rushed into the lobby, then into Beck's room. Harry was already there; he had a teddy bear in one hand and balloons in the other. Cami and Eric were in the room as well. When I walked in and saw Beck sitting up, drinking juice, my knees buckled. I held onto the edge of her bed, tears already in my eyes. Cami and Eric left to give us space. Beck opened her arms for me. I flew into them and squeezed.

"Quinn, it was—"

"I know," I said, wiping tears from her eyes. "It's all over now."

Harry timidly approached and gave Beck the teddy bear, then tied the balloons to her bed.

"You're such a cliché," Beck chuckled, pulling him down to kiss her.

"I'm sorry we weren't there," I said.

Beck and Harry stopped embracing so we could all see one another.

"I'm sorry I pushed you both away," Beck said. "I made some stupid mistakes that night."

"And none were your fault." I put a hand on hers. "That reminds me."

I reached into my pocket and pulled out the teal *B* earring.

Beck started to cry again. "You found it."

"Of course I did," I said. "Did you really think we wouldn't figure out who did this to you? I'd go to my grave for you, Beck."

"I love you both so much," Beck said with a sad smile.

"Right back at you." I winked.

"I love you," Harry said, kissing Beck on the cheek.

*Jon Willis was posthumously convicted for the murder of Marki Pickett, Sarai Matthews, Christine Gateman, and the attempted murder of Rebekah Wood and Quinn Levi. Abigail Willis's death was ruled a suicide, and Harry Newman was let off with no charges against him. Rink Matthews was released and given a formal apology by the Boiling Springs police department.*

I capped the glue stick I used to stick the news clipping on a page in my notebook. The case was finally closed. Beck got to leave the hospital the day after she woke up. She only remembered Jon Willis picking her up from the party and attacking her at his house. She didn't know Gilly was the one who tried to kill her. And I wouldn't ever tell her the truth.

Harry convinced himself Gilly had actually killed herself. He'd never asked about why she had a gun raised when he hit her, probably to put it all behind us. Jon and Gilly were both dead. The murderers of Boiling Springs were dead. At some point, we had to leave the past in the past.

"So you really went back there? You burned *everything*?" Beck pressed me, her eyes watching me.

The Saturday after the news released the statement about Jon Willis, I told everyone I went for a walk and ended up at school. The caution tape by the woods had been taken down, and people were freely going in and out of them again.

"Yes," I told Beck. "I did."

I explained the whole moment, how I breathed in the cool air, how it felt like the events from the night before Halloween had just happened yesterday. I was still haunted by the vision of Jon collapsing and dying from his gunshot wound—the one I'd inflicted upon him. Even more so, I was haunted by the scene of Gilly getting hit by Harry's car. The way her body had fallen to the road, torn and bloody. I didn't hate Harry for it, though. Gilly didn't fit into this world anymore.

Gilly's life had been harsh to her. The tragedy in her blue house had only been the start. I blamed Jon Willis for the rest of her pain. Gilly had needed help, and he'd never gotten it for her. Instead, he'd fed into her crimes because she was his only child left alive. I'd underestimated how far a parent's blinders could reach.

"Do you still miss her?" Beck asked.

"I don't know, I think a part of me will always still love her, even after everything." Even after discovering she would have shot me dead. She would always be my first love, and it wasn't easy to ignore how long I believed she really did love me. We would always have our season together. I couldn't help but wonder if that seed of evil live inside Gilly before everything, or had it festered beginning with the death of her mother and brother?

My mind pulled me back to the story I told. I saw myself walk over to the storage room by the bleachers. Watched as I pulled out the barrel Rink and I had used to burn Christine's evidence. That evidence could have kept him out of jail and maybe even prevented Jon and Gilly's deaths, but maybe nothing would have ever come of it even if we had gone to the police. Jon Willis had proven his power to me the night he died. If he could cover up his daughter's multiple murders, he could cover up anything.

I told Beck I had brought a shot bottle of Fireball from mom's liquor cabinet and some matches. I thought back to the image I was describing, the girls in the photo beginning to curl together until the fire nearly burned my hand. I visualized myself dropping it into the barrel and letting the flames eat the group up, burning their younger lives into ash.

I took the plastic part of the ring pop Gilly had given me out of my pocket and tossed it in the barrel. It reminded me too much of a Gilly I wasn't even sure was real. Lastly, I took Christine's pocket-notebook out. Inside was a collection of poems, but only one mattered.

*In the grove of trees, branches dancing*
*There is a girl, gray eyes sad and weeping*
*So much grief, but she goes on prancing*
*Get into the fetal position, to continue sleeping.*
*Ignore the calls of distant evil*
*Live in the company of tragic people*
*Lift off for oblivion, a group's upheaval*
*You won't believe it true, but believe it in the steeple.*

She'd written the poem about Gilly, for me, as a warning. It'd been a clever way to tell me without actually having to say it—but Gilly had gotten to the notebook first.

It had been easy sneaking back into Gilly's house before the police raided it for everything. I debated taking the carousel and the hunter's knife, but I left them. Jon Willis's fingerprints were on both, along with Gilly's. It was *credible evidence.*

I dropped the notebook in the barrel and poured Fireball over it, making sure it was saturated. When it was, I lit a match and dropped it in the barrel. The flames started out small, then licked their way up the notebook's sides. My ring pop melted slowly. I waited until both were completely disintegrated before I shoved the barrel back into the storage room.

I walked back home, passing a newsstand with Jon Willis's face on the front covers of the magazines. Gilly's face was also on the covers, but smaller than his. My heart burned when I looked into her blue-gray eyes.

"He's scum," the newsstand worker said. "Killing his daughter's friends like that."

What I wanted to say was "Screw Gilly Willis, the last dead girl," but I held my tongue. I walked away, anger and hurt mixing in the pit of my stomach all at once. Hopefully, one day, I could convince myself that it was Jon Willis all along and *not* Gilly. The rest of the town was fooled, after all. I would patiently wait for the day that I could also fool myself.

# EPILOGUE

November 30, 2004

*The one person holding me together right now is Beck. After she woke up, I have refused to leave her side, until today. I let her and Harry have some much-needed alone time. I've become codependent on being their third wheel, but neither ever complain about it. They know I'm still in pain, but it goes much deeper than that. The guilt is what truly keeps me latched onto them.*

*I can't bring myself to hate Gilly Willis. Loathing her as deeply as I loved her is impossible. She's not a monster, to me. In fact, I'm not sure what she is or was to me. I never truly got to know the real her, the side that also had darkness and lies as building blocks. But I guess we're even; she will never know the real me either.*

*I never burned the photograph of Gilly and her friends. I stare at them; they stare back, and we sit there trying to figure each other out. How did they get to a point where they became the "trouble" Rink claimed they were?*

*But here we are again, diary. You've become as much of a crutch to me as my best friends. Christine was onto something when she wrote everything down about the case. I should've kept this from the start. Not that you'll remember, anyway. As soon as I'm done here, all will be erased. You know the routine by now.*

- Quinn Levi; Gilly's girlfriend. Beck's best friend. Liar.
- Quinn lied to the investigator about what really happened in the fall of 2004.
- Gilly never tried to kill Quinn when she found out that Gilly was the murderer. She was going to let Quinn go. But Quinn, enraged, couldn't stop herself.
- After shooting Jon Willis, Quinn pushed Gilly into the road when she saw Harry's car coming. There was never a standoff on opposite roadsides. Quinn killed both Jon and Gilly Willis, all in the same night.
- Quinn is a murderer, just like her girlfriend, who she'll probably love forever.

# ACKNOWLEDGMENTS

This book has been something I cherished since I first got the idea for it. I have always been a fan of mysteries and thrillers, which I feel has led me up to this point of writing one. *All (Dead) Girls Lie* came to me after the pandemic. I have gotten to know it year after year, hoping one day I would see it on a bookshelf. Now, she's getting her moment!

I want to thank my wonderful editor V. Ruiz for taking a chance on this book. I'll never forget my excitement when you requested for me to send it over to you. I also want to thank Rebekah Borucki and everyone at Row House Publishing for helping me achieve my longtime dream of becoming a traditionally published author.

Thank you to the UNCW creative writing department and all the friends I met there. You gave me community and a home. I will be forever grateful for my time spent on the rocking chairs in Kenan Hall with you all.

Thank you to my family, who get as excited about my writing as I do.

And if you've made it to this point, thank *you* for reading my debut novel.

This is only the beginning.

## ABOUT THE AUTHOR

PIPER L. WHITE is the author of two young adult novels, *Flicker* and *Flare*. Her debut poetry chapbook, *Barefoot in the Woods*, was published in May 2022 by Bottlecap Press. She holds a BFA in creative writing from UNC Wilmington, where she also got her certificate in publishing. Her other work can be found in literary magazines such as *Atlantis*, *Full House Literary*, *Carolina Muse Arts*, and *The Crow's Quill*, among others.